P9-DTO-320

An inviting smile . . .

She leaned her head onto his shoulder and asked in a soft voice, "I wanted to get to know you better but I forgot to ask questions."

"What did you want to know?"

"Why you run around with us all but you really don't. Do you prefer being alone?"

"Not really," he answered. "I have a job and I have to help at home and I have a lot of homework. I'm just kind of busy."

They were standing still and he had his arm around her waist. The sun had gone and the sky was getting dark. She knew if she just stood there and smiled up at him he would get the idea to kiss her. She just knew that he was going to kiss her any minute now.

**Other Scholastic books
you will enjoy:**

A Winter Love Story
by Jane Claypool Miner

Winter Dreams, Christmas Love
by Mary Francis Shura

Forbidden
by Caroline B. Cooney

Unforgettable
by Caroline B. Cooney

WINTER LOVE, WINTER WISHES

Jane Claypool Miner

SCHOLASTIC INC.
New York Toronto London Auckland Sydney

If you purchased this book without a cover, you should be aware that this book is stolen property. It was reported as "unsold and destroyed" to the publisher, and neither the author nor the publisher has received any payment for this "stripped book."

No part of this publication may be reproduced in whole or in part, or stored in a retrieval system, or transmitted in any form or by any means, electronic, mechanical, photocopying, recording, or otherwise, without written permission of the publisher. For information regarding permission, write to Scholastic Inc., 555 Broadway, New York, NY 10012.

ISBN 0-590-48152-5

Copyright © 1994 by Jane Claypool Miner.
All rights reserved. Published by Scholastic Inc.

12 11 10 9 8 7 6 5 4 3 2 1   4 5 6 7 8 9/9 0/0

Printed in the U.S.A.   01

First Scholastic printing, November 1994

Dedicated with much love
to Davy DuVivier

WINTER LOVE, WINTER WISHES

Chapter 1

"Of course it's a silly idea." Brittany shrugged and reached over to take another black walnut from the gunnysack between Teddy's knees. "But maybe a boardinghouse will give my mother something to interest her for a while. Certainly in Madison, Wisconsin, there are plenty of kids at the university who would be interested in boarding. She's tried gardening, volunteering, and sewing. Running a boardinghouse is at least something with people. She's alone too much since Dad died. She doesn't need the money, but . . ."

"It's a dumb idea," Teddy grumbled. "You should have stopped your mother but instead, you actually encouraged her."

"Willow was the one who thought it would be fun," Brittany protested.

"You both said yes and that's because you're both boy-crazy. Willow's sixteen and she wants to meet older college guys. Besides, she's always been an airhead. But you — you're too smart to believe any college man would be interested in a fourteen-year-old. At least I hope you are."

Brittany went on cracking nuts, ignoring her best friend Teddy's grumbling. What would he know about who would or would not be interested in her? After all, she was a very sophisticated fourteen.

Brittany was in the swing. She had to lean forward and hammer the walnut on the cement floor where Teddy was sitting. "I need my kneecaps," Teddy warned. "Sit on the floor like me. And remember you can't play the piano without fingers."

"I've been cracking black walnuts since before you were born," Brittany answered. Her haughty voice seemed to float over the top of Teddy's dark, curly hair.

Teddy looked up and grinned. Sometimes he looked exactly the same as when she'd first met him in kindergarten nine years before. His wide-spaced blue eyes always looked as though he knew a secret and his smile was always almost a grin. She frowned and tried to look very superior. Of course, she had to hit her finger just when she was trying to impress him with her maturity! She bit her lip to keep from crying out but Teddy noticed anyway. Teddy didn't miss much.

"I'm three days younger," he said. "Even the great Britt couldn't hold a hammer at the age of three days. Does that hurt? Want some ice?"

She allowed herself the privilege of putting her bruised finger in her mouth but she shook her head no to the ice. Teddy got up and strolled into the kitchen anyway. He was back with a bowl of ice before she could protest. She stuck her finger in the bowl and said, "I just thought it would be nice to make walnut cookies for the boarders."

"Boarders!" Teddy's tone was derisive. "I thought you were making them for me. Let the silly boarders go to 7-Eleven for their cookies."

"A boardinghouse may seem like a silly idea but as long as we're doing it, we're going to do it *right*. Anyway, Mother asked me to make cookies. You know Mother — she can be enthusiastic."

"So can you," Teddy said. He tapped the nuts methodically, hitting them lightly on the seam where the two halves joined. That was the way Teddy did things — quietly and efficiently. Some people said they were best friends because they were so opposite.

Brittany smiled at his concentration over the nuts. When they were younger they had no secrets. But now that she was fourteen and becoming a woman, there were things she couldn't share with him. After all, young women matured much earlier than boys, and there was a lot more than three days' difference in their emotional age. Teddy was still a baby in so many ways — happy to crack walnuts on a Saturday morning and maybe take a bike ride in the afternoon.

"Want to ride out to the lake after lunch?" he asked. It had always been like that between them — two heads, one mind, her mother called it when they were younger.

"I told you, I have to wait here for the new boarders."

"You *want* to wait here," Teddy said matter-of-factly. "You want to see what they look like. You're not much better than Willow these days."

"What's that mean?" Brittany pretended to be hurt but secretly she was pleased that Teddy could see she was entering a new phase and assuming some of the same interests as her older sister, Willow.

"Doesn't mean anything," Teddy answered calmly. "Just a statement of fact. You and Willow let your mother go for this boardinghouse idea simply because you both want to meet new boys."

"That's not true!" Brittany's cheeks were flushing. Was she so easy to read?

"It's true," Teddy said. "I guess I'll see if Jason wants to take a bike ride."

He was off the porch and on his bike before she could protest. She supposed he was mad at her but he would be over it before the day was up. One thing she could always count on was Teddy's cheerful ability to forgive and forget.

She moved from the swing into a bamboo chair that she pulled into the sunlight. Then she stretched her face toward the pale warmth. September in Madison, Wisconsin, was usually cold but today it was warm. Brittany sighed and closed her eyes, trying to imagine that she was on the beach in California or Tahiti or someplace exotic. Madison was all right but it certainly wasn't exotic.

As she let her imagination play, she saw herself as an Aztec princess stretching her hands up to the heavens asking the sun god for mercy. Her lover lay across the sacrificial stone and the cruel priest held a knife in his hand, ready to cut out his heart. But she — Summeriti, daughter of Montezuma — would save him from his cruel fate.

"Trying to catch sunbeams?" A man's voice broke into her daydream.

Brittany jumped up, flushing with embarrassment, and looked at the young man who was standing on the steps that led from the street onto the porch. "Hi," she said and held out her hand. "I'm Brittany Winston. Are you Carlos Montoya?"

He took her hand and shook it as he laughed and said, "Nope. I'm Dan Evans from Wyoming. I'm a couple of days early. Hitched a ride out with a friend of a friend. Thought I'd get a chance to sightsee. Is it all right?"

"Certainly," Brittany was mentally going over the plans and directions her mother had made. Where did this one go? Was he the one they were putting on the third floor? She simply couldn't remember. "I'll have to check the battle plan in my mother's office," Brittany said. Then she added, "Don't mind me. It's just that this is our first experience operating a boardinghouse, and my mother and sister have gone to Chicago today. Shopping. My sister's getting some new school clothes. My turn's next week. So anyway, I'm in charge and we were only expecting one person today. He's from Mexico."

"And his name is Carlos," Dan teased. "So what's this battle plan? You expecting trouble with your paying guests?"

"It's just a manner of speaking," Brittany said. She was afraid her answer sounded too short. On the other hand, her other answers had definitely been too long. She told herself to get herself together and act as if she were competent. "Won't you follow me?"

Dan followed her into the house, slowing down to look around in amazement at the furniture and paintings in the living room. "It's beautiful," he said. "What kind is it? I mean, I've never seen stuff like this before."

"My mom and dad collected all the furniture and art before he died," Brittany explained. "It's mostly American but some European and it's all around 1900–1920. This is a Craftsman house."

"I see."

It was obvious to Brittany that he didn't see at all. She was used to that. "This house was designed by a famous architect who was part of the Craftsman movement. That was an important time between Victorian and modern. Craftsman houses are scattered all over America. My folks bought this one about twenty years ago and restored it."

"It's not exactly modern," Dan said. "But it's not old-fashioned either."

"That's right," Brittany answered crisply. "It's a *transitional* period in architecture. We

7

get students from the art and architecture departments over here a lot."

She led him through the living room to the dining room. Dan stopped and stared at the huge walnut table that dominated the room. "Sixteen chairs," he counted. "Wow!"

She was busy studying her own reflection in the huge mirror over the sideboard. Was she pretty enough to catch the eye of a college man? She knew that her head of bright red curls attracted a lot of attention, but she wasn't sure she was exactly pretty. And she wished she were taller and more filled out. In short, she wished she looked older and maybe a bit like her sister, Willow.

"Sixteen chairs. That calls for a lot of company, doesn't it?" Dan asked.

"That's what gave my mother the idea of a boardinghouse," Brittany explained. "We used to have parties when my father was alive but since then, Jessica — that's my mother — hasn't bothered. So she decided it would be fun to have some students living here with us."

"I hope it isn't too much work for you and your mother," Dan said. "Do you have any brothers and sisters to help? How many boarders are you taking in?"

"It won't be any trouble," Brittany explained. "We have a woman who's doing the cooking and cleaning and my cousin is moving in from the country. She's going to help out." Brittany frowned because she knew she was talking too much again. She should be asking him about himself, not chattering like a little kid. "So what made you decide on Wisconsin for college?" she asked.

"I hear it's a great school," Dan said and grinned. When he smiled he was kind of good-looking, Brittany decided. But he wasn't exactly impressive or anything like that. He had brown hair and brown eyes and wasn't very tall. He just looked sort of ordinary and like a nice guy.

"How old is your cousin — the one coming in from the country?" Dan asked. "She in college?"

"No. She's in high school. She wanted to go to a city school and we needed help, so it worked out."

"Wanted a better academic program?" Dan guessed.

"Nope. She wants a better athletic program," Brittany answered. "Seems she's so good at sports she's been playing on the boys' team. She wants a better team to play with."

Dan laughed with surprise and asked, "Basketball?"

"Basketball and track," Brittany answered. For the hundredth time since they'd received the letter asking if Anna could come and stay, Brittany wondered what kind of a girl would pack up her whole life and leave her friends and family just for a better basketball court. From the beginning, she and Willow had been cautious about this mysterious cousin they'd never met but their mother had written back the next day and offered room and board in exchange for "light housekeeping." That was mostly to turn down the offer of money that accompanied the request.

"Even with help, you'll have your hands full," Dan said sympathetically.

"I just told you, *I'm* not going to work." It was annoying the way everyone assumed that they had chosen to open this enterprise because they needed the money and that they would have to scrub floors themselves.

"Not at all?" Dan asked doubtfully.

"Not at all," Brittany answered. "Unless you call showing you to your room work."

They were in the kitchen now and Dan was obviously impressed by the size of it. On one wall, they found a copy of an old blueprint and people's names written into the floor plan. "There I am," he said, pointing to a room on the third floor.

"You'll get used to the stairs," Brittany assured him.

Dan laughed aloud and said, "The stairs won't bother me. I'm fresh off the ranch. I'm in good enough shape to climb stairs, I reckon."

"So you're a real cowboy?" Brittany asked. She tossed her head a little bit and smiled in her most grown-up way. She didn't care what Teddy said, she was mature for her age and a lot of college boys weren't so grown-up. Maybe Dan . . . she had a brief vision of herself riding the range with Dan beside her. They were on matching palomino ponies and Wyoming stretched behind them just as far as she could see.

Dan laughed. Brittany flushed and she knew he was laughing at her for flirting. He wasn't really her type anyway. Though he was nice-looking, he wasn't really handsome and he spoke with a kind of cowboy drawl. Besides, he wore glasses and had a small mustache. She didn't like to think about kissing anyone with a mustache. She frowned at her own thoughts, worried he could read her mind. "Follow me," she commanded and led him quickly up the stairs to his room.

The room was a large one with big windows that looked out to the lake. Dan sighed and picked the bed closest to the window. "At least I'll be able to see a ways out," he commented.

"Being cooped up all winter will be hard for me."

"So what's your major?" Brittany asked.

"Animal husbandry," Dan answered and then laughed. "That's eastern lingo for a major in cowboying."

"I'm majoring in drama," Brittany offered.

"In high school or junior high?" Dan asked.

That was so insulting she decided not to answer. After all, she was in the ninth grade. "You'll have to eat supper out tonight," Brittany answered haughtily. "I have to meet the bus to pick up my cousin."

"Want me to go with you?" Dan offered. "I could drive that car out there."

"No, thank you," Brittany answered. One of the things she and her mother and sister had talked over carefully was how important it would be not to be too friendly with their guests — at least until they were better acquainted. Besides, her mother had left her money for a taxi. That would be fun. She decided she would call Teddy and ask him to go with her. They could get hamburgers in the diner next to the bus station. Teddy loved those burgers.

Chapter 2

"So, did you meet your dream man?" Teddy asked.

"That's a ridiculous question," Brittany snapped. Then she told the truth. "The first guy was a cowboy from Wyoming. Nice, but hardly anyone's dream man. I think he may be good to have around though. He's already promised to fix the squeaking stairs and he nailed down the carpet runners before he unpacked his bags."

"Sounds like a good man," Teddy agreed as he reached for the catsup. "Wonder if he knows what's in store for him with you helpless women."

"You really ought to outgrow woman bashing," Brittany said. "No one is going to talk to you if you don't."

"Okay. I'll rephrase — you helpless *persons*. How's that?"

Brittany ignored him.

"Carlos — the boy from Mexico — seemed really surprised that I didn't carry his bags for him. I guess rich people in Mexico have a lot of servants or something."

"So, is he moving out?" Teddy asked hopefully. He and Brittany had a ten-dollar bet that none of their eight boarders would stay past Christmas. Brittany knew that Teddy was already spending that money mentally.

"Of course not," Brittany laughed. "He was perfectly charming about it. In fact, he was perfectly charming about *everything*, even though he said he had the flu and was exhausted from his flight."

"It's not that far from Mexico City to Madison," Teddy said.

"He came from Switzerland by way of San Antonio. I didn't get all the details but I don't think he's been in Mexico for weeks. He looks as if he has loads and loads of money."

"Maybe if I whine, he'll give me some," Teddy said. "You know, stand outside your door each evening with my cap in my hand, all hunched up and pitiful."

"You're ridiculous," Brittany laughed. "He's really handsome. Movie-star handsome. Like sort of a combination of Cary Grant and Brad Pitt." In his own way, she thought Carlos was just as handsome as her secret love — Lars Peterson. Although Lars was blond and blue-eyed and Carlos had black hair and black eyes — they actually looked a little bit alike. Both had straight noses and high cheekbones and they both had wonderful smiles. But she had no intention of telling Teddy that Carlos looked like Lars. She'd never even mentioned Lars to Teddy. No one knew she was crazy about the handsome senior.

"So you're in love?" Teddy teased.

"Nope. He's too old for me. And he really did expect me to carry his bags up all those stairs."

Brittany frowned and looked away. "That bus should be here any minute. Ever been to Saint Olaf's?"

"Here comes the bus," Teddy said as he stuffed the remainder of his french fries in his mouth.

"I went to Saint Olaf's once when my father was alive," Brittany said. "I was about six or seven. It's all Norwegian. Even a lot of the signs are in Norwegian. They are all farmers and really old-fashioned.

"Look for a tall girl," Brittany said. "There she is," Brittany pointed to the tall, young woman who stepped off the bus. "I've got her photo."

"Whew!" Teddy said admiringly. "How old did you say she was?"

"Fifteen."

"She's close to six feet," he said. "She can carry her own bags. I'm excess baggage."

It was true. Anna Goethe was at least a head taller than Teddy and she were. Last time they measured, they were both five feet six so Anna had to be at least five feet eleven. No wonder she was good at basketball.

As Brittany drew close to her cousin, she suddenly felt very shy, as though she were talking to someone from a foreign country.

Anna's pale blue eyes seemed distracted and remote, and there were wisps of light brown hair that blew out from under her knitted wool cap. She was wearing a man's wool tweed overcoat and carrying a funny old plastic purse that must have belonged to some old lady. She wore white tennis shoes and black knit stockings and her gloves were bright blue.

Brittany tried to keep her dismay from showing as she said, "Hi, Anna. This is my friend Teddy and I'm Brittany. How was your trip?"

Anna nodded her head and Brittany wasn't sure whether that meant the trip was good, or simply over. Then Anna held out her hand and Brittany shook it.

As she shook her cousin's hand, Brittany noticed that Anna's hands were about twice the size of hers. It made her feel small, and a little frightened somehow. She wasn't sure what to say so she said nothing.

Teddy tried to take Anna's battered old suitcase but Anna waved him away as though he were a small annoyance and she wouldn't let the taxi driver put it into the trunk either. So Teddy rode in the front seat with the driver and Brittany and Anna rode in the backseat with the battered old suitcase wedged between them.

It was quite dark as they pulled away from the station and Brittany was relieved of the burden of pointing out the sights. She did manage to mention that they were driving past the capitol building and when Anna said nothing, she added, "Madison is the capital of Wisconsin, you know."

"I know." Anna's voice was soft and a little flat. There was something about it that made Brittany want to cry but she wouldn't have said that Anna sounded sad. Just different. Brittany shook her head in the darkness and wondered at the strangeness of life. This young cousin from 250 miles away seemed ten times more foreign than the young men from Wyoming and Mexico.

Chapter 3

Willow liked the idea of a boardinghouse and she thought at least two of the new boarders had definite possibilities. Carlos was very, very handsome, and there was a young man named Justin who was just darling.

Willow spent a lot of time during that first week experimenting with new hairstyles. She was seriously considering cutting her strawberry blond hair and getting a short, curly cut. She thought she might look prettier and she also thought that the shorter hair might make her look more grown-up.

None of her girlfriends thought she should cut her hair though and when she tried pinning it up in back, the reflection that stared back at her in the mirror didn't look any older. After a week's consideration, she decided to keep her hair in the same shoulder-length blunt cut.

On the Saturday morning before school started, she took the car into Madison for a hair appointment and told Joel, her cutter, she'd decided not to change anything, just take off a little. He stood behind her and looked at her reflection in the mirror, running his hand through her thick, smooth, strawberry blond hair. "A woman's glory," Joel said. "I'm glad. You're a beautiful girl and your hair is important to your beauty. Let the others go cute — you've got style."

Willow was pleased by the compliment although it would have been nice to go back to school as a whole new Willow Winston. She was a junior this year and it should be her best year in school. She already had her whole year planned.

Willow was certain she would be a cheerleader again. If she'd made the team in her sophomore year, then she was a certain winner in her junior year. And she wanted to get at least a B average in classes. She frowned lightly as she thought about school and grades. B's were hard enough for her, but Brittany never seemed to do any homework and she brought home A's. Life wasn't exactly fair.

Willow smiled at her reflection in the mirror . . . her wide cheekbones, turquoise eyes, and dark, arched brows and full mouth. Even with her hair all wet and skinned down as Joel cut it, she was good-looking.

Willow decided this year she would have one special boyfriend. She hoped it would be Lars Peterson. Lars was everyone's favorite guy and she really liked him and she was beginning to think he really liked her, too. He was always friendly when he saw her and usually stopped to talk.

Lars was smart. They said he was working hard on his grades to get a full scholarship to college. They said that was the reason he didn't have a special girlfriend. He always had lots of girls around him but he didn't date a lot. They also said he saved the money that he made on Saturdays at the drugstore for college. She didn't know Lars well enough yet to be certain that the stories she heard about him were true but she did know that everyone seemed to like and respect him.

So maybe Lars is the one, Willow thought. Maybe he's my special love. She sighed and twisted slightly in the chair. Of course, Lars was still in high school and she really thought it would be neat to date a college man. Some of the other girls in the senior class went out with students from the University of Wisconsin and now that they had the boarders, there was a possibility she might do the same.

Dan was sweet but he wasn't exactly her idea of a dream man. He was too plain and honest to be very romantic. But he was a nice guy and he had helped her with the groceries yesterday. Her deal with her mother was that she had to drive to the grocery store in exchange for using the car. She'd liked it when Dan helped her.

Carlos was the handsome and charming one, though. He was always kissing her mother's hand and that seemed sort of weird but he said nice things. Yesterday he called her, "Beautiful Willow." She liked that but it made it hard to take him seriously.

Justin Marks was darling. He was about nineteen and he had dark curly hair that fell into his eyes. He hadn't really said anything at all but he was a definite possibility. He was adorable and he was young. Willow didn't know any more than that but she was hopeful.

"So, how do you like having all those people around your house?" Joel asked.

"Too early to tell," Willow said.

"Your mother already looks stressed," Joel offered his opinion. "I think sometimes Jessica lets her enthusiasm run away with her. And Brittany, of course, Brittany thinks they're all just great. Brittany wouldn't let me cut two inches off that mop of curls she calls hair. You Winston girls — the one with good hair wants it cut and the one with too much hair wants more."

"Brittany would look better with short hair," Willow agreed. She frowned when she thought of her younger sister. It was not going to be easy having Brittany at Madison High as a freshman. Brittany was so . . . unusual. She said and did whatever she wanted and never really cared what other people thought.

"She asked me if I could do dreadlocks," Joel said, then shuddered. "I said no and she couldn't have them either. That Britt — she's a case." And then he laughed and shook his head just remembering her.

Willow smiled. People were always laughing at Brittany. They thought she was cute. Maybe in her own way, she was. "You should see my cousin," Willow said. "She's really funny-looking."

"She's coming in?" Joel asked.

"Mom asked her if she wanted a haircut and she said no."

"How does funny-looking look?"

Willow wanted to answer his question. She would have liked to describe how awkward and strange Anna looked but she knew it would be very bad manners to do so. She felt guilty for even bringing it up so she picked up a magazine and began thumbing through the pages, as though she was really interested in the fashion photos.

"She from Mars or what?" Joel teased. "Green radar equipment coming out of her ears? Long, furry teeth?"

"She's just very quiet and aloof," Willow said. "She'll look better when she gets some new clothes and stuff, but she's still weird to me. I'm taking her shopping as soon as I get out of here."

"You're a sweet kid," Joel said and patted Willow on the shoulder. Willow winced inside, knowing that she was only taking Anna and Brittany shopping because her mother was forcing her to do it. She knew she was what people called well behaved but she wasn't certain she really deserved the title *sweet*. In fact, if there were any way at all of getting out of the upcoming shopping trip, she would have taken it.

Chapter 4

Brittany was offered two choices. Her mother said, "We could go to Chicago to shop in a month. You'd have to wait until the boarding-house is under control. Or you can pick out your own clothes here in town. I just can't face a Chicago trip this week."

"All alone?" Brittany longed to express her own fashion taste this year. Her mother and Willow were always well dressed but they were so conservative. Brittany figured her own style should be more dramatic — maybe she could find a cape with a hood. Besides, she doubted that the boardinghouse was going to be under control anytime soon. It was basically pretty confusing to have all those extra people around. "Not alone," her mother said. "I'll give you money and Willow and Anna can go with you."

"But I get to pick my own clothes?" Brittany insisted.

Jessica nodded. "You can help Willow help Anna, too. She needs some new clothes for high school."

"It will take more than new clothes," Brittany said. Anna was so strange-looking that she didn't even want to be seen with her at the mall. It wasn't just that she was tall — there were plenty of tall kids at Madison High — it was that she seemed to shrink inside herself.

"You girls are being nice to Anna, aren't you?"

"Mom, she's really weird. She doesn't *want* to be friendly. And she looks like — like something out of the pages of my history book. No one looks like that but Anna Goethe."

"New clothes will help," her mother said briskly. "I'll give your money to Willow and you two can help Anna make some choices."

"Don't give *my* money to Willow!" Brittany protested.

"Willow is older."

"It's not fair!"

"If you say one more word, you won't go at all!"

Brittany didn't say another word because

she had long ago learned to recognize the stretched-to-the-breaking-point tone in her mother's voice. She guessed her mother would escape totally today and go paint in the fields or something. Ever since her father died three years ago, her mother had found ways to be alone when she was really stressed, and had found painting soothing. Sometimes she felt really sorry for her mother but today wasn't one of them. Today she just felt like her rights had been taken away and given to Willow just because of an accident of birth. Just because Willow was two years older didn't mean she was a bit smarter. In fact, Brittany happened to know that her reading and math scores were higher than Willow's. But she also knew better than to mention that to her mother.

Willow drove because she had the license. Anna sat in the front seat of the Acura, all hunched up and silent and Brittany sat in the back, staring out the window and wishing she was already eighteen and going off to college. Better yet, she would use the college fund her father left her to take a trip around the world. Eighteen was old enough to travel alone and it *was* her inheritance, wasn't it? She imagined herself standing on the front porch with her duffle bag packed, waving a casual hand to her mother and sister, saying, "Don't expect a card till Easter. I'll be busy looking at the pyramids and swimming in the Mediterranean." In her daydream, her mother and sister were weeping and they were very, very sorry they'd been so cruel to her.

When they parked, Willow said, "Let's go to Hunsaker's first. They have the most departments. And let's look at skirts and sweaters for Anna first."

"I think I'll go check the Mystical Dragon first," Brittany said. "Give me my money."

"No money," Willow answered. "I just have one credit card. Mom said we should stick together."

"Do we have to hold hands?" Brittany asked, teasing.

Anna looked so nervous that Brittany thought she might like to do exactly that. When Willow led them into the skirts and sweaters department, Anna looked as though she might bolt and run. She stood still though and let Willow pick out things that she liked.

Brittany watched as Willow pulled out one and then another skirt and sweater that were very cute and collegiate and totally unsuitable for Anna. Most of them looked as though they would be too short and Anna didn't say anything but she shook her head quickly and Willow put them back.

After about thirty minutes of getting absolutely nowhere, Brittany said, "Why don't we split up? Willow, you can wait for us at the Food Emporium. Anna and I will pick our own clothes. Then all you'll have to do is sign the credit slip."

Willow shook her head. "No, I promised."

"Then at least cut me free," Brittany said. "I'm only making Anna miserable."

"You behave yourself," Willow said. "We're sticking together."

Brittany shrugged and plopped herself down in a chair. "Why don't you look for something for yourself?" Willow asked.

"I wouldn't be caught dead in this stuff. It all looks like it's out of a forties' movie called *Junior Miss* or maybe *Junior Mistake*." Brittany was being deliberately nasty because she knew this was Willow's favorite department in her favorite store.

Willow ignored her and pushed Anna into agreeing to try on a plaid skirt and a pink sweater. As Anna walked away, Brittany said, "She's going to look like the Bride of Frankenstein in that, you know. Pink is *not* her color, it's yours."

"You are just being impossible," Willow said.

"She's in the wrong department. She's too tall and these clothes are too cute. You'll probably put her in a poodle skirt next."

Willow looked as though she might cry and that made Brittany madder than ever. Willow never fought back — she just crumpled and then that made *her* the bad one. It wasn't fair.

Sure enough, Anna came out of the dressing room and handed the skirt and sweater to Willow, saying, "No good."

"I thought you'd show us," Willow said. "That way, we could at least see what to try on next."

"I'd rather not have any new clothes," Anna said.

"Mother said I *had* to buy you clothes," Willow countered. Brittany wondered if Willow might really cry. It could happen. Anna looked as though she might start running and run all the way home. Brittany had been in the worst mood of all when they started out but now things were so bad she was almost getting interested. The whole day was a blueprint for disaster designed by Jessica when she gave Willow the credit card and told them to stick together. They had absolutely nothing in common except a few genes. What was it about mothers that made them think up unusual torture treatments like this one?

But Willow surprised her. Instead of insisting that Anna try on more clothes, she said, "I've got an idea. Why don't we split up? You and Brittany can go alone and pick out your own clothes. I'll wait for you in the Food Emporium."

"Could we?" Anna said hopefully.

"I don't see why not," Willow said. She was glowing now and Brittany was surprised to see that her sister was actually smiling at her. Willow was always beautiful with that long strawberry blond hair and those big blue-green eyes. When Willow smiled, her dimples showed and the whole room seemed to light up. Brittany was almost tempted to smile back.

Then she noticed that the smile was actually grazing her shoulder and going beyond her. Her sister wasn't smiling at her — she was pretending for an audience. Brittany turned to see who Willow was really aiming all that candlepower at and saw a group of high school students behind her. In the middle of the group was her own secret love — Lars Peterson!

Willow waved and floated past her little sister and big cousin as though she'd never met them before. Brittany and Anna watched as

Willow joined a group of about ten teenagers and they moved away laughing and talking.

Brittany wished with all her heart that she could run over to Willow and insist on being included but that was impossible. In the first place, they were nearly all seniors and Willow was only a junior herself. All social protocol would be broken if she tried to include Anna, a sophomore. Besides that, she hadn't been very nice to Willow this morning.

Brittany sighed. She knew it was hopeless but it would have been nice to be included in the group. Just to be close to Lars would be wonderful. She never really had been. She just admired him from a distance and he didn't even know who she was. Lars was tall, blond, handsome, and nice. He was the most popular boy in the senior class and most girls would give a lot just to get a smile from him. He didn't date anyone but they were all hoping that one of these days, he would select someone special. Brittany suspected that Willow was hoping that she would be that someone special.

Of course, a lot of boys already liked Willow. She *was* beautiful and sweet and nice. But Brittany hoped that behind those wonderful blond good looks of Lars Peterson was a man who would rather have an interesting woman — a woman who had a thirst for life — someone like her. Brittany didn't see any reason at all why Lars wouldn't want her if she could just get to know him. She was planning to make that her freshman project.

As she was thinking all these thoughts, she blinked and when she opened her eyes, Anna was gone. Brittany shrugged and went to the Mystical Dragon where she tried on some purple boots that laced halfway up the calf and told the salesgirl to hold them. Then she made her way to the Retro Express where all the clothes were dramatic hand-me-downs from the sixties or earlier. She loved a cotton wrap-around skirt from the fifties but it was not really warm enough for winter. She picked out a pair of tie-dyed bell-bottoms and a large, scarlet wool hooded sweater with heavy pearls sewn on as a fake collar. She also put aside a long, black velvet skirt and a black satin shawl with embroidered roses and fringe. For school, she found a pair of white wool pants and sweater that looked like they came from a ski movie. She could tuck the pants inside her boots and look really different from anyone else.

When she'd reached her financial limit, she found Willow alone in the Food Emporium. "What happened to your friends?" Brittany asked.

"They were on their way to the lake," Willow answered. "I couldn't go because I had you."

"That's not my fault," Brittany pointed out. "Besides, if they'd really wanted you, they would have invited you to come later." When she saw the hurt look on Willow's face, she quickly added, "I found my clothes."

To her surprise, Willow came quietly and paid for everything without any arguments. Brittany figured she must be in a good mood because of meeting her friends. Willow had clearly forgotten their argument. Brittany loved her new clothes and that made the shopping trip a success.

They went back to the Food Emporium and Brittany had Chinese noodles with a taco and a Dr Pepper. As she munched, Willow complained, "Mom is really going to be mad at me for letting you buy those secondhand clothes. And nothing you can wear to school."

"I'll wear everything to school," Brittany said.

"That stupid shawl?"

"I'll save the shawl for special events and for our Thursday evenings." When they'd planned the boardinghouse, her mother decided that each Thursday would be a social evening when all the boarders would be invited along with some other guests. They were having their first Thursday evening next week.

"I know Mom is going to blame me that you bought those weird things. It isn't fair."

"You had a responsibility," Brittany said solemnly and she sucked Dr Pepper as loudly as she could just to annoy her sister. "You abandoned your post just to be with Lars Peterson."

"You . . . you brat!" Willow actually raised her hand but Brittany knew she would never hit her. It was fun to drive Willow up the wall because when Willow got there, she never knew what to do.

"What is he like?" Brittany asked.

"Who?"

"You know who."

"I had many friends in the group," Willow pointed out.

"There was only one Lars Peterson in the group. What's he really like?" Brittany coaxed.

But her sister either didn't know what to say or didn't want to talk about him. She said, "He's nice."

"Everyone knows that."

"That's all there is," Willow said. "He's nice and he doesn't talk much. Why do you care?"

"I know you're crazy about him," Brittany

answered quickly. Better to attack than retreat, she figured.

The conversation stopped when Anna joined them. She was carrying a small shopping bag from the women's budget department of Hunsaker's Department Store. She said, "I told them to charge it to your mother's account, just like you said and they did. I hope I didn't spend more than she intended."

"I doubt that you could in that department," Brittany said. Willow frowned at her to shut her up, and Anna opened her shopping bag and pulled out a pair of navy blue polyester slacks and a navy blue wool and polyester sweater. "They were long enough and they were practical," Anna said proudly.

Brittany and Willow looked at each other in dismay. The clothes Anna picked were too old for their grandmother. While Willow's clothes were a little too cute and collegiate and Brittany's clothes were definitely wild, no one — absolutely no one — would wear the pants and sweater like the ones Anna purchased. What would their friends say when they introduced this cousin?

Chapter 5

Anna had a hard time concentrating on what was going on the first day of school. Everything was so much bigger than it had been in her old school that it was like being dropped into a different world.

Teachers were polite enough when she asked her way but they seemed too busy to give really good directions. Anna was lost most of the morning and she missed one class entirely because it was in room 3E and she was only able to find rooms 3A and 3D. She never did figure out where the letters B, C, and E were.

Once, Anna saw her cousin Brittany talking to a group of boys and she almost went over to say hello but she didn't. Brittany seemed to be having so much fun and if she went over, her cousin would feel responsible and leave her friends. So, in the end, Anna just hung around the hall until the period was over and she could go to her next class.

At lunch, she found the cafeteria without any trouble because everyone was rushing toward it. She stood in line by herself and didn't really mind because there were a lot of other kids who didn't seem to know anyone, too.

When she got her tray, she looked around for Brittany or Willow and all she could see was an ocean of heads bobbing back and forth. Though she stood quite still and looked carefully, she couldn't see any redheads at all. Brittany and Willow didn't seem to be there.

She went over to a table and sat down at the end and began to eat her sandwich. When she tried to open her milk, she realized she didn't have a straw and so she went back to the line. This time the line was much shorter and she could see that her cousins were a few people ahead of her. She moved up closer.

They didn't see her but she got close enough to hear what Brittany was saying. "I don't care what Mom says. She's strange and I'm not going to eat with her."

"I can't do it," Willow wailed. "She's the funniest-looking girl in the school. Did you ever see such big feet? She must wear those tennis shoes because they're all that fit."

"You have to eat with her," Brittany said.

"I'm meeting Teddy and you're the oldest, and we can't be nasty."

"We could take turns," Willow offered. "You eat with her today and I'll eat with her tomorrow. At least till she makes friends of her own."

"She'll never make friends," Brittany said.

Anna backed off quietly so they wouldn't know she'd been anywhere near earshot. She drank her milk directly from the carton and finished her sandwich in two bites. By the time the Winston girls had their food, Anna was ready to leave the cafeteria.

"Wait a minute," Brittany called.

But Anna turned and left, pretending she hadn't heard them. She would never let them know she'd heard them and she'd never, never eat lunch with them or try to be friendly again.

She went directly to the women's room where she washed her face and combed her hair. As she combed her soft, light brown hair, she looked in the mirror. She was tall but she was glad she was tall. It made her a good basketball player and that was the most important thing in her life.

Did being tall make her funny-looking? Or was it that she wasn't wearing any makeup at all? But she would feel silly in eye makeup and she suspected she would look silly, too. She stared into her own clear blue eyes and looked at her high forehead, wide cheekbones, and pointed chin to see what was so funny-looking. As far as she could see, she looked normal enough. So she wasn't little and cute like Brittany or beautiful like Willow, but that didn't make her funny-looking, did it?

She frowned at her reflection, blinking back tears, and told herself not to be silly. Lots of people had a hard time the first few days of school. It was bound to be difficult at the beginning. Pretty soon she would find some guys to play basketball with and things would be better. Then her silly cousins could go their own way and she'd go hers. She was an independent person and she was going to act like one.

Chapter 6

The next day, Jessica said she wanted to put Anna in Brittany's room. "Over my dead body!" Brittany yelled and left before anyone tried to talk her out of it.

When she came out an hour later, her mother tried again. "I know we planned to put Anna with a boarder but she is your cousin," Jessica reasoned. "And you girls are about the same age."

"She's almost Willow's age," Brittany argued. "Put her in with Willow."

"She'll be better off with you," her mother said briskly. "You have more . . . more empathy."

"I have absolutely no empathy," Brittany protested. "I am a spoiled brat. And I'm sloppy. Anna will hate it."

"It's true you're a spoiled brat," Jessica

agreed complacently, "but you have a good heart."

"I do *not* have a good heart!" Brittany slammed out the door and practically ran down to Teddy's house to complain about the latest foolishness at the Winston house. Teddy was doing his homework but he listened to Brittany complain for a while before he said, "I really feel sorry for Anna. She seems like a good enough kid and you girls aren't very nice to her."

"That's not true."

"You told me about the shopping trip yourself."

"That was a disaster," Brittany agreed. "But I tried to help her with the dishes last night."

"And when she said no, she could manage, you went off to read a book."

"Let's change the subject." Brittany knew he didn't really know that — it was just a lucky guess.

"Okay. How's your dreamboat Carlos?" Teddy asked.

"He's not my dreamboat. But he's a nice guy. Very smooth. He actually kissed my mother's hand before he went to class today."

Teddy laughed and asked, "What did your mother do?"

"She blushed. Imagine a woman my mother's age blushing when a college student kisses her hand." Brittany turned and asked Teddy, "Do you suppose she thought up this whole idea because she's looking for a boyfriend? Maybe she's interested in younger men?"

Teddy shook his head. "Your mother thought up this idea to fill the space in her life. She'll keep thinking up weird things until she finds something she really likes to do."

"You really do believe the boardinghouse is temporary?"

"Probably all be gone by Thanksgiving — Christmas at the latest," Teddy promised. "You got your algebra done?"

"You don't? Where were you this afternoon? Jason, Mitch, and I waited for you. We were supposed to do it together."

"Can you keep a secret?" Teddy asked.

"Of course I can."

"You never have before," Teddy reminded her.

"So you told me that secret about your money buried in the tin can and I told a few people. So that was in the fifth grade."

"And the whole fifth-grade class dug up my grandmother's backyard garden. And what about the time you decided to tell everyone about the journal I was keeping, and Mitch got hold of it and started quoting my poetry."

"You're writing poetry again?"

"Not really. Some song lyrics, that's all."

"You're in love?"

Teddy looked at her with disgust and said, "Forget it. You would tell if I told you and I've decided not to tell anyone till it's time."

"You're building a boat?"

"Why would you think that?" But his tone of voice told she'd hit on something. He sounded a little freaked.

"I just got this picture of you sailing away. All of us waving on the shore and you saying, 'It's time to go.' "

"You really are weird," Teddy said. "There's no ocean anywhere near Madison."

"I got it — didn't I?" Brittany asked with triumph. "I am *psychic!* You're building a boat to sail away in the springtime. Going across the Great Lakes to the Saint Lawrence Seaway and then to the South Seas?"

"Let me see your homework," Teddy said.

"Nope. You missed the study session."

"Mr. Switzer said we could work together."

"You aren't going to tell me, are you?"

"What did you get for number seventeen? Was it twenty-four-x?"

"Yes. Where are you building the boat?"

"Just hang it up, Britt. I'm not telling you

anything about anything and there are no boats," Teddy said.

Brittany changed her tactic. "If I tell you a secret that no one knows — a secret that I'd rather die than have anyone know — will you tell me yours?"

"I already know your big secret," Teddy said.

"You do not."

"Sure I do."

Brittany stood up and put her hands on her hips as though they were both five years old again. How many times had she and Teddy argued like this about nothing? But tonight she was feeling a little bored with the game. She would rather go home and watch television than banter with a child.

"Your secret is that you are in love with Lars Peterson," Teddy said.

"That's ridiculous!" Brittany yelled.

"Probably is," Teddy agreed, "but it's also very easy to see. Every time he walks by, you melt."

"I do not." Brittany pulled on her coat and stormed out of the room. She slammed the door, too.

Brittany walked so fast she was practically running toward her home. The short block seemed to take forever because the first really

44

cold weather of the season blew icy air onto her uncovered head and face as she marched along the familiar street. The few tears that squeezed out of her eyes ran down her cheeks and burned as the frost hit her cheeks. She was furious with Teddy, of course. He had no reason to humiliate her like that. But she was also furious at herself for letting her feelings for Lars show so plainly.

She wondered if everyone could tell how crazy she was about the handsome senior? Did Willow know? Did the kids in her class know? Did they all think she was ridiculous? And what about Lars? Did he even notice the skinny little freshman with the bright red hair and the big green eyes? And if he noticed her, did he think she was a fool?

When she got home, Anna was holding the telephone in her hand and she said, "It's for you."

Brittany took the phone and barked into the receiver, "I don't want to talk about it, not ever again."

"I'm sorry, Britt," Teddy said. "I didn't think you'd freak that way. I won't tease you again."

"You're too young for me," Brittany said suddenly. It was something she'd been thinking for over a year now and she blurted it out loud. "I don't want to be best friends anymore."

"I'll tell you my secret," Teddy offered.

"I don't care."

"I'm taking dance lessons on Thursday afternoons. I don't want anyone to know because they'd think . . ."

"They'd think it's weird and so do I." Brittany wanted to hang up but she had to ask, "So what has that big secret got to do with ships?"

"I've tried out for the lead part in the school play, *The Good Ship Grease*. It's a musical. Mostly R and B but some tap and some rap music."

"You won't get the lead. You're only a freshman."

"Well, I tried out. And there's more. I've definitely decided that I'm going to have a career in show business. Dancing, writing songs, singing, you know."

"That's ridiculous."

"Just don't tell anyone," Teddy warned. "I figure *everyone* will think it's ridiculous until they see how good I am. Then they'll think I'm talented. You know how that works."

"So your plan is to get the lead part and keep it a secret until opening night? You're not tall enough. You're not old enough. You're not . . ."

"I'm not Lars Peterson," Teddy interrupted with a hurt voice. "But Lars isn't trying out for a part and as a matter of fact, there is a shortage of male dancers and singers at Madison High. I think I might have a chance."

"About as much chance as I have to get a date with Lars," Brittany said crisply.

"Wish me luck," Teddy demanded.

"All right. Good luck. You're nuts but good luck."

"See you tomorrow in algebra. Right?"

"Right." Brittany hung the phone up thoughtfully. Getting rid of Teddy as her best friend wasn't going to be so easy but it was definitely in her plans for her freshman year. She couldn't afford to be seen with a goofy kid who thought tap dancing and singing was the way to be popular. She needed some grown-up, sophisticated friends. Someone more on her wavelength.

Chapter 7

Willow tried not to see Anna sitting alone in the cafeteria. She wanted with all her heart and soul to join a group of senior girls who were sitting along the left wall. She would be welcome because several of them were very friendly to her. And they were friends of Lars Peterson so there was always the possibility that Lars would join them.

Willow knew what she wanted to do, but today it was just too hard to pretend not to see Anna. She looked around quickly, hoping that Brittany would release her from this unpleasant duty but Brittany was nowhere in sight. She sighed and slipped into the seat beside her cousin and asked, "Hi, how are you doing?"

"Fine," Anna answered.

"Did you get to all your classes?" Willow knew it was a week late to be asking the question but she had to say something. This morning, while Anna was out running, her mother laid the law down — telling them that they had to be nice to Anna and that was that. It was all Brittany's fault, of course. It was Brittany who told her mother that Anna ate alone every day and that was when Jessica made them promise. Count on Brittany to talk too much at the wrong times.

But at least if Brittany were here, she would have filled in the big holes in the conversation. Willow repeated her question, "Your classes all right?" It wasn't just that Anna was strange-looking that made it so difficult, it was also that she was so silent.

"My classes are fine," Anna answered. She ate the last of her peas and carrots and stood up, saying, "I heard there was a basketball court close by. Where?"

"You mean here on campus?"

"No." Anna shook her head. "The boys have that one at lunch. Someone told me there was a court east of the school. About two blocks?"

Willow shrugged and sunk a little into her seat. She could see Lars Peterson looking over their way and it was just too embarrassing to be seen with Anna. So far, no one had said anything about her cousin but she knew that people must notice the silent, large, overgrown girl with the short, wispy hair and weird clothes.

Willow wished she had really helped Anna find some decent clothes. Since that disastrous shopping day last Saturday, Anna had worn the navy blue slacks and sweater three days and a white cotton blouse that was probably her mother's with some black slacks the other two. And she always wore those dirty white tennis shoes. She must wear size twelve shoes, Willow thought.

Anna left quietly and Willow wished she had the nerve to get up and join her friends. But she would feel too weird now that Lars was sitting with the others. All the girls were so silly about him. Brittany practically melted into the floor every time she saw him, and she didn't want him to think she was just another silly girl.

Willow ate all of her dessert, even though she had promised herself she would only taste it. She felt sorry for herself sitting there all alone and she hoped no one noticed that she didn't have any friends to eat with. Nevertheless, a still, small voice within told her she'd put herself in this difficult position. She could have ignored Anna. Or she could have asked Anna to join her and the others. Willow sighed. She'd tried to be nice and ended up all alone. It wasn't fair.

She finished her dessert and stood up. If she walked slowly by her friends maybe someone would invite her over. That way, she wouldn't feel so pushy. But no one even looked up as she walked by and she was soon outside the cafeteria with nothing to do but go to the library and study for the remainder of the lunch hour.

In the library, Willow sighed and slumped into a chair, thumbing through a magazine. It didn't really help to think about the boarders.

Still, the boarders were kind of interesting. Carlos was the most handsome and he always seemed to be flirting with her. He called her beautiful every time he saw her. She wasn't sure it meant much to him but it was nice to hear.

The other one who was always nice to her was Dan — the one from Wyoming and he really was a help around the house. Dan was always offering to fix things. Justin always spoke to her when they met. Justin was a definite possibility.

Of course, the best boy of all was Lars even though he was just in high school. He was definitely nice and he was the best-looking boy in school. Everyone said so.

Willow sighed and drew a heart on the cover of the magazine and then she drew an arrow through it and wrote *W loves L P*. When she realized what she'd done she swiftly ripped the cover off the magazine. She folded it up and put it in her pocket and hurried out of the library. How embarrassing it would be if anyone had seen that childish stunt!

Lars Peterson was waiting outside her fifth-period study hall! He was leaning up against the wall with his hands in his pockets, and he looked so casual and so relaxed that Willow envied him. She clutched her books to her chest as she smiled and said, "Hi. What are you doing here?"

"Waiting to say hello to you," Lars said and then he smiled and said, "hello."

He was gone in a split second and Willow stood in the hall looking at his departing back. What was that all about?

Willow wasn't sure if he was kidding or serious but she was certainly a lot more cheerful than she had been earlier. One thing she knew — she would have to start being a nicer person if she wanted to have Lars for a boyfriend. He was always courteous, hardworking, and studious. During her study period she decided to get an A on her history exam and be nice to Anna. She was going to start changing her ways this very evening.

Chapter 8

Anna found the basketball court easily but there were a group of three men already on it. They were obviously older — maybe college age or maybe more. She was disappointed but decided to hang around a few minutes and watch them play.

One guy was really good. He was so good that she decided he might be a professional player. She stuffed her hands in her pockets and stood absolutely still, hoping her presence would go unnoticed.

The man was so aggressive, so fast, and so smooth that the other two guys laughed and complained constantly. The one-man team never said anything.

He moved like a machine and Anna watched him with hungry eyes. That's how she wanted her body to move. That's why she'd moved to Madison. That's what she was going to learn.

Standing still, with the cold wind blowing on her face, she began to jog in place. It was fascinating to see the way the extraordinary player — they called him Joe — moved. She was so engrossed in watching him that she almost missed the chance to stop the ball when it came her way. But she caught it and tossed it to them.

Joe looked at her then and smiled, saying, "Thanks."

She nodded and the game went on for a few more minutes and then the two guys started complaining that it was snowing. It wasn't snowing but it was a very cold day for the first of October, and the wind did cut into Anna's neck and face as though it were ice needles.

She wanted to leave but she couldn't resist watching a little longer. When the two men quit, Joe dribbled up and down the court with his left and right hand a few times and then he tossed the ball directly at her. Anna caught the ball and threw it back. He tossed it back and called, "Can you score from there?"

She tossed the ball directly into the hoop and he grinned and said, "Come on in."

She moved into the middle of the court and he tossed a few more balls to her. She made every basket, easily and fast. Then he moved in to block her and she tried to dribble and move around him. It was hopeless. He grabbed the ball and tossed it over his shoulder, hitting the rim of the basket without even turning to aim.

"You're Joe Andrews, aren't you? You're on the university team," she asked.

"Yeah. What's your name?"

"Anna Goethe."

"Well, Anna, you need a little work on your defense," he said and moved around her as though she weren't there. Too late, she lunged after him and almost fell. He laughed and said, "Let's see you dribble."

She dribbled the ball up and down the court, using her right hand first and then her left. "Pretty good," he said. "Now speed it up and behind you."

Anna understood what he wanted but she'd never really tried to dribble the full length of the court with the ball behind her. She lost the ball about halfway down the court. He shook his head and grinned. "Sloppy performance. Let's try some jump shots."

For the next few minutes they tossed the ball back and forth and jumped into the air, making baskets from every point on the court. After Anna made a very long shot, Joe grabbed the ball, kept it, and came over to her. He had the ball tucked under his arm and he was more than a foot taller than she was. For Anna it was a strange experience to be looking up at someone.

He asked, "You've heard of me?"

Anna nodded. "Everyone has." Joe Andrews was the point guard for the University of Wisconsin basketball team. He'd been the major point man for two years, and the papers were full of stories about what pro team would get him when he graduated in June.

"How old are you, Anna?"

"Fifteen."

"You *are* good. You on the high school girls' team?"

Anna nodded. "I played on the boys' team in Saint Olaf's last year but I'm going on the girls' team here at Madison High."

"Why? You're good enough for the boys' team."

"The coach says I'll have a better chance at scholarships if I play women's ball. He also thinks we can win the state championship if I'm on it."

"Maybe he's right about the scholarships," Joe said. "This court is too cold to be any use anymore. Want to come toss some after school? I get an hour alone every Monday and

Thursday on campus. I've got a partner today but next Monday you could help me practice."

"Really?"

"Sure. All I need is someone to pace me and run after balls. I can help you and you can help me."

By now their noses were red. She smiled and nodded.

"Four to five on Monday and Thursdays," he said. "I'll give you some pointers on your defense."

"Really?" She realized she'd just asked that but she couldn't think of anything any smarter to say. If it hadn't been so cold and she hadn't been so sure she'd just played ball, she would have thought she was dreaming.

Joe nodded. "You could make something of yourself with some help. You *do* want to be an athlete, don't you?"

"Yes."

"I thought so," Joe laughed and said. "You've got that lean and hungry look. I remember it well."

"I'm tall enough for women's ball already," Anna said. "I'm five feet eleven."

"Good. See you Monday," Joe said. "Wellbourne Courts. Ask anyone."

Anna nodded and turned and jogged back to school. She was thirty minutes late to class and was assigned two nights' detention but she didn't care. This was Thursday. She could make up the detention tonight and Friday. By Monday, she'd be on a real college court playing basketball with Joe Andrews. Life was startling but wonderful.

She was so happy that she actually smiled and waved at her cousin Willow when she passed her in the hall. Willow slowed down and asked, "Where are you going?"

"Detention."

"You've got detention?"

"Yes. I was late to class."

"That's too bad," Willow said. "Don't forget that this is Thursday."

"Yes, this is Thursday." Sometimes Willow and Brittany said things that Anna simply didn't understand. They were such strange girls — they never seemed to be interested in anything of value. They talked back to their mother. Neither of them cared about school — although Brittany seemed to do well enough. And they certainly didn't like to work. As for sports — she could see the first day she came that neither of her cousins knew anything at all about sports.

"We're having our first Thursday evening — you remember. Thursdays are supposed to be sort of parties," Willow reminded her.

"I'll have homework," Anna said quickly. There was no way she was going to stand around feeling shy with a bunch of strangers.

"You *have* to be there," Willow said. "Everyone agreed. And Mom will really expect you to be there because you're a relative."

"I'll speak to Aunt Jessica," Anna said.

"It won't do any good at all," Willow said confidently. "Mom has her mind made up and when she gets these ideas, she holds on to them until she gets a better one."

Willow seemed to be walking away but then she slowed down and said, "I think I'll come to detention with you. We can walk home together later."

Anna was surprised until Willow called out to a tall blond boy, "Hi, Lars. What did *you* do to deserve detention?"

"No homework," Lars admitted. "I got to watching the NFL ball game and came to school empty-handed."

"Shame on you," Willow teased.

"What about you?" Lars asked.

"Oh, I'm innocent," Willow answered quickly. "I'm just keeping my cousin company. Are you sitting there? I'll sit beside you. You don't mind?"

"Not if you let me do my homework," Lars

answered. "I can leave when I get it done."

Willow chose a desk close to Lars and Anna sat on the other side of her. Anna didn't know Willow's friend and Williow didn't introduce her but she didn't really care. It was enough to have Joe Andrews know who she was. She opened her history book and started reading, trying to ignore her cousin's giggles and laughter. She didn't really care when Willow ignored her but she felt a little sorry for the tall, young man who obviously wanted to get his homework done.

When Willow and Lars left together about twenty minutes later, Willow said, "I'd better get on home and help Mom with her Thursday evening."

Anna nodded. She didn't want to walk home with Willow anyway. She wanted to jog home because she could use the extra training. If she was going to be practicing basketball with Joe Andrews, she could use all the training she could get.

Anna tried to concentrate on her history but her mind was really in the future. She skipped from dreading tonight's social ordeal to joyously anticipating next Monday's basketball opportunity. Finally, detention was over. She closed her books and packed them into her shoulder bag.

She breathed a lot easier when she left the closed building and stepped into the cold outdoors. It was almost dark as she jogged along the streets toward the Winston home. She loved this particular time of day when everything was in half light. She often felt as though she were free from all obligations when she was jogging. She hoped she would be able to capture that feeling on the run home, but try as she might, she couldn't shake the dread of the evening's ordeal.

Chapter 9

Brittany wore her long, black velvet skirt and her black satin shawl to their Thursday evening. No one else was very dressed up but she didn't really mind. She had checked her reflection several times before descending the staircase to the living room where everyone was gathered and she thought she looked dramatic and grown-up.

Carlos came over to her, saying, "Brittany, you look lovely. So sophisticated."

Jessica smiled brightly and said, "There you are, Brittany. I am hoping to persuade you and Willow to give us a little music."

"Mother!" Both sisters protested in unison.

Under her breath, Willow said to Brittany, "You look silly in that secondhand stuff."

"I think I look great. So does your boyfriend."

"Overdressed," Willow pronounced.

Brittany shrugged. She thought everyone else was underdressed. Jessica had on a simple navy dress with red and white trim at the bottom of the skirt and navy and red flats. She looked fine for an older woman.

Willow — well Willow was definitely casual but she looked wonderful in black tights and a big white peasant overblouse with a black turtleneck sweater underneath. The younger woman boarder who was Anna's roommate, Victoria Brown, was wearing jeans and a red sweater. She was pretty enough but she seemed to complain a lot and she certainly wasn't as pretty as Willow.

As for Anna . . . Anna looked horrible in her black slacks and white blouse. She'd done something to her hair — maybe wet it and run a comb through it to pull it back. And she had on some funny black shoes that looked too small. Anna looked miserable and she probably was. She sat on a straight-backed chair in the corner and answered questions with yes or no a couple of times. After that, no one tried to talk to her.

Brittany hoped that the party would perk up enough so that she and Willow wouldn't have to perform and she tried to keep the conversation moving. First, she took some nuts and cookies over to the two newest boarders,

Harry and Larry Zimbalist. "You guys sure you aren't twins?" she asked once again. They were exactly the same height, had the same profiles, and dark brown curly hair. In fact, they looked so much alike that she couldn't really tell them apart except when they were together — she could see that one had a lot more freckles.

"I'm a year older," the one with the most freckles answered. "But we're freshmen together because I was sick for a year."

"So you must be young," Brittany said and then she blushed. Sometimes she blurted out things that sounded so — so unsophisticated. Even if she was wearing long black velvet, they would think she was just a child.

"I'm seventeen," one answered. "Harry's eighteen."

"Next week I'll be nineteen," Harry added. "For one month, I'm two years older than Larry."

Brittany laughed and settled down in a chair beside them. At least they were somewhere near her age and they seemed cheerful enough. She spent the next fifteen minutes asking them questions and they answered promptly but they didn't exactly know how to keep a conversation rolling. They didn't joke or ask her questions, they just answered hers as politely as if they were talking to someone's grandmother.

Finally, Brittany stood up and said, "At least from now on I'll know that Harry is the oldest." She didn't add that he also had the most freckles. But she knew she'd be able to keep them apart and that was something. Still, she couldn't just spend the whole evening with them so she looked around for someone else to talk to.

Dan was sitting on a dining room straight-backed chair that was pulled into the living room, and he didn't look like he was having a whole lot of fun. Brittany decided to join him. She pulled in another dining room chair and sat down beside him. "So how's it going?"

"Okay," Dan answered. "Your sister's having fun."

Brittany sighed. She could tell by the tone of his voice that Willow had made another conquest. And the infuriating thing was Willow's complete indifference to the reaction she was producing as she moved through a room. Brittany often saw boys' faces at school. There was something about the way Willow was so cool and self-controlled and beautiful that drove men into desperation. Once or twice, she'd even seen that look on Teddy's face when Willow walked by him and obviously didn't know he was alive. So sometime in the last week, Dan had fallen for Willow and, of course, Willow didn't have a clue. What's more, if she did, she wouldn't have known what to do about it.

Brittany followed Dan's gaze to the corner of the room where Willow sat with Carlos on her left and Justin on her right. Justin was telling a long story and Willow was smiling and laughing, dividing her attention evenly between the two men.

Brittany shrugged. She was used to people thinking Willow was beautiful. Willow was beautiful. "Willow's easy to please," Brittany said. "Now, I'm fussy. I only like certain people." She turned toward Dan, hoping he would see that she was flirting and flirt back but he was still looking across the room with a preoccupied stare.

Brittany said, "I think I'll go see if Mother wants anything." Dan didn't even seem to notice she left him.

Brittany found her mother sitting in a conversation area near the window. She was talking with Victoria Brown.

Victoria paused midstream to include Brittany in her conversation, "Now here's a girl with real style. Bellamy, I love your velvets.

Did you find them in Madison? They're so California. I'm from California, you know."

"I'm Brittany. My skirt came from the Retro Express. It's in the mall. But everything there is secondhand so maybe it did come from California." As usual, Brittany felt she'd answered a simple question with a complicated reply. They should have some way to take words back, Brittany thought. Catch them and censor them like they do when you call on the radio with the thirty-second delay.

"I don't see how you bear to wear anything this light," Victoria said. "I'm absolutely freezing. I told my dad I wouldn't be able to stand the weather but he *insisted* an Eastern education would be good for me." She laughed and raised her arm to rattle the bracelets on her arm. There were ten or twenty of them — all glass-beaded and probably from India. "I told him that if he wanted me to have an Eastern education he should send me back to India but he sent me to Wisconsin. Isn't that a scream?" Victoria laughed and laughed and the others looked on, wondering what they'd missed.

Anna was the first to go to her room. She stood up abruptly at eight-fifteen and said, "I have homework and I have to get up early." Then she turned and practically ran out.

Victoria frowned after her and said, "Strange girl. I hope she remembers to clean the bathtub."

"I think Anna is very neat," Jessica said.

Victoria sighed and looked out the window as though she were enduring a great hardship just being there.

Dan stood up and stretched and yawned and said, "Thanks, Mrs. Winston. I guess I'll turn in, too."

By nine o'clock, the Zimbalist brothers were gone. So was Victoria, and only Carlos and Justin, Willow and Brittany, and her mother remained. Jessica moved to the couch and patted the seat beside her. Brittany came over and sat close to her. Jessica asked, "How do you think it's going?"

"I think Thursday evenings are too old-fashioned," Brittany answered honestly. "Just because people live in the same house doesn't mean they have anything in common."

Jessica nodded thoughtfully. "We need to make it more like a real party. Next Thursday, I'll insist that you and Willow sing and play. And I'll invite some other people. You can ask Teddy and I'll ask a few of my friends."

"I don't want to ask Teddy," Brittany said. "Teddy's too young for me."

Jessica smiled and patted her daughter's

hand. "Did you enjoy talking to Harry and Larry?"

Brittany said, "They aren't exactly great conversationalists."

"They are computer nerds," her mother said.

Brittany laughed. "I never thought I'd hear you call anyone a nerd."

"That's what they called themselves."

"At least Willow had a good time," Brittany said enviously. "She's had Justin and Carlos hanging over her all evening."

"Willow will always have young men around," her mother said philosophically. Then she patted Brittany's hand again and said, "And one of these days, you will, too."

But Brittany didn't find "one of these days" very comforting.

Chapter 10

When Willow woke on Friday morning, the first thing she thought about was Carlos. He certainly was handsome. She loved the way his eyes crinkled when he smiled. And she loved the way he called her, "Beautiful lady."

Sometimes she thought Carlos was flirting with her and sometimes she thought it was just the way he was. But whether he was serious about her or not, he was fun to be around. And Carlos had asked her to go to the movies tonight. Now, if she could just get her mother to say yes.

Willow went to the dresser and began to brush her long blond hair. She smiled into the mirror, watching to see if *her* eyes crinkled. But her face remained smooth and her blue-green eyes looked back at her with the same peaceful look as when she was just staring at herself. Willow knew people thought she was beautiful. She'd heard that all her life.

Sometimes she wished she looked more like other people, so that she would know that people liked her just because she was herself. But this morning she was grateful for her special good looks. It had kept Carlos and Justin interested in her last night and she'd had a good time. It was fun to have two older men competing for your attention.

Justin was not as polite as Carlos and his manners were much more ordinary, but he was full of laughter and he was always teasing. He'd called her a "golden girl" and whispered that one of these days he'd catch her alone. As he whispered, his breath grazed her neck and sent shivers up and down her spine. She would have liked it better if his breath hadn't had alcohol on it. Justin seemed to like to drink a lot. She guessed he'd had three or four glasses of wine last night. Willow wasn't sure where he got it because her mother was strict about not serving the students. She and Carlos and the others drank ginger ale.

Willow showered, brushed her teeth, and selected a deep turquoise sweater to wear over her black tights and turtleneck. Then she picked up her black-and-turquoise sequin earrings that hung almost to her shoulders and put those on. Then she took them off and decided that she wanted to look nice but she didn't want to look too dressed up. She wouldn't want Carlos or Justin to think she'd dressed up just for them.

When she got to the breakfast table, Mrs. Shelley, the cook, was putting hard-boiled eggs on the table. Each morning, there was a big spread on the Winston dining table: hard-boiled eggs, English muffins, biscuits or toast, cheese, and fresh oranges and bananas. Breakfast every morning and four week nights of dinner were included in the fee her mother was charging.

Willow walked quietly into the dining room and the one boarder who was there, John Johnson, obviously didn't hear her. She watched as he slipped four pieces of toast, two eggs, and two bananas into his bookbag. Then he sat down and ate another four pieces of toast, cheese, three eggs, and two oranges for breakfast.

Willow stood in the doorway and watched him eat. Only two days ago, she'd found Jessica puzzling over the grocery bills. Her mother frowned and shook her head, saying, "I didn't really expect to make a lot of money, but at this rate we're actually losing. I can't have that."

Willow cleared her throat and walked into

the room. John Johnson didn't even look up and when she said, "Good morning," he just nodded his head. She had never really talked to him and she wondered if Jessica would expect her to say something to him about how much food he was taking. She decided that wasn't her place but she was going to tell her mother when she got a chance.

John Johnson talked with his mouth full and Willow found that very unpleasant so she chose a seat as far away from him as possible. She opened a magazine, which was on the kitchen magazine rack, and started reading a story about losing weight by cutting out desserts. She thought the article was interesting and was very disappointed when she turned the page and found the ending was missing. Someone had cut out a coupon.

Willow stood up and went into the kitchen where she asked Mrs. Shelley, "Could you not cut coupons out of the magazines until they're ready for the trash?"

"I didn't cut coupons," Mrs. Shelley said crossly. "He did." She pointed to John Johnson who was walking out of the dining room. "He cuts them out of everything. Cuts them off of the food packages, too."

"But that's silly," Willow said. "He isn't even buying groceries."

Mrs. Shelley shrugged and turned back to her work.

That afternoon, when Willow came home, she found Jessica in her studio out behind the house. Her mother was working on a big canvas and seemed pretty absentminded, but she put the paintbrushes down when Willow said, "I really want to talk to you. Come inside, it's too cold out here."

"There are too many people in the house," Jessica answered.

"The kitchen is empty," Willow answered. "Mrs. Shelley isn't due back for an hour."

They went into the kitchen and made themselves a cup of tea. Jessica sat down at the little round kitchen table and said, "We never sit here anymore. I miss it. There's always lots of people around."

Willow was worried that her mother was already losing interest in the boardinghouse. If that happened, Carlos and Justin and all the other college boys would move away. Willow wasn't ready to let that happen. "But I think the people are good for you," Willow said. "It makes life more interesting."

Jessica smiled at her daughter over the steaming tea and said, "Makes *your* life a lot more interesting. I agree. Of course, no one is making eyes at me."

"Carlos flirts with you. He kissed your hand yesterday."

Jessica laughed. "Carlos flirts with Brittany. For all I know, he's been flirting with Anna behind our backs. How is she doing? Does she have any friends yet? Did she make the basketball team?"

"All right. I just wanted to tell you that I saw John Johnson packing a huge lunch off of the breakfast table and taking it to school in his bookbag. He was really eating a lot. I figured if you were worried about not making money on the boardinghouse, you'd want to know."

"Thank you. I'm not exactly worried but I'll have to figure out what to do so we can at least break even. I can't believe he's really eating so much that it makes a difference."

"You'd believe if you saw what I saw."

But her mother clearly wanted to move on to pursue another topic. She said, "I'm more worried about Anna than what John is eating. How much can one person eat? Anna is our relative and our responsibility. How's she doing?"

Willow dropped her eyes and said, "All right, I guess."

"You guess. That means that poor girl is all

alone. Neither you nor Brittany has a charitable bone in your body."

"I'm nice to her when I see her," Willow protested. She felt guilty because she knew she was avoiding Anna as much as possible.

"You know I'm counting on you girls to be decent, friendly people," Jessica said rather sternly.

Willow flushed. "Mother, I'm really trying," Willow said. Then she added, "And I'll try harder. Mom, Carlos asked me to go to the movies tonight. Okay?"

"Not okay. He's at least twenty years old and you are sixteen. Definitely not okay."

"He just asked to be friendly. I mean it's not a real date or anything. It just sort of came up in conversation that I hadn't seen *The Lonely Rider* and neither had he so we decided to go. Very casual."

"Then you can take Anna along."

"Mother!"

"And Brittany. And I think I'd like to see it, too. That's right, we'll *all* go. What time should we be ready?"

"That's ridiculous!" Willow wailed.

But at dinner that night, when her mother told Carlos that she and Anna and Brittany wanted to see *The Lonely Rider* also, he smiled and said, "I'm a very lucky fellow to be able to escort so many beautiful ladies. Wonderful!"

As it worked out, Anna said she had to study and Brittany was going somewhere with Teddy so only she and her mother went to the movies with Carlos. He sat between the two of them and the only time his hand even brushed Willow's was when he reached for some of her popcorn.

Chapter 11

"So how was your Thursday evening bash?" Teddy asked Brittany at school the next day. They were eating lunch together and they were alone.

"It was weird," Brittany answered. "You're invited next week."

"You talked to the college boys?"

"Some," Brittany admitted. "Willow was the popular one though. I guess she always will be."

"Not necessarily," Teddy said. "You may grow tall and beautiful in time, my dear."

"She's not tall," Brittany said. She wasn't sure why she was having this conversation. Mostly, she didn't like to discuss the difference between her looks and her sister's. It wasn't that she was ugly, it was that Willow was especially beautiful. The contrast kind of shook people up. Long ago, Brittany had gotten used to that "and here's the little sister" look that people got when they met them both at the same time. Mostly, she preferred to have her own friends and her own activities. It was just easier to be accepted for herself that way.

"So how's your theatrical career?" she asked.

"You haven't told anyone?"

"No. But how do you think you're going to keep it a secret? Once you start rehearsing, everyone will know. I mean, they'll put your name in the school paper or something."

"No one reads the school paper," Teddy answered.

"But people will know. Anyway, why do you care?"

"I care because I care," Teddy answered. He reached for her cake and asked, "You don't want this?"

She pretended to stab his hand with her fork and said, "You're afraid Mitch and the others will say you're weird, right?"

"Right."

"But when they see you in the show, they'll say you're weird anyway and maybe they'll even be harder on you because you kept it a secret."

"I'm going to be terrific in the show."

"Did you get the lead?"

"Won't know till Monday but I know I got a good part."

"How?"

"Everytime the drama coach sees me in the hall, he says, 'Hi there, Myers.' He never knew my name before and he wouldn't know it now if I hadn't made a great impression."

"Nothing like confidence," Brittany said, and she smiled her most brilliant smile at Teddy. The smile was actually aimed at Lars Peterson who was walking by their table but he missed it.

As Lars turned the corner, Teddy said, "Let me guess. Lars the Magnificent just walked by and you tried to dazzle him but fizzled. Am I right?"

"I don't know what you're talking about." Brittany bit down on the cake she was eating so hard that she hurt her teeth on the fork.

"You're getting a lot like your sister," Teddy said.

"And you're getting so I never know what you're talking about."

"Willow's got this awful trick of smiling over your shoulder. You're supposed to think it's for you but it's really for some poor guy twenty feet away. Now you're doing it."

"Get over it." Brittany said and stood up

abruptly, pushing her chair back so fiercely that it tumbled over. To her dismay, Lars came over and picked it up for her.

She blushed and said, "Thanks."

"It's okay," he answered and then smiled at her. When he smiled she forgot to breathe. That made her feel dizzy and a little goofy. She was actually grateful to Teddy when he broke the silence.

"How you doing, Peterson?" Teddy asked, as though they were the best of friends. "Think we're going to have a good basketball team this year?"

Lars kind of frowned and shrugged. "I don't know. I hope we do better than last season. We need some bigger players."

"Yeah," Teddy agreed. Then he actually clapped Lars Peterson on the shoulder and said, "But you fought the good fight. You did your best."

"Sports isn't about doing your best," Lars answered. "Sports is about winning." Then he laughed out loud and said, "At least that's what Coach Contraro says."

"We'll do better this year," Teddy encouraged him.

"Your sister going to be a cheerleader again?" Lars asked Brittany.

"Yes," Brittany answered, and then she added, "And so am I. At least, I'm going to try out for cheerleader."

"Good girl," Lars said and then he walked away.

Brittany was grateful that Teddy waited until Lars was out of hearing range before he said, "That was really stupid!"

"What's stupid about trying out for cheerleader?"

"You didn't even think of it till the great Lars stopped to talk to you. What would you want to be a cheerleader for?"

"What do you want to be an actor for?"

"That's different," Teddy said. "I've got talent."

"Well, maybe I've got talent, too."

"And I'm doing it because I really want to do it — not just to compete with my sister for a guy."

"I don't know why I even talk to you," Brittany said. "I don't think I will anymore." She turned and left.

Chapter 12

Willow woke at seven on Saturday morning and she went downstairs, hoping to have a quiet cup of chocolate and some toast before the crowd arrived. Mrs. Shelley was due at six-thirty and probably wouldn't want any interference, but she could take her breakfast on a tray into the little day porch off the kitchen.

Willow tiptoed down the stairs, grateful that Dan had fixed the squeaky ones. But when she went into the kitchen John Johnson and Victoria were together around the empty stove.

"There's no coffee," Victoria accused Willow with a frown.

"Where's Mrs. Shelley?" Willow asked.

"She's late," John Johnson complained. "And I'm due at my job in thirty minutes. Breakfast is part of my arrangement, you know."

"I know," Willow said. "I'll try and scramble some eggs."

"And toast, yogurt, juice, and cheese," John Johnson reminded her.

"Hi." Brittany walked into the kitchen, rubbing her eyes. "You're up early."

"Good," Willow said. "I'm glad to see you." If the truth were told, she had never been so glad to see anyone because Willow had never cooked in her life. As long as she could remember, they'd had a cook and though Jessica always talked about how the girls should learn to cook, she'd never actually allowed them to try.

Willow pulled Brittany aside and said in a whisper, "You've got to help me. Mrs. Shelley isn't here and they are hungry and cranky."

"I can't cook," Brittany protested. "And neither can you."

"You can do the toast and coffee. I'll tackle the eggs." Willow insisted.

"This is not my job," Brittany said. "I'll just make myself a cup of tea and go back to bed. Mrs. Shelley will be here soon."

John called over to Willow, "You'd better hurry with those eggs. If I don't get my breakfast, I won't pay my board for today."

"That is the tightest human being I have ever met," Brittany said in a fairly loud voice.

"Yesterday, I saw him stand and wait for a nickel's change from the paperboy for ten minutes. And then he wrote the expense in his notebook."

"Quiet," Willow said. "And get the English muffins out of the freezer. If we give them muffins it will make the eggs seem better."

Brittany burnt the English muffins and Willow put too much cheese in the scrambled eggs, but they were able to feed the first group of boarders pretty fast. John Johnson left for work on time and though he grumbled, he didn't threaten to stop paying his bill anymore.

Carlos was the next one down and came directly to the kitchen, asking, "How can you two women be so beautiful so early in the morning?"

"We have to cook your breakfast," Willow explained. "Mrs. Shelley isn't here."

Willow did a better job on his eggs because these didn't have any shells in them. However, Carlos took one look at the English muffins and asked for wheat toast. Brittany tried not to look hurt.

As Brittany carried the muffins into the kitchen, she looked around and asked, "Where *is* Mrs. Shelley?"

"Who's left?" Willow worried. "Just Anna and Mom — they can cook their own eggs."

"And Dan and Harry and Larry," Brittany reminded her.

Willow groaned and carried the heavy black skillet over to the sink to clean it. As she did so, Dan walked into the kitchen and said, "Let me do that." He took the heavy skillet from her and starting scraping the fried eggs off the bottom and sides.

Willow handed him the liquid soap but he shook his head and said, "Never wash an iron skillet. It will rust."

Willow smiled and asked, "Then how do you clean it?"

"It will come clean with the spatula and scraping," Dan explained. "Then you can rinse if off and put it on the stove to dry fast. The heat of the fire disinfects it."

"Did you learn that on the ranch?"

Dan nodded. "Where I come from, everyone can scramble eggs. You girls are really something."

Instead of defending her eggs, Willow laughed and batted her eyes and told Dan how clever he was. Brittany watched in dismay as her older sister tricked the poor young cowboy into making breakfast for himself and the Zimbalist brothers as well as Willow and Brittany. When they were all finished, he went back into the kitchen to help clean up.

Anna came in from her run about the time they were cleaning the table. She pitched in immediately. She and Dan had the kitchen spotlessly clean in just a few minutes. Willow and Brittany watched as the two of them moved efficiently through the mess they'd created.

By the time Jessica came downstairs, there was no sign of an emergency and she was served by her daughters with grace. When she finished her second cup of coffee, she said, "You girls managed very well."

Willow looked at Brittany and Brittany burst out laughing. Willow tried to ignore her sister's outburst but couldn't and she started laughing also. Jessica looked from one to the other and asked, "Am I missing something?"

"We had help," Willow admitted. "Dan helped us some."

This understated admission sent Brittany into more peals of laughter and she hooted, "Some! Dan did it all. Before he got here, it was a disaster. And then Anna came in and helped, too. We did our best but it wasn't good enough."

Jessica smiled and stood up, kissing them both on the cheek. "You did your best and that's all that's required." Then she moved to the telephone, saying, "Now, we'd better check on Mrs. Shelley."

There was no answer and Jessica looked worried as she said, "If she's not coming in, we have to think about lunch. And this is Saturday — the day the sheets are all changed. Oh, dear."

"I'll do what I can," Willow said doubtfully. "But I don't think we should try cooking again. Maybe order pizza?"

"We're already losing money on food," Jessica said. "But I suppose in an emergency . . . and this is our first month so it's natural that there would be a few hang-ups."

"A few hang-ups!" Brittany snorted. "I'd say the next hang-up will be us — get it?"

But no one seemed to be in the mood for her jokes. Willow just frowned and her mother didn't seem to hear. "I promised Teddy and the guys I'd work on algebra this afternoon," she said and headed for the door.

"Where are you going?" Willow asked.

"Out. I didn't sign up for a short course in homemaking," Brittany answered.

"You can't do that," Willow said. "You're a part of this family."

"My part of this family doesn't care if the boardinghouse succeeds or not," Brittany explained. "You're the one who's getting all the attention from the men and I'm too young to compete."

"You're too selfish," Willow said.

Jessica looked over at them absentmindedly and said, "Cooperation is helpful. Quarreling — while always unpleasant — is absolutely out of the question at the moment. *What* are we going to do? Do you think we could get a replacement for Mrs. Shelley?"

"On a Saturday morning?" Brittany asked. "I don't think so. Remember what happened when you put the ad in. You didn't exactly have a lot of takers."

"True," Jessica agreed. "I guess I'll have to cancel my appointments and we'll all three pitch in. Maybe Anna can help. Will you call her, Brittany?"

So Brittany went upstairs and took Anna away from her homework. She listened quietly as Jessica explained their problem and then she nodded. "You don't have to cancel your appointments, Aunt Jessica. And Brittany can go to Teddy's. And Willow can — Willow can study. I can do it all."

"My dear child, you don't have to do it all. It will be fine if you just help." Jessica seemed a little shocked at Anna's suggestion.

"I can do lunch," Anna insisted. "I'll make a salad and spaghetti. That's easy enough. And

I can change the sheets. You go on out."

"I'll help Anna with lunch," Willow said. Then she added softly, "She can tell me what to do."

"I want to do it alone," Anna said. "Please let me, Aunt Jessica. It's important to me to do it this way."

In the end, the three Winstons went about their regularly scheduled day and Anna called them down to lunch at exactly noon.

As Jessica unfolded her napkin and surveyed the beautifully prepared meal, she said, "This looks marvelous, dear. The table is beautifully set."

"Better than Mrs. Shelley." Brittany agreed. She tried the spaghetti and added, "And you're a better cook."

All of the boarders who were there agreed that lunch was good and Carlos called it "magnificent." Anna seemed pleased with the praise and actually allowed Dan and Willow to help her carry dishes back to the kitchen.

Willow looked around and said, "Wow! This kitchen is clean already. How did you do that?"

"I wash pans as I go," Anna explained.

"That's the way we do it on the ranch," Dan said. "I'll just go get my toolbox and fix that cabinet over there." He pointed to the cabinet over the refrigerator.

"What's wrong with it?" Willow asked.

"It sags," he answered. "Look along the bottom. See how it's out of line with the others?"

"This is an old house," Willow said. "Lots of things sag."

"Shouldn't," he answered shortly and left.

When they were alone, Anna asked Willow, "Do you think your mother would give me Mrs. Shelley's job if I asked?"

"Why would you want it?" Willow answered. "It's not costing you anything to live here." Then she thought she saw a hurt look cross Anna's face. "Not that you're not welcome. You *are* welcome, of course."

"Of course," Anna said.

If Willow hadn't known better, she might have thought that Anna was being sarcastic.

"Anyway, I'm sure that Mrs. Shelley will want her job back. She'll probably call and have a good excuse," Willow added.

"Yes." Anna agreed and turned to leave the kitchen. Willow stood, looking at her cousin's disappearing back, wondering why Anna wasn't friendly. She should be a little more grateful for the opportunity to go to school in Madison. After all, they'd practically taken her in.

That afternoon, Jessica Winston called the home of Mrs. Shelley several times but there was no answer. Finally, around three o'clock, Jessica decided to drive over to the woman's house. She was back in thirty minutes and looked very angry as she said, "She was home all right. Perfectly healthy. She's quit. Without any notice at all. She says it's too much work. I offered her a raise and she turned it down."

Willow's heart sank. If they didn't find help fast, her mother would close down the boardinghouse. And if she closed it down, Willow would probably never see Justin or Dan or Carlos again. That would never do.

"Anna wants the job," Willow said.

"Anna? Our Anna?"

"Yes. She asked me about it earlier today," Willow said.

"Why would she want a job?" Jessica asked.

"Maybe she wants to buy new clothes."

"We can't have that," Jessica frowned. "And I've already offered to buy her clothes."

"Why can't we have that?" Willow asked. "She did a great job at lunch."

"I would feel like the cruel stepmother and you — my darling daughter — would be the ugly stepsister."

"I don't see why you even make jokes like

that," Willow said. "Anna is never going to be Cinderella — that's for sure."

Jessica looked at her older daughter and shook her head and smiled. "There are all kinds of Cinderellas and the world is full of surprises."

Chapter 13

Anna rose at five on Sunday morning and
jogged for an hour before she went into the
Winston kitchen to prepare breakfast. When
Aunt Jessica came down at eight, breakfast
was on the table and she seemed very pleased.
"You really are wonderful," she said.

At lunchtime, they all went to a restaurant
near the college, and everyone was very
cheerful to be out of the house and all alone.
"Isn't this cozy?" Jessica asked. "Just the
family?"

She closed her hand over Anna's and said,
"If we close the boardinghouse down, you can
stay. You're family."

"You don't have to close the boardinghouse," Anna said quickly. "I'd really like to
have Mrs. Shelley's job."

"You're in school and you have your athletics," Jessica said. "What do you want the
money for?"

"For college," Anna said promptly. "If I don't get an athletic scholarship, I'll need money. And you pay very well." She thought it was best not to mention to Jessica that she planned to send some money home to her younger brothers.

"How will you do the work?"

"I'll jog at five-thirty instead of six-thirty. That will give me time to do the breakfasts. I can change the sheets and do quite a bit of cooking on Saturdays."

Jessica shook her head. "Mrs. Shelley had her hands full working mornings and dinners. You simply can't do it all."

"I'm stronger and more efficient," Anna argued. "There will be plenty of time to do dinners, and I'll do laundry and housecleaning on Saturday. It won't be a bit more than I did at home. When I was on the farm I got up at four-thirty to help with the milking. Please, Aunt Jessica."

"What about your basketball practice?" Jessica asked. "How will you work that in."

"I'll make dinner plans in advance. We don't eat until six-thirty. I can do it."

"She wants to," Willow urged.

"I don't know," Jessica said. "Somehow, the prospect of having a relative come home from school and work so hard while my girls play just feels very, very peculiar."

"I won't be playing," Willow answered. "I have my cheerleading practice after school four nights a week. And there's homework. I promised to bring up those C's in Spanish and math to B's."

"What about you?" Jessica asked Brittany. "What will you do while your cousin works so hard?"

"I'm going out for cheerleading, too," Brittany answered promptly. "So I'll be practicing every day, too."

"I'll help Anna with dinners," Willow said. "I need to learn how to cook."

"I'm against it," Jessica said but there was a softness in her voice that indicated she was about to give in.

"Let me try it for October and November," Anna urged. "Then you can decide for certain."

"I have to do something," Jessica said. "I can't just give our boarders all their money back and tell them to run along and find some other place to live. Maybe if we try it for a few weeks . . ."

"It will get easier," Willow said. She turned to Anna and said, "We're all counting on you."

"I'll try," Anna promised.

Chapter 14

Teddy was waiting for Brittany in the cafeteria at lunch. She took one look at his face and said, "You got the part?"

"Not the lead. The second lead. But it's a great part."

"A star is born," Brittany said. "Have you told anyone else?"

Teddy took her arm and squeezed. "You promised not to tell and I want you to keep your word. I don't want to go through months of teasing from the guys."

"You should be proud of your accomplishment," Brittany chided.

"I will be when I accomplish something. Meantime, let's eat alone. I want to tell you the plot."

"*The Good Ship Grease* has a plot?"

"More or less — mostly less, I guess."

As they sat down at a table with their trays

of food, Teddy began to relate the plot, scene by scene and tell her all of his lines. When he finished, she laughed and said, "You already know your lines."

"It's not the lines that are important. I've got one song and two solo dances. It's a good part."

"I think it's a wonderful part," Brittany agreed.

Teddy looked grateful and smiled at her. When Teddy smiled, he looked very happy and that made Brittany happy, too. Just then, Anna walked by their table, carrying her lunch tray.

Brittany waved and called to her but Anna kept on walking, pretending she didn't see them. Teddy asked, "You and your cousin had a fight?"

"I thought we were getting along really well," Brittany said. "I helped her with the breakfast setup this morning, and Willow and I talked Mom into giving her Mrs. Shelley's job."

"Your cousin is a celebrity in my gym class. All the guys are talking about how she plays basketball. Coach Contraro thinks he's going to win the women's championship."

"Is she really that good?"

"She is," Teddy answered. "Some guys in third period were taking bets that she'd be All-

Star Captain this year. Your pal Lars was one of them."

"Which way did he bet?"

"He bet on Anna. I bet she wouldn't."

"How much?"

"Five dollars," Teddy said complacently as he bit into his tuna salad sandwich. "I figure if I win that five from your dreamboat and the ten from you, I'll be a rich man by Halloween."

"I think you're developing a gambling addiction." It seemed to her that Teddy and Lars were getting kind of friendly. She longed to ask Teddy more about Lars but she didn't dare. Every time his name came up, Teddy referred to him as her dreamboat or her secret love. It made it impossible to discuss him and keep the conversation casual.

"Speak of the angel," Teddy said. "There's your dreamboat now, talking to your sister."

Brittany tried not to notice the way Willow was flirting with Lars. She thought that life was especially cruel to have sent one special boy into her life and then made him closer to her sister's age. She didn't fool herself into thinking that she could really compete with Willow in a general way but she did have some hope that Lars would appreciate her unique qualities. Of course, when she watched Willow and Lars together, laughing and talking, it was hard for her to remember exactly what her unique qualities were.

"Cheer up," Teddy said. "They're not going to run off and get married or anything."

"I don't know what you're talking about."

"Whenever you don't want to know what I'm talking about, you get very, very stupid," Teddy said complacently. "Are you going to eat that cake?"

"No."

He forked the cake off her plate before the syllable was out of her mouth and started an entirely new train of thought as though it was what they'd been talking about all along. "So the way I see it, you and Willow talked your mother into letting your downtrodden cousin do all the work around there. She wanted the job to buy new clothes — that's very doubtful, you know — and your sister wanted to keep the boardinghouse open because she thinks Carlos is cute."

"And Justin. She likes Justin, too."

"So you went along with the deal because if *she* has Justin and Carlos, you still have the cowboy and the nerds. Or is it because of Lars Peterson?"

"None of the above. Lars is *your* friend, not mine. And the cowboy likes Willow, too. In fact, he's really crazy about her. And the nerds hardly ever come out of their room except to eat."

"So you should be nice to me," Teddy said. "I'm absolutely the only man on your horizon."

"You're not a man — you're a child and I haven't got a horizon. Could we change the subject, please?"

"I'm a little sick myself, just thinking 'bout that cousin of yours working like some Cinderella so you two dimwits can play man-crazy. Willow's bad enough — I don't expect much more of her — but you don't even have any men after you."

"That's it," Brittany said and she stood up. "I'm not speaking to you ever again."

She left the lunchroom without looking back. Teddy could be the most obnoxious boy in the world and she was really sick and tired of his criticizing her and what she was doing.

"You'll be sorry when I'm a star," Teddy called to her. She kept on walking.

That afternoon, she went to the first cheerleading practice. She felt kind of silly lined up with the group of girls waiting for the two cheerleading coaches.

Miss Nelson, their algebra teacher, looked up as Brittany's turn to sign up came. She frowned and said, "Brittany, what are you doing here?"

"Trying out for cheerleading. What are you doing here?"

Miss Nelson sighed and said, "I have to sponsor some after-school activity. This is mine."

"Were you a cheerleader in high school?" Brittany asked curiously.

"Of course not." Miss Nelson looked insulted at the question. Brittany understood how she felt but she couldn't help feeling sorry for the cheerleading squad for being stuck with her as a sponsor.

Brittany signed her name and said, "I've never been a cheerleader before. This should be fun."

Miss Nelson looked at her quietly and said under her breath, "If I were a smart girl like you, I'd find some other way to work out my sibling rivalry."

Brittany blushed. "It's not really about Willow. I mean, I know she's good but I'm good at some other things. . . ."

"Yes, you are. So what is this about?"

Brittany couldn't imagine telling Miss Nelson the truth. There was no way she was going to admit to this brilliant woman that she'd signed up for cheerleading to be closer to Lars Peterson. So she shrugged and said, "I just thought I'd see how the other half lives."

Miss Nelson looked over at the roomful of girls with a mixture of amusement and dismay. "It's not easy, you know. The ones who make it will work very hard. And they really care."

"I'm a hard worker," Brittany said cheerfully. She moved on before her teacher could ask her if she really cared.

It was the other sponsor who worked hard that afternoon. Miss Nelson stood with her arms across her chest, looking bored as Mrs. Mahoney led the new girls through the basic cheers. Most of them seemed to know a lot of the routines already and Brittany felt foolishly out of step. When one young woman she barely knew said, "I guess you have a head start on the rest of us. Since Willow is your sister, I mean."

"Willow and I don't practice cheers together," Brittany answered crossly. In her heart, she knew that Willow would have been more than happy to help her if she'd asked. But it had never even occurred to her that she was going to be trying out until that rash moment when she'd blurted it out to Lars Peterson. Now, she had no one to be angry at but herself.

She was proud of Willow when Mrs. Mahoney asked her to demonstrate the more advanced cheers. Brittany had never really paid attention before and she watched with awe as Willow did her backbends and flips. She was really good.

As she huffed and puffed through her beginner routines, Brittany realized she had never really thought about the amount of talent and hard work that went into her sister's cheerleading activities. She'd always just thought it came along with the Willow package — pretty girl — cute costume — clever routines. Now that she was expected to imitate some of the intricate maneuvers, she saw that there was a lot of athletic ability involved.

Brittany stumbled through the routines, knowing that she was definitely not predestined for a slot on the Madison Markers. There were several girls who were better athletes and had better timing than she did. By the time the hour was up, Brittany was happy enough to put her ski jacket on and get out.

Willow caught up with her in the hallway and invited her to come to Charlie's for a Coke with the other Madison Markers. "I can't," Brittany answered. "I've got too much homework."

"I shouldn't." Willow sighed. "Anna had basketball practice tonight and I should go home and help her."

"Let your conscience be your guide."

Willow laughed and said, "That's not a lot of help. Tell Anna I'll help her clean up, will you?"

"Sure." Brittany watched as her beautiful sister moved away in a group of laughing, chattering kids. It seemed to her that whenever she saw Willow around school this year, she was in the center of a large group. Sort of like a movable party. For the first time in her life, Brittany wondered if Willow was happy with all those people around all the time. It seemed a strange way to live.

Brittany walked home alone, breathing in the cold fall air, and thinking about other people's lives. How could they be so different? And what would it be like to be someone else? She tried to put herself in other people's places, tried to see the world as they saw it.

First, she tried to imagine what Miss Nelson's life was like. She was a woman about the same age as her mother. She'd never been married or had children. All she did was teach algebra and geometry to kids who would rather be doing something else. Was Miss Nelson happy? Brittany knew she took a lot of trips in the summer — mostly to foreign countries. Did Miss Nelson just put up with ten months out of the year to kick up her heels in Spain?

She tried to imagine what Willow's life was

really like. Even though they had always been sisters and they lived one room apart, Brittany decided it was easier for her to understand Miss Nelson's life. She quickly moved on to Mrs. Mahoney and just as quickly decided that Mrs. Mahoney was impossible to understand.

Who was left? Anna? But Anna was a true mystery. And those boarders who were living in their house. Everyone of them was as different as they could be. About the only one who seemed easy to understand was Dan. He was a nice guy who liked to be helpful and he was in love with Willow. No mystery there.

Good. She could understand Dan and maybe she could understand Teddy most of the time. Maybe boys were easier to understand than girls. What about Lars? Could she understand him?

Brittany sighed and jammed her hands into her jacket pockets. It was getting cold and she was getting depressed just thinking about Lars. She would never understand a boy like that. He was too perfect.

She was in a bad mood when she entered her house and her mother put her in a worse one. Questions. Questions. "How was cheerleading practice?"

"All right."

"Did you do well on your history test?"

"All right."

"Did you have a good day at school?"

"All right."

"Did you and Teddy have another quarrel?"

"No."

"Good. Did you remember to invite him to our Thursday evening?"

"Why are we doing this?" Brittany asked crossly.

"I'm trying to start a conversation," her mother said pleasantly. "You are obviously cross about something and I'm not quite sure what you are doing. Picking a fight, maybe."

"I mean, why are we having these stupid Thursday evenings?"

"I thought they would be a pleasant way to get to know our guests." Her voice said that she was determined not to quarrel with her younger daughter.

"You can never really know anyone," Brittany said. "And you certainly aren't going to get to know anyone by sitting around talking about nothing like we did last week."

"That's why I asked you to invite Teddy," Jessica said. "Willow has asked some young man and it will make things more interesting."

"Who did Willow invite?"

"I'm not sure. You can ask her when she gets home."

"Was it Lars? Lars Peterson?"

"Yes — that's right. Do you know him?"

"Of course not," Brittany answered. "I don't know anyone at all. I don't know Willow. I don't know you. I don't know anyone."

"Oh, dear," Jessica smiled. "It sounds as though you and Teddy *really* quarreled this time. Why not get your mind off unpleasant things and go help Anna in the kitchen."

"She's another one," Brittany said. "I don't understand her at all."

"She comes from a different background," Jessica explained patiently. "If you girls will just give her a chance, I'm sure you'll enjoy each other. She's a very pleasant person and she's clearly an excellent athlete."

"Maybe," Brittany said.

"Brittany, go see if you can help in the kitchen," her mother said. "I'm not up to solving the riddle of life before dinner."

Chapter 15

Willow dressed very carefully for her mother's Thursday night, choosing a soft pink silk blouse with full long sleeves, white stretch pants, and her white boots. She experimented with a pink ribbon to pull back her hair and then discarded it, settling for her regular hairstyle. She wanted to look great but not too dressed up.

Lars was going to be there and that made all the difference. She wondered what he would think of the collection of unusual characters her mother selected as boarders. She worried that Brittany would be silly and drive him away. She even worried a little bit that he would be jealous of Carlos, or Justin, or Dan. When Lars saw how they all flirted with her, would he think *she* was silly?

At exactly seven o'clock, Willow descended the stairs and she was there to answer the bell when Lars rang at five minutes after seven. He stood there in the doorway, smiling and looking very pleased to be there. He was carrying a bunch of chrysanthemums and said, "My mom thought your mom might like these. They're the last of the season."

So it was easy enough to bring Lars into the living room and introduce him to Jessica, who immediately went to the kitchen for a flower vase and then took Lars under her wing, asking him about his mother's garden.

Things seemed to be going pretty well until Carlos came over and sat down in the chair next to her. He took her hand in his. Then he leaned forward, introducing himself to Lars, "Carlos Montoya, at your service. Are you going to be living here with the charming Winston ladies?"

Lars looked surprised at the question and shook his head quickly. "No. I know Willow at school. That's all."

"Ah, you are classmates," Carlos said. "Fortunate but not so fortunate as I. *We* are housemates."

Willow was really embarrassed and she knew that her cheeks were about as pink as her blouse. What right did Carlos have to come over here like this and act as though he owned her? And his language sounded really funny and old-fashioned when she heard it through Lars's ears.

Lars looked pretty uncomfortable, as though he wasn't certain what to do or say next.

Jessica tried to make things go better by saying, "Carlos has been in the United States for only a few weeks. He's from Mexico."

"Really?" Lars asked.

Dan spoke up, "You know, Montoya, you don't sound Mexican. I've been around lots of Mexicans and they don't talk like you."

Carlos laughed and looked directly at Dan. "Do you think I am an imposter?"

Now it was Dan's turn to color and shift in his chair. "I'm not accusing you of anything. I'm just saying you sound different than the guys I've worked with in Wyoming."

"I suppose I do." Carlos turned to Willow and said, "Willow, it was such a wonderful movie we saw the other night. I think the hero looked like your friend here. Don't you?"

Willow didn't know what to say and so she smiled and stood up, saying "I'm going to get a Coke. Anyone else want anything?"

"I'll take a diet 7-Up," Jessica said. Her tone of voice told her daughter that she was very amused by the attention Willow was getting. As Willow made her retreat, she tried to remember that she usually enjoyed having a lot of male attention. It was only because Lars was there that she was flustered.

What was it about Lars that made her feel different? She wasn't sure but she thought it was because he seemed more real than the others. Carlos was so extreme and Dan was such a cowboy that they almost seemed like they were acting parts. So she could act a part herself. But Lars was different. She knew him well enough to know he was serious about school, worked hard, had a Saturday job at the Payless Drug Store, and tried to do things right. He was . . . steady. Having him see her with the others was embarrassing because she was afraid it made her seem immature.

When she came back with the drinks, Carlos was gone and Lars was in the corner talking to Brittany's friend Teddy. The two of them were standing close together, as though they were best friends. She didn't even know they knew each other. They were clearly deep in a conversation and Willow wasn't sure she should interrupt. On the other hand, Lars had come to see *her*, not Teddy.

She handed Jessica her 7-Up and said, "I haven't said hello to Teddy."

Jessica raised one eyebrow and smiled with that smile that drove Willow crazy. Then she turned back to the conversation she was having with Dan. Willow went over to Teddy and Lars and said, "Hi, Teddy, I really haven't said hello to you this evening."

"You never say hello to me, Willow. Why would you start now?"

Willow stopped dead in her tracks and stared at Teddy. Why had he said that? She had never done anything to him to make him be so mean. Then she saw he was smiling and so she supposed she was to take it as a joke. She managed a small laugh and didn't know what to do next. Should she stand and wait for one of them to offer her a chair? Should she move on? Or maybe she should just sit down on the floor between them and demand to be a part of their conversation. That's what Brittany would do, she knew, but she wasn't sure she was brave enough.

"We were just talking about your cousin," Lars said. "I'd like to meet her. Is she here?"

"Anna?"

"Yes. Is she here?"

Willow was surprised and she looked around the room slowly. Where was Anna? When she didn't see her anywhere, she said, "She's supposed to be here but she's kind of shy."

"See if you can find her," Lars urged. "I really came to talk to her if I can."

Now Willow *knew* what she was supposed to do! She had clearly been dismissed and it hurt. As she turned away, she wished she had never invited Lars Peterson to the party. Why hadn't she been satisfied with the attention from all the other young men? She'd had a great time last week with Justin and Carlos and Dan all after her.

Willow went into the kitchen and tried to get herself together. She didn't want anyone to know she was upset. She would hate it if Lars knew how insulted she was because she was certain it had not been his intention to hurt her feelings. As she opened the refrigerator and tried to take out ice, she told herself what she had already figured out — that Lars wanted to talk to Anna about sports. There was nothing wrong with that.

"Let me help you." Dan's drawl told her that he was in the room and watching her struggle with the ice cubes.

He came over to the refrigerator and pulled the ice cube tray out with one flick of the wrist. She smiled at him and said in a light, flirtatious voice, "You're wonderful, Dan. I don't know what we did without you. You're such a big help around here."

He looked very pleased and grinned as he

said, "But I don't have party manners, do I? I guess I was rude to Carlos."

"Don't worry about that," Willow assured him. "Carlos will get over it."

"He already has," Dan admitted. "The minute you left, he told me that he was educated in Europe. That's why his accent is so funny. And I apologized."

"That's wonderful," Willow said and smiled her most dazzling smile. She and Dan walked back into the party and she did her best to look as though she was absolutely enthralled with his description of how he built a fence around ten miles of ranch.

They sat together for the next half hour, and she let Dan do all the talking as she encouraged him with flirtatious laughter, smiles, and interested questions. Once in a while, she noticed what Lars was doing out of the corner of her eye. She saw when Brittany joined Lars and Teddy and she saw it when Brittany brought Anna back to them.

While Dan described the first time he roped a calf and branded it, Willow watched Anna standing tall and awkward as she talked at length with Lars. Then Lars and Anna shook hands. Clearly, they'd come to some sort of agreement but Willow couldn't imagine what it could be. She wondered what that handshake was all about.

"So what do you think?" Dan asked.

Willow blushed. She hadn't really been listening and she wasn't sure what he was asking her. She took a deep breath and hoped she was giving the right answer as she said, "I think whatever you think."

"Good," Dan said. "We can go this Saturday."

Willow nodded her head, having no idea what she'd agreed to but guessing that it would be all right. She got up then and left Dan to circulate around the room a bit.

She found out what she'd agreed to a few minutes later when Dan came over to her and Jessica and asked, "Did Willow tell you about our apple-picking expedition on Saturday?"

"No," Jessica answered. "What's going on?" She directed the question to her daughter.

"Let Dan tell you," Willow said quickly. She was somewhat relieved that she'd only agreed to apple picking, much as it didn't interest her. But it might have been a lot worse, she told herself and she also promised herself that in the future she would really pay attention to the person she was supposed to be listening to. But even then, she was watching Lars as he shook Anna's hand again and stood up to leave.

"There's a lot of apples left on the hilltops," Dan said. "And I miss the countryside. Anna told me that we could pick all the apples we can carry for five dollars a bushel."

"What will we do with a bushel of apples?" Jessica asked.

"Apples for the table. Home-baked apple pies. Applesauce and baked apples," Dan answered promptly. "Anna said she'd like to make apple butter. Willow and Brittany can help."

Jessica nodded and said, "All right. On Saturday we pick apples. Sounds like fun." She turned to Lars and Teddy who were waiting to say good-bye and asked, "How about you fellows? Want to pick apples on Saturday?"

"I will," Teddy said promptly.

"I have to work," Lars answered. "But thanks for the invitation. And thanks for tonight. I enjoyed it."

Lars was driving Teddy home and Willow was only included in the general good nights. As he left, Lars smiled and said, "See you in school, Willow."

There was a lump in her throat as she nodded good-bye. One thing she'd learned this evening for sure. Lars wasn't interested in her. He'd talked more to Teddy and Brittany and Anna than to her.

And where were Carlos and Justin? They'd both left at about eight o'clock, claiming they had to go to see a friend. Half the others hadn't even bothered to show up. She smiled at Dan. Reliability had its virtues.

"Well, I think this evening was a success," Jessica said. "What do you think about our Thursday evenings, Willow?"

"I think they're a drag," Willow answered. "I didn't have much fun and half the boarders skipped out totally. I don't see why we have to do these things. It's a lot of work for Anna."

"I'm glad to hear you're concerned about Anna," Jessica said. "You and Brittany can help her clean up." Then she smiled a small smile and added, "I think we can cancel the Thursday evenings indefinitely, don't you?"

"Teddy won't come back. Probably Lars wouldn't either, would he, Willow?" Brittany asked.

"Mom's already canceled Thursday evenings," Willow pointed out. "You don't have to sell her on it."

"You're just mad because Lars talked more to me than to you," Brittany said.

"That's all in your imagination," Willow answered. "I have no special interest in Lars Peterson. He's just a friend."

"You girls get in there and help before Dan and Anna have it all done," Jessica said. "I'll help, too."

They had the kitchen in spotless order by ten o'clock. On their way to their rooms, Willow couldn't resist asking Brittany, "What did Lars want to talk to Anna about?"

"Running," Brittany said. "He wants to run with her. She said yes. I'm going, too."

"Going where?" Willow asked.

"Going to run. But right now, I'm going to bed," Brittany answered. "Got to set my alarm for five o'clock. I'm meeting Lars at five-thirty for a nice, long run."

Chapter 16

Anna's alarm gave off one little beep and she punched in the buzzer and jumped out of bed. She dressed and opened the door to her room very quietly, being careful not to wake her roommate. As she crossed the hall, a board creaked, and she made a mental note to ask Dan to fix it. No sense waking up the whole house.

She didn't really think about it consciously but she was especially quiet as she neared Brittany's room. When Brittany had invited herself along for the run, Anna wanted to protest. Brittany would slow them down even though she promised she wouldn't. She was looking forward to running with Lars and she knew Brittany wasn't really serious about running.

She got out of the house without waking anyone and was standing, jogging in place, when she saw Lars running down the street toward her. She fell in beside him and they ran a block without saying anything. Then he asked, "Faster?"

"Go as fast as you want."

"Really?" He kind of half turned and grinned at her. It was still very dark outside but the streetlight threw patterns onto his face and she could see his expression. He looked happy.

As she ran, Anna thought about her life in Madison. It was her custom to let all the negative emotions she was feeling well up inside of her the first few minutes of her run. It was a way of dealing with all the stress she dealt with during the day. And just because Lars was with her, she wasn't going to give up that survival skill.

Running with Lars shouldn't be that different from running alone, Anna thought. She sort of pretended that she was alone and let herself think as she always did.

She thought first about her schoolwork and how she was doing quite well. Her grades were A's or B pluses, so far. And sports were all right, too. She had her friend Joe Andrews to play serious basketball with after school and the girls' basketball team wasn't too bad. She hoped Coach Contraro would get a better team together before the actual season began. But she knew that high school sports were for everyone and he had to give them all a chance.

Joe was coaching her and he said she should block everyone out of her mind and just compete with herself. He was right about that, she knew. She was going to be as good an athlete as possible and let the rest of the team do what it would. "Don't waste your talent whining," Joe said. He was right about that, too.

So she was okay with the reasons she'd come to Madison — sports and school. That was good but the truth was, she hated it here. The Winstons were just not her kind of people. Like that party last night. She hated that and she had to go because she was "a part of family."

Aunt Jessica was pretty careful about doing the right thing. She was nice, of course, but sometimes she caught her aunt looking at her with such an obvious dismay that she knew she didn't know what to do with this tall, athletic niece. It was Aunt Jessica's niceness that was the hardest to take in a way. She obviously meant well but she kept offering to buy clothes. Last week, she'd even suggested that Anna get her hair cut by her stylist. It was clear that her aunt thought she should look like and be more like her cousins.

Certainly, she was a lot *different* from her cousins, but at home, Anna had never felt like a freak. She didn't want to be like Brittany, who seemed young and foolish. Or Willow who seemed shallow and not too smart. She supposed they were both nice enough to their own kind of friends but they certainly hadn't been very nice to her.

Of course they were better now that they knew she wasn't going to try and horn in on their social life. Willow was actually pleasant now that Anna was doing all the work around the boardinghouse. Willow wanted to keep the boardinghouse open and so she was helping Anna some.

Anna felt the cold air in her lungs and it felt as though she was breathing in pure power. She tried imaging that — the air as power and her lungs as circulating the power. Joe used a lot of mental imaging to improve his game.

She felt her mind begin to quiet, just as she knew it would and she relaxed and let her body take over. Anna loved this part of the running when she felt as though she'd lost track of her thinking and was simply racing along with the wind, moving as though she were a part of the morning itself. She was comfortable. She was happy and there was nothing about her that felt out of synch or like a freak. At that moment, life was good.

They ran further than she'd ever run before and she began to worry about time. She motioned to Lars that she had to turn around and he immediately complied. The trip home seemed to go twice as fast and when they got back to the Winston house, she said, "Thanks. That was great."

"We could have gone further."

"I have a job," Anna explained. "I have to shower and get breakfast on the table for ten people. I have about thirty minutes to do it in."

"That's impressive," Lars said admiringly.

Anna smiled at him and asked, "See you tomorrow?"

"Same time," Lars said.

She held out her hand but he clapped her on the shoulder and said, "This is great, Anna. Thanks a lot."

"Got to go." She turned quickly and moved into the house. She didn't want Lars to see how touched she was to have someone actually treat her as though she was all right the way she was.

When she got into the house, Brittany was waiting for her in the kitchen with fire in her eyes. "Why didn't you wake me?" she asked.

"I didn't know you expected me to," Anna retorted quickly.

"Well, I *did* expect it," Brittany answered and then she quickly amended her statement. "I mean I didn't *expect* it but it would have been nice."

"I'm sorry," Anna said. She walked quickly past Brittany and added, "I have to shower and get going on breakfast."

"Can I help?" Brittany asked.

Anna was surprised by the offer and automatically began to turn it down. Then she smiled and said, "Thanks. You could turn the oven on to three hundred fifty degrees and set the table. That would be great."

"It's the least I can do for a fellow runner," Brittany said. "I'll be there tomorrow for sure."

Chapter 17

"So did he ask you or did you just invite yourself?" Teddy asked.

"You were there," Brittany answered. "I volunteered to tag along. But they both said I would be welcome."

"They're both polite," Teddy observed. They were in the library after school and Brittany was supposed to be helping Teddy with his algebra homework. But, as was often the case, they found a hundred things to talk about besides math.

"I don't see *why* I wouldn't be welcome," Brittany said. "I mean, it's not like they had a date." She laughed out loud at the thought of Lars and Anna as a romantic couple.

"He came to your party especially to meet her," Teddy argued. "And he told me he planned to ask Anna since he saw her running past him one morning. Must have been the first day she got here. Seems he needs a long-legged partner."

"I may not be long-legged enough to keep up all the way but I said they could go on ahead."

"You'll slow them down — at least at first. They're both so polite and well behaved. They're a lot alike, you know."

"Lars and Anna?" Willow laughed at the idea.

"I know it sounds funny to you," Teddy said. "But that's because you don't really see either of them."

"Of course I see them. I see them all the time."

"But you don't *see* them."

"You are the most infuriating person I know. All we ever do is argue and I don't know why I even agreed to help you with this math. You don't have any interest in math at all. You'd just as soon flunk as not."

"I'd rather not flunk," Teddy said calmly. "I'd rather learn just enough to get a C. I'll get A's in everything else so it will work out."

"That's disgusting," Brittany observed. "And I do see people. I have an understanding heart." Even as she repeated her mother's words, she felt a twinge of guilt. She might have an understanding heart but something was certainly off base with her and cousin Anna.

"When you see Anna, you see only a tall, awkward social embarrassment," Teddy said. "When you see Lars, you see only a dreamboat. You're wrong about them both."

"Anna *is* tall and awkward."

"When she's around you," Teddy agreed. "You and that dim-witted sister you're always imitating. But on the basketball court she's a ballet dancer. A swan."

"And what's Lars?"

"He's a nice guy. A striver. Someone who wants to do the right thing. Wants to be good at what he does. Not your type at all. Not your sister's type either."

"You make him sound so dull."

"He is, compared to thee and me, my dear."

"Since you took acting, you're impossible." Brittany closed the conversation and opened the math book to the next chapter. "You have twenty minutes until rehearsal. No more talking. Only numbers."

"What about cheerleading practice?"

Brittany shrugged and said, "I'm dropping out. I don't want to be a cheerleader anyway."

Teddy nodded. "Good thinking. And I'll bet

you five dollars you never get up early enough to go running with those two either."

"You make them sound so dull, I don't know why I would want to," Brittany answered. "Now could we do a little algebra please?"

"Just a little," Teddy agreed.

Chapter 18

Brittany overslept the next morning, but on Wednesday she was waiting for Anna when she came downstairs at five-thirty. She said, "I'm ready to go."

Anna looked surprised but nodded her head and they went to the front door together. They stood outside on the porch and waited for Lars. Brittany said, "I am absolutely freezing."

"Jog in place," Anna answered. "It warms you up and gets you moving." She began to move very lightly from one foot to the other, as though she were skipping rope.

Brittany jogged beside her, complaining, "I'm keeping time with the chattering of my teeth."

Anna said nothing and when Lars came running down the street, she moved off the porch and stood, jogging on the sidewalk, waiting to fall in beside Lars. Lars smiled and said, "Hi, Anna. Brittany, you coming?"

Brittany's teeth were chattering so that she just nodded her head. Lars said to Anna, "I guess we'll start a little slower today."

Anna nodded and Brittany flushed. "Hey, you guys, do your thing. If I can't keep up, I'll go at my own pace and you can pick me up on the way back." She was angry when she saw the look of relief on their faces.

"You sure you don't mind?" Lars asked. "We've been running really fast."

"Well, go ahead and run," Brittany said. "I'm a fast runner, too. Or at least I was in the sixth grade. I beat everyone."

"Good," Lars said. Then he smiled again at Anna and said, "Let's go."

They did. Brittany ran as fast as she could for about a block but they ran twice as fast. By the time that she'd gone three blocks, they were tiny specks on the horizon.

Despite the fact that she was running fast, she was still cold. The air hurt her lungs and she had a spot that was rubbing on her heel that she knew would soon be a blister. Brittany stopped abruptly, turned, and started running back the way she came.

When she got back home, she made herself

a cup of tea and carried it up the stairs to her bedroom. Once she was there, she climbed into bed and sat up, resting her cup of tea on her knees, as she stared into space. She wasn't exactly thinking. She was just digesting the fact that if she ever attracted Lars it would have to be because of who she was. She obviously wasn't going to be a star cheerleader or a runner. Lars would just have to love her for herself.

She was still wearing her red jogging suit and she pulled the blankets around her tightly. With the warmth of the house, the tea, and the blankets, she warmed up quickly. Nevertheless, she had no real interest in getting up and getting dressed for school. It was only six o'clock in the morning and she was already exhausted. She sighed, drank the last of her tea, put the empty cup on the table beside her, and turned her body around so she could lie down. She still had her knees as close to her chin as she could manage as she drifted off to sleep.

Chapter 19

At first, Willow didn't want to go apple picking but when her mother said, "Good, you can stay home and make sure the boarders are happy. Get breakfast and do the laundry," she changed her mind.

As it turned out, the only boarders who came along were Carlos and Dan. Teddy's mother dropped him off early and she also loaned them her big jeep van. Everyone helped with breakfast and the rest of the work was postponed till Sunday. When all seven climbed in, and Jessica got behind the wheel, Teddy said proudly, "Plenty of room left for apples."

It was a cheerful group and not too far outside of Madison, Dan began to sing songs he'd learned on the ranch. He had a deep, mellow baritone that was so good it surprised them all. He sang "Home on the Range," "You Are My Sunshine," and "Get Along, Little Dogie."

Then Carlos sang a Mexican song that he said was a ranch song. Though none of them could understand the words, it was clear that he was telling a long, complicated story. Carlos had a loud voice and he wasn't a bit shy, but he couldn't sing as well as Dan.

Brittany thought Dan looked pleased when Carlos lost his way in the song and had to backtrack. She was certain he was happy when Jessica asked him to sing another song from Wyoming. Dan sang a song about a man named Tom Dooley who was condemned to death. It was kind of sad and for a second, when he finished, everyone was silent. Then Jessica said, "Thanks. You have a beautiful voice, Dan."

"You must all come with me to Mexico at Christmas," Carlos said suddenly, surprising all of them. "In my town, the villagers all sing every night. Each home has a guitar and they know many, many songs. Will you come visit at Christmas?"

"Sure we will," Teddy said. "We can charter a plane."

"I don't think we need to charter a whole plane," Carlos began and then he seemed to understand that Teddy was making a joke. "You are joking but I am serious," Carlos said with a slight hurt in his voice.

"Look over there," Jessica said quickly. "Those are Brahman bulls. First we've seen today. We must be getting close to Gays Mills."

Jessica went on talking about livestock and the landscape they were traveling through and the rough spot was smoothed over. Willow wondered if Carlos was really serious about inviting them all. He seemed rich enough and he was a nice, generous person when you got to know him.

She longed to ask questions about Christmas in Mexico but she knew her mother would be horrified if she did. Her mother would never approve of anything that looked like "fishing for an invitation." Still — it would be wonderful to go to Mexico.

Willow shut her eyes and tried to imagine what Mexico was really like. Was it like the tourist posters she'd seen, with bright flowers and colored peacocks everywhere?

She pictured herself standing beside Carlos. She was wearing a lace mantilla and then she pictured a tall, dark, handsome man lifting the lace veil and bending over to kiss her. Carlos — with his black eyes, his flashing smile, and that soft mustache. What would it feel like to be kissed by someone with a mustache? Willow smiled at the thought.

They pulled into a tiny little town with one gas station, one small store, and one block of offices that included a newspaper, a lawyer, and an insurance agent. Willow turned to the back and said to Teddy, "You'd better wake up Brittany. We're here."

Teddy poked Brittany with his elbow and said, "You can wake up now, we're here."

"Where?"

"We're in Gays Mills." Teddy bent over her and took her face in his two hands and said, "Snap out of it, kid. You're in Gays Mills, Wisconsin, two hours outside of Madison with your old friend Teddy and your loving family. Get your thoughts collected and put them all back in your head. The dream is over. Wake up to real life."

Brittany stretched and yawned. "Get your hands off me," she said. "I wasn't asleep."

"No, you were just drifting," Teddy agreed. "Daydreaming and drifting. No doubt thinking about your dreamboat Lars."

"Where are the apples," Brittany asked.

They turned down a dirt road where a handwritten sign said APPLE PICKING, and Willow was glad. She always hated it when Teddy teased Brittany about Lars. He made her younger sister sound so silly, for having a crush on Lars, that it made Willow feel like maybe she was silly, too. But her own crush on Lars was just perfectly natural, Willow told herself. Lars and she were about the same age and they had a lot in common.

"We have to find the tallest hill in the orchard," Dan said. "That's where there won't have been any frost."

"First we have to find the farmer and pay him," Jessica said.

"And get ladders and sacks," Dan agreed.

Anna led the way and though she'd never been here before, she had obviously been to farms like this one before. They decided that five bushels would be more than enough even though the farmer said they could have all the apples they wanted for three dollars a bushel.

"Five is enough," Jessica said. "One for Teddy's mother, one to give away, and three for the Winston household."

"Let's take six," Anna urged. "We can pick out the best ones to eat," she said, "and I'll cook the rest."

"Sounds like a lot of apples to me," Willow said. "I don't like applesauce at all."

Anna looked as though she might say something to her cousin, but she just picked up a ladder and a gunnysack and two bushel baskets. She started climbing the tallest hill and the others followed.

"I guess she wants to work alone," Jessica said, "but I need a partner. Someone who can give me a boost onto this ladder." Jessica looked suspiciously at the triangular ladder she was carrying.

"We can go two to a tree," Teddy said. "I'll go with you."

"You may have to help me," Jessica said doubtfully, "I'm not a great tree climber."

"Not to worry," Teddy replied. "My great grandfather was a monkey. Jake Simeon, he was called."

Jessica laughed and they stopped at a tree about fifty yards from the crest of the hill. They leaned their ladders against the tree so that they were facing each other and prepared to go to work.

Willow looked brightly at the remaining party and said, "I'd like to work in partners, too."

"I'll help you," both Dan and Carlos spoke simultaneously.

Brittany stood back and glared at them as they went through the process of deciding who got to climb the same tree as Willow. Willow knew that Brittany's feelings were hurt but she didn't see what she could do to make things any better. If Dan and Carlos both wanted to work with her, then that was the way it was. Besides, it was kind of fun to have both of them act so silly. It made her feel important.

Finally, Willow couldn't stand the look on Brittany's face another minute and she said, "I've got a better idea. Let's all four work together. We can get lots done that way and it will be more like a party."

"I'll just take my own bushel basket and go by myself," Brittany said.

"That wouldn't be any fun," Willow answered and she bent to pick up all three gunnysacks. Willow knew that Brittany was really very angry but she also knew that Brittany wouldn't say or do much except glare at her. Long ago, Jessica had taught them never to quarrel in public. Brittany might be angry enough to knock her down but that definitely came under the classification of inappropriate behavior. She would be grounded for a month.

Brittany settled for frowning at Willow when the men weren't looking and standing as far away from her sister as she could get without attracting special attention.

Willow led her little group over to a place beside a small running stream and started picking apples up off the ground under the trees.

Dan said, "Don't bother with those. Pick the ones on the tree and be careful they're not bruised or you'll ruin the whole lot."

"How can I tell if they're bruised?" Willow asked helplessly.

"I'll show you," Dan said. He propped the ladder up against the tree and put his arms around Willow's waist to give her a boost onto the ladder. "Just make sure you get some stem when you twist," he said.

"How can I do that?"

"It's easy," Dan said. "It's the natural place for an apple to break from the limb. Remember that an apple was once a flower and the stem was once its little branch."

Willow stayed in the tree long enough for the others to get up there and then she looked down at the ground and decided it would be a more comfortable place. She slowly backed down the ladder and jumped to the ground.

"Three people in one tree is plenty," Willow called up to them.

It wasn't long before Carlos came down off his ladder and bit into one of the apples. He held the apple out to Willow and asked, "Want a bite?"

She took a bite of his apple and then laughed and said, "I've got lipstick on your apple."

Carlos carefully rubbed the lipstick off the

apple and smiled down at her and said, "I wouldn't want your mother to catch me with your lipstick on my face, would I?"

Willow's heart beat just a little faster and the blood rushed to her cheeks. She believed if Carlos was making jokes like that, he must have kissing her on his mind. Maybe he wanted to kiss her right now and this was his way of hinting at it. Did she want to kiss him?

She had to admit she did. For many weeks, she'd been thinking mostly about Lars Peterson and dreaming that Lars would be her only boyfriend but compared to Carlos, Lars seemed a little dull and a little young. How much more exciting and fun it would be to have a boyfriend like Carlos. Someone genuinely cosmopolitan and well traveled. Someone with great manners and a good education. Someone older.

She took a deep breath and asked. "Want to take a walk? Look around the farm?"

"I think I'd better get back to work," Carlos said. "You don't like to climb trees?"

Brittany jumped down from her tree and landed at their feet. Willow thought her sister acted like a ten-year-old sometimes. She said, "I never could climb trees, could I, Brittany?"

"You couldn't do much," Brittany answered quickly. "Play with dolls and look pretty.

Except for that, you were useless."

Willow was shocked at Brittany's response. Carlos threw back his head and laughed as though Brittany had made a great joke, but Willow didn't think it was funny at all. Not at all.

Chapter 20

Willow looked so distressed that Brittany would have felt guilty if she hadn't been so mad. What right did her sister have to spoil the whole day? First, she had all the guys wanting to pick with her. Then she quit picking. Now she was trying to lure Carlos away altogether.

"I have to have another bag," Brittany said. "Give me yours, Willow."

"I was going to use it."

"You're not doing anything," Brittany said.

"I'll stay down here and you guys can throw them down to me," Willow said.

"You asked for it," Brittany answered and quickly climbed up the tree again.

Brittany hit her sister on the head once and on the shoulder twice. The second time she hit her on the head with an apple, Willow shouted up at her, "You did that on purpose."

Brittany stopped hitting her then, not because she was over being mad, but because Willow's voice sounded as though she might cry. She knew her sister from way back and she knew that beneath that flirtatious beauty mask was defenseless Willow who would cry if you picked on her.

Eventually the bushel baskets were filled and everyone went back to the van, where Anna was waiting for them. She'd finished first, of course, and she'd also picked up a cardboard box in the field and filled it with apples that were "too good to leave behind."

Brittany was still mad at her sister and it made her crosser to see how happy Teddy looked. He had no business deserting her that way in the first place. "Your mother is a great tree climber," Teddy told her. "I almost fell out a couple of times but Jessica never missed a step. Once, she caught my ladder."

"I'd think all that tap dancing you're doing would improve your athletic ability," Brittany snapped. The minute the words were out of her mouth, she wished she could retract them but, of course, that was impossible. Radio stations had thirty-second delays but human conversations didn't.

Teddy glared at her.

"Tap dancing? What tap dancing?" Jessica asked.

Brittany glared at Teddy. It was dumb to keep a secret like that anyway. She waited to see what Teddy would say to her and she was ready for a big fight. But Teddy just shook his head and turned to her mother. "I'm in the school musical and I've got a singing and dancing part. I was keeping it a secret until I was sure I was going to be good. And I don't think it's good luck to talk too much about things like that."

"I'm sure you will be wonderful," Jessica said quietly and quickly tried to change the conversation by asking, "Would you like to stop by Hugo's on the way home and get hamburgers?"

"Do you have the lead in the play?" Willow asked. "I thought Bill Sawyer had the lead."

"He does," Teddy said, "I play the second lead."

"What's your role like? Are you funny or what?" Willow asked.

Brittany's heart sank. So Willow had heard the conversation and now it would be all over school. Willow would tell a few people who would tell a few people. It would turn into exactly what Teddy wanted to avoid. "He doesn't want to talk about it," Brittany interposed.

Teddy turned and looked at her coolly. "I won't make a big deal about that now. So don't you make a big deal either, Brittany Winston."

Her heart sank as she heard his tone of voice. She had never heard Teddy sound so cool, remote, and she knew that he was really mad this time. She didn't dare say anything else and listened helplessly as Teddy answered a million questions from Willow.

Chapter 21

"Those folks you live with, they treat you all right?" Joe asked Anna as they finished their practice.

"They're nice," Anna said. "But different. They do things I never even thought of."

"Like what?"

"I have to wear a costume to their Halloween party," Anna said. "Aunt Jessica thinks I should go as a queen. She wants me to wear a powdered wig and a hoop skirt."

Joe laughed. "Is that the worst thing?"

"Yes, it is."

"That doesn't sound so bad to me. It's the other stuff that sounds kind of off. Sounds like you're working very hard. And they don't do much, do they?"

"They're busy," Anna said. "The girls have a lot of friends and they study. Willow works hard on school and her cheerleading. And Aunt

Jessica has a lot of interests. She's a painter. They just don't know how to do housework."

"So you do all the housework? Sounds weird." Joe turned and tossed the ball one last time against the backboard.

Anna watched wistfully as the ball rolled around the edge of the rim and dropped in. She wished she could do that. She would learn if she practiced long enough — and if she was truly talented. Was she that good? Joe thought she could be.

"How about friends?" Joe was frowning at her now. "Do you have any friends?"

"I asked for the job," Anna reminded him. "I'm saving almost five hundred a month. That means I'm going to save my first year of college tuition in my sophomore year of high school. That's good."

"You'll get a scholarship," Joe dismissed her need for money with a shrug of his shoulders. "What about friends, Anna?"

"You're my friend."

"I'm an old married man and you're a kid."

Anna laughed. "I do have another friend. His name is Lars Peterson and we run together every morning."

"Do you see him at school?"

"I see him but we don't spend time together." Anna frowned and quickly changed the subject. She wasn't sure exactly why Lars was so friendly early in the morning and he avoided her at school, but she thought she understood. He was one of the most popular kids and ran around with the most popular crowd. Whenever she saw him, he was surrounded by other kids — usually girls. Lars always waved or smiled or said hi but he never came over to talk to her. Anna never went over to him. She was a definite outsider.

"It's all right," she assured Joe. "My life is going well."

"Just because you're ambitious doesn't mean you have to live a miserable life," Joe said. "You told me yourself you're studying till eleven at night. That's too late for a growing girl."

Anna laughed and said, "I think I *am* growing. And so does Aunt Jessica. You should have heard the way she said it though, 'My dear, I do believe you've gotten taller since you moved here.' "

Joe laughed and said, "You could go to the Halloween party as the tallest person in the world. Wear high heels and a top hat with a tuxedo."

When Anna didn't laugh, he suggested, "I was always a pirate with a fake mustache and red bandanna around my head."

"You're talking about when you were a little kid. This is different."

Anna sighed and continued, "She'll make me go, no matter what. And I think she's taking me on Saturday to rent a real fancy costume. Something with hoop skirts."

"How about we dismantle this hoop and you wear a basketball uniform?" Joe teased.

"I wish I could."

"You can wear my uniform if you want," Joe offered. "And I've got an old hoop in my room. At least it's a costume you'll be comfortable in."

"Would you let me borrow your jersey? The one with the number 123 on it?"

"Why not?"

Anna laughed. "I could tell Aunt Jessica that I already have a costume with hoops."

"I'll bring it on Thursday. Get you a nice new one."

"They have no idea I even know you," Anna said.

"That's good," Joe said. "Everywhere I go, people ask me dumb questions. I like being a star but I'm not much of a celebrity."

"If you sign with the Jets you'll have to get used to it," Anna reminded him. Only Anna and his wife knew about the offer he'd received last week from the Jets. It would mean leaving college basketball early but he was thinking about taking the opportunity.

"If I sign with the Jets I can afford to buy my wife some things. Alicia's been waiting for three years while I play college ball. She deserves the best so I guess I'll learn to be a celebrity. That is, if I make the grade."

Anna laughed at the idea that he might fail.

She had to run all the way home in order to get there in time to prepare dinner but she didn't mind. Practicing with Joe on Mondays and Thursdays was the high point of her week. She knew she was a very, very lucky person to have been picked out by the star. He took a lot of time and trouble teaching her things and, besides that, he seemed to like her.

As Anna chopped the celery and onions to put in her stew, she reminded herself that things were going quite well. She had Lars to run with in the mornings and Joe to coach her two afternoons a week. She had a job that wasn't too hard, she was saving money, and her grades were fine.

Anna sighed as she dropped the onions and celery into the pot. No matter how much she tried, she couldn't get over the idea that the Winstons were displeased with her. While Willow and Brittany tolerated her around the house, they still avoided her at school.

Aunt Jessica tried to be nice when she thought about it but things generally went better when Aunt Jessica was busy elsewhere. Right now, she was busy with another painting class at the university.

Anna got dinner on time and there were only nine at the table. Jessica was in class and so was Dan.

John, Justin and Carlos, the Zimbalist brothers, and Victoria were there, as was Brittany. Willow came in just as she was putting the stew on the table. Willow said, "Sorry, Anna. I know I promised to help but my practice ran over."

"That's all right," Anna said. She reminded herself that Willow only helped to be nice and that it was her job. As she set the stew down, she looked at her table and decided that it was a good-looking dinner. She wished Aunt Jessica were there to see how pretty everything looked. There were crystal candlesticks, a shining silver dish for pickles, and the best china. While she was happy enough to have Aunt Jessica gone when she was in the kitchen, she liked to have her there for dinner.

Conversation went better when Aunt Jessica was there. With just the girls and the boarders, conversation often took on a dull, distant politeness. Aunt Jessica had a way of keeping the talk going. Without her, things were much less pleasant.

Victoria, her roommate, began to complain. Everyone was used to the complaints by now but they effectively stopped all other conversation. "Stew again?" Victoria asked.

"We had it *ten* days ago," Anna defended her menus.

"I like stew," Brittany said.

"So do I," John Johnson said and helped himself to a second portion before the bowl got too far down the table.

"Delicious," Carlos pronounced.

The Zimbalist brothers didn't say much but they never did. They ate exactly alike — attentively and quickly. Then they said, "Excuse me, got to get back to work," and left the table.

Victoria complained, "Those two are the least sociable young men I've ever met. I wonder what they'll be like when they're forty."

"It's pointless to wonder what anyone will be like twenty years from now," Brittany said. "The world will be so changed."

"This salad is wilted," Victoria complained. "Did you make it this morning?"

Anna nodded quietly and Victoria went on, "I told you not to do that. The lettuce leaves get too wilted. Can't you spend a little more time on preparation of this food? It's practically inedible." As she complained, she took a second portion of stew and began to chew as she talked, "Apple pie for dessert? I suppose you made that yesterday?"

Anna said nothing but Brittany was ready to fight. "All the finest restaurants make their salads earlier in the day, my mother says so. And apple pie is better if it sets one day, my mother says so."

"Your mother certainly has a lot to say considering she's never around," Victoria retorted. She stood up abruptly and said, "I'll have my pie later. Save some for me."

Everyone relaxed when Victoria left the table. Carlos began to talk about Halloween in the United States and how different it was from the Day of the Dead in Mexico. "In the countryside, the families still prepare feasts for the departed spirits and they go to the graveyards and have picnics on that night."

Brittany shivered in delight and asked, "Did you ever see a spirit?"

Carlos laughed. "I was never allowed to go to the picnics and seldom allowed to go to the villages. Most of the villagers work for us, you know."

"Exactly how rich is your family?" Brittany asked.

Willow kicked her under the table but Carlos just laughed and said, "Things are different in Mexico. My family owns a lot of land but they might not be called rich by American standards."

"How much land?" Brittany asked.

"Hectares or acres?"

"Acres," Dan said promptly.

Carlos appeared to be making some mental calculations and then he shook his head and said, "Three million."

"You mean three thousand?" Brittany asked.

He shrugged and said, "Perhaps. I'm not good at those calculations."

Justin stood up and slapped Carlos on the shoulder. "Well, old buddy. Three thousand or three million, it's more than my family owns. No mortgages either, I bet."

Carlos just smiled and Justin followed Anna to the kitchen, saying he would help with the pies.

Anna carried a tray of pie slices out to the table and filled the tray with dirty dishes to carry back. As she entered the kitchen, she saw Justin putting something into the cabinet and wondered what it was. He took the second tray of pie slices out for her but didn't bother to return with dirty dishes.

When they were all finished, Anna cleaned up quickly and as she did so, she noticed the brandy decanter, which was out, was empty again. Strange. She wondered if she should fill it again or check with Aunt Jessica first. That would make the third bottle of brandy in the first month of school, yet no one ever seemed to drink.

She made a mental note to discuss it with Aunt Jessica when she had a chance to talk with her again. She began to scrape the dishes and put them in the dishwasher. As she worked, Victoria came into the kitchen and asked, "Where is my pie?"

"I think there's a piece in the refrigerator," Anna answered. She turned away from her roommate, hoping to avoid a long list of complaints. She'd had enough of that earlier that evening.

Victoria went to the refrigerator and looked inside. "Is this it?" Her voice was hard and unpleasant and began to rise in volume as she started into her round of complaints. "This is ridiculous! I told you that you were supposed to save it and you keep this — this sliver for me! You are the worst servant I have ever seen! You don't even try to take orders, do you?"

Anna kept on scraping dishes, and didn't

reply. She was used to this kind of complaining although it seemed to her that Victoria was getting worse each day. Anna tried to pretend she was deaf and let her roommate rant and rave without replying.

"I don't know why the Winstons even let you live here! They obviously don't know how bad you are even though I've tried to tell Jessica several times. And another thing — you didn't make my bed this morning. You're supposed to make my bed when you make yours. You're getting worse and worse!"

Anna turned slightly to put a salt shaker in the cabinet and she was startled to see her aunt Jessica standing behind Victoria. Aunt Jessica put her finger to her lips and shook her head to indicate that Anna shouldn't let Victoria know she was there.

Victoria raved on, "It's ridiculous for her to let someone as obviously incompetent as you be in charge. She could at least put those lazy girls of hers to work also! Now, get me some ice cream and some cookies!"

Aunt Jessica stepped out of the shadows and said, "No ice cream. No cookies. Nothing. Get upstairs and pack your bags, young lady. No one speaks to Anna like that."

Victoria asked, "How long have you been there?"

"Long enough to tell you to pack your bags."

"You can't turn me out because of an incompetent girl."

"You're out of here. Tonight."

Victoria looked frightened. "You can't turn me out at night like this. What can I do? Where can I go?"

Aunt Jessica muttered something under her breath and then said, "You can go to a hotel. I'll pay for up to a week in the Budget Motel. That will give you time to find someplace else. Only don't give us for a reference."

"You'll have to give me my rent back for the month," Victoria said.

"I'll give you the money just to get rid of you," Aunt Jessica said. She went to her purse and pulled out two bills. "Here we are. One month's refund. Now, Brittany and Willow will go with you to help pack your bags. I'll call a taxi for you." She turned to Anna and said, "You sit down and have some ice cream and cookies. I'll be right back."

When Aunt Jessica returned, Anna said, "You can deduct the money from my pay this month."

Aunt Jessica's eyes began to water and she blew her nose, then she hugged Anna and kissed her on the cheek. "My darling child, I'll do nothing of the kind. I just ask you to forgive me."

"There's nothing to forgive."

"My girls tell me she'd been picking on you ever since she arrived. They were sick of her long ago, and to do her credit, Brittany tried to tell me again last week." Aunt Jessica frowned and said, "So did Dan. I guess I just didn't want to hear. Can you forgive me?"

"There's nothing to forgive," Anna said.

Aunt Jessica kissed her again and said, "Things will be different now. You'll have your own room. And I'm giving you a raise. I'd insist you quit the job but I know you'd think that was a punishment, so I've told my girls that one of the three of us will help you every evening. We'll work in shifts."

Anna wasn't sure whether that would turn out to be good or bad news but she knew that Aunt Jessica meant well. In fact, it seemed as though Aunt Jessica really wanted to make her happy, so she thought it might be a good time to ask. She asked, "Aunt Jessica, could I ask you a favor?"

"Anything, dear. Anything."

"Could I just skip the costume party?"

"Oh, my dear," Aunt Jessica shook her head and laughed. "I didn't mean *anything*. You *must* come to the costume party. Everyone will be expecting you."

"Well then . . ." Anna wasn't surprised and, in fact, she had just used the request as an opening ploy. "Would it be all right if I pick out my own costume. All alone, I mean?"

"As long as it's flattering," Aunt Jessica said doubtfully.

"I'll look good in it," Anna promised. "And it will even have a hoop."

Chapter 22

Willow dressed very carefully for the Halloween party. She had selected her costume three weeks earlier and she believed the costumer as he told her, "You will have the very best."

Now, as she stood back and looked at her reflection in the mirror, she decided she had been smart not to powder her hair or wear a wig. Though Jessica wanted everyone to be "authentic," Willow decided that letting her own natural strawberry blond hair be piled on top of her head in huge curls was authentic enough.

Marie Antoinette wore powdered wigs but she also carried a stick to scratch under the wig. Willow knew that because her history teacher had told her. She wasn't wearing a wig and she wasn't carrying any fancy sticks. Instead, she would be carrying Anna's special apple cake out of the kitchen as she said, "Let them eat cake." That was authentic enough even to please her mother.

Her dress was white embossed satin with a low-cut front and an outside corset in pink satin with deeper pink laces. Her shoes were pink satin flats and she wore a pink carnation tied to her wrist. She was also wearing her mother's diamond earrings, and that made her feel very beautiful as well as authentic.

As she gazed at her reflection, she wondered if Carlos would think she was beautiful. He always said she was, even when she was wearing a simple T-shirt and leggings, but Carlos was so polite, you never knew whether or not he really meant it. She twirled around, practicing moving in her huge skirt. It sure slowed you down to carry all these petticoats and hoops. No wonder the rich women had so many servants.

Willow tried bending over from the waist and discovered she couldn't. If she wanted to pick up her fan, she would have to unlace her corset first. She laughed out loud because she felt so awkward.

"What's funny?" Brittany asked.

Willow jumped back and frowned. "You're supposed to knock."

"I forgot. Will you help me with this?" Brittany turned so that Willow could fix the clasp on a rhinestone necklace she'd borrowed from Jessica.

"I still don't think you should wear this with a ballerina costume," Willow grumbled. "It's not authentic and Mom wants us to be authentic."

"You're wearing her diamond earrings," Brittany answered. "So she said I could wear the necklace. How do I look?" She twirled around twice, almost falling on the second round.

Willow smiled. "You look gorgeous — like a pink angel. And your legs look pretty in those pink stockings. I think you're growing up."

Brittany wasn't sure she liked the patronizing tone in Willow's voice but she decided to accept the compliment and let it go. No sense starting the night off on a sour note. "You look beautiful," Brittany said. "Of course, you always do."

"Do you like the pink shoes?"

"I love the pink shoes," Brittany said. "Do you like my pink shoes?"

"I love your pink shoes," Willow assured her. Then they laughed because they were wearing exactly the same kind.

"It's time to get downstairs," Brittany said. "Do you think I should descend twirling or on my tiptoes?"

"If you're smart, you'll walk. Anyway, I didn't know that dancing was your secret desire. You never said anything about it."

"It isn't," Brittany said complacently. "I've given up secret desires altogether. I tried cheerleading and then I tried running. Now I'm trying to be myself. I just wore this because I thought it would look good."

"I'm glad you gave up cheerleading," Willow said suddenly. "You're so good at so many things and I — I'm good at cheerleading."

Brittany turned to stare at her older sister. Was she actually saying what she was saying? "You're the one who has all the friends. You're the one who is beautiful. You're the one . . . you're the one I've always known I couldn't compete with."

"Give me a break," Willow said. "Who gets straight A's without studying? Who is everybody's favorite?"

"Are you crying?" Brittany asked. "If you're crying I'll have to laugh at you. Anyone who can look like that and feel sorry for herself is very, very funny. Besides, you'll spoil your makeup."

Willow sniffled and said, "You go first."

The Winston girls descended the stairs and moved into a sea of costumed figures. Willow looked around quickly, spotting Teddy in the corner with Lars. Teddy was wearing a top hat and tuxedo and carried a cane. She knew he was supposed to be Fred Astaire but he looked pretty silly. Lars was wearing overalls and chewing on a straw. She supposed he was dressed as a farmer. Willow sighed and turned her back on the two high school boys. She was glad she was over her crush on Lars — he was just too, too young.

Justin, Carlos, and the Zimbalist boys were all standing in a cluster around the punch bowl when Willow wafted toward them, holding her hoop skirts carefully out of the path of traffic. "Hi," she said. "Having a good time?"

"Better, now that I've fixed your mother's punch up." Justin held his glass high and said, "Cheers."

"You didn't put alcohol in that punch, did you?" Willow asked.

"Just in his own glass," Dan whispered. "He's got a bottle stashed behind the TV."

"Mom will be really upset if he gets drunk," Willow said. "She's invited several old friends and some of them are from the university."

"Willow, you look beautiful," Justin said. Then he reached out and grabbed her wrist. "Come here, I want to show you something."

"Not now," Willow said swiftly and pulled her arm away from him. "I've got to mingle. I promised Mother I'd mingle."

"Come on, Willow. Just take a little walk with me to the kitchen. We can mingle in the kitchen."

But Willow was smarter than that. "Dan, you see what Justin wants to show us in the kitchen," she ordered. "Carlos, you and I can mingle."

She placed her hand on Carlos's arm and took him over to a group of older people from the university. "Hello, Dr. and Mrs. Henry. Dr. and Mr. Jones. May I present my friend Carlos." When they looked confused she laughed and said, "You don't recognize me? I'm Willow. The older daughter."

"Willow?" Dr. Jones said as she frowned into her drink. "I was feeling old when I pinched myself into this Barbie doll costume but now that I've seen you, I *know* I am old. My dear, it seems like yesterday that I was holding you on the swing set you had in your backyard."

"The swing set has been gone for a long time," Willow said gently. "But you look terrific in that Barbie doll outfit."

"Is everyone here?" Dr. Jones asked. "Have they all seen me? Can I take off these shoes yet?"

"You can take them off," Willow laughed. "Everyone is here except my cousin Anna and she won't notice." She wondered if Anna was hiding in her room or just late because she'd worked so hard getting the party ready.

As they moved from group to group, Willow was careful to be her most charming and most grown-up. She felt it was something she could do for her mother. Certainly, Brittany and Anna wouldn't be socially graceful enough to circulate. And Carlos was so attentive and handsome by her side. It made Willow feel just wonderful to have him there, smiling and laughing and saying just the right things as she took him from group to group.

At one point, her mother passed her and whispered, "Thanks, Willow, you're really a big help and I'm proud of you."

"Where's Anna?" Willow asked.

Jessica's eyebrows raised and she asked, "You didn't see her dramatic entrance?"

"No."

"Or hear the oohs and aahs?"

"Does she look wonderful?" Willow could hardly believe that.

"In her fashion, my dear." Then Jessica laughed and said, "I should have known something was up when she said her costume had hoops."

"What's she wearing?"

"Go see for yourself," Jessica said. "She's

over there with Lars and Teddy and a crowd of other young people."

Willow maneuvered Carlos around the room until they were in a position where they could climb a few stairs and look down on the group surrounding Anna.

"I just want to see what she's wearing," Willow explained.

"Your wish is my command," Carlos said and helped her up the few stairs until she could lean over the rail and look directly down into the group. As he did so, he leaned over her and Willow could feel his breath on the back of her neck.

Willow shivered and moved slightly so that she was closer to him. Carlos didn't seem to notice but he slipped one arm around her and held onto the banister so that he could look down as well. Willow was so aware of his closeness that she could barely concentrate on the scene before her. She expected that at any minute he would slip his arm around her waist and draw her into an embrace. Yes — she was certain that Carlos was going to kiss her and she shivered in anticipation.

"Cold?" he asked. Again, his warm breath touched her bare arm and shoulder as though it were a caress.

"Not cold," Willow said. "But I can't see Anna."

Perhaps he would lift her and after she'd been lifted, perhaps he would turn her around in his arms and let her slide down into an embrace. Perhaps . . .

"She's wearing a basketball uniform," Carlos said. "And she's carrying a basketball hoop."

"There's nothing particularly special about that," Willow said. Her voice was filled with disappointment, not because of Anna's costume, but because Carlos had moved away from her.

She turned and looked up into his eyes, hoping against hope that the sight of her face so close to his would tempt him into the kiss she dreamed about. But all he said was, "Nothing special. Now, you my sweet Willow are so very special, so beautiful that I must be the envy of every man in the room. Perhaps we should go back and find some of your other admirers so that my life won't be in danger."

Willow frowned. Carlos was going to take her back to Dan and the others without even kissing her. She knew that Carlos really liked her so she could only suppose he thought she was too young or too innocent to kiss.

Chapter 23

"What's he really like?" Teddy asked for the third time.

Anna smiled and looked into her punch glass. "He's just a real nice guy. He helps me, that's all."

"And he actually coaches you every Monday and Thursday?" Teddy asked. "I just can't believe it."

"Is he — is he like a boyfriend?" Brittany asked. She knew it was a dumb question but she was still in shock at seeing her cousin in Joe Andrews's jersey.

Teddy turned and scowled at her. "Count on you to ask something silly. And you think you're a feminist."

Brittany actually smiled at him. If he was at the stage in his anger toward her that he was making sharp digs again, that meant he was probably going to forgive her for telling everyone about his acting part. She breathed the first really relaxed breath she'd breathed all evening. Even after Teddy said yes to her question about whether or not he was coming to the party, she hadn't been sure he was ready to forgive her. And life without Teddy was hard to think about.

Anna shook her head and said quickly, "Joe's married. He just thinks I have talent." She wished she could leave the party now but she supposed thirty minutes wasn't quite long enough to count as "putting in an appearance."

"Is he going to sign with the Jets? I read in the newspaper that he'd had a great offer. Two million for the first year." Someone she didn't know asked the question.

"I don't know. We don't talk much."

"When and where do you practice?" another stranger asked. This one was wearing a long red wig and a funny bulbous nose with a clown-painted face.

Anna looked around the group that surrounded her and tried to remind herself that they were just friends of Aunt Jessica's. She knew that this was a Halloween party and everyone was dressed up to look funny on purpose, but she couldn't shake the feeling that she was surrounded by weird, threatening strangers. She began to sweat and she could feel the palms of her hands going cold and clammy. I'm frightened, Anna thought, and it was a strange idea. She knew she was shy but she'd never actually been frightened by anything in her life. Yet she was frightened by this bunch of people who seemed to be crowding too close, taking her breath away.

"Want to go get something to eat?" Lars asked.

She nodded her head quickly in agreement. Lars took her hand and pushed his way through the group. He held her hand until they were in the kitchen and then he dropped it and turned to laugh at her. "I thought you were either going to break and run or faint. Which was it?"

Anna shook her head and poured herself a glass of water. "I've never actually been frightened before," she confided. "It was very strange."

"They were strange," Lars said. "I can't believe the excitement that uniform caused. Who spotted the numbers first?"

Anna shrugged. "It was a dumb idea. And now if anyone comes to watch me practice with Joe, that will be ruined. Of course, it's almost over anyway."

"So he *is* signing with the Jets," Lars said. Then he said very seriously, "Don't worry,

Anna. I won't say anything to anyone. I'm your friend."

Anna smiled. She trusted Lars. He had clear blue eyes that were steady and serious. She always felt good around him.

Lars said, "I thought you and I might be on the same team this year. We could use you." Then he laughed. "Or maybe Coach Contraro would dump me and give you my spot."

Anna shook her head. "I talked it over with him and with Joe. They both think I'll be better off playing with the girls' team."

Lars frowned. "You can force him to let you on the boys' team, you know. Everyone knows you're good enough."

Anna took another glass of water and drank deeply. "He would have let me try out for the boys' team but he thinks the girls have a good chance for the state championship and I'll have a better chance for scholarships if I play with them."

"I don't know," Lars said. "Seems like if you play with the boys and do well, you'll get a lot of publicity. Colleges will be fighting over you."

Anna smiled and shook her head. "Publicity isn't what I'm after. I just want to play ball."

Lars looked at her quietly and seemed about to say something else then he asked, "You all right now? Want to go back in?"

"You go on in," Anna said. "I'll just hang out in the kitchen for a while."

"I'll stay with you," Lars said.

"You don't need to," Anna answered promptly. "I'm fine now."

At that moment, Willow came into the kitchen and said, "There you two are. Anna, where did you meet Joe Andrews? And why have you kept him a secret?" As she asked her cousin those questions, she smiled at Lars.

When Anna didn't answer, Willow didn't seem to notice because she went right on and asked Lars, "Don't you want to come out and hear me sing? I hate to perform in public but I promised my mother that I would. So I guess I have to do it and I'd feel a lot better about it if you were listening. Good to have a friend there, you know."

Lars looked indecisive and Anna spoke up. "Go ahead, Lars."

"Why don't you come along?" Lars asked.

"No. You go ahead. I want to check on the soda supplies."

"She's heard me sing too many times," Willow assured him and took him by the hand and led him out of the kitchen.

Anna went into the side porch where Jessica kept extra supplies and brought out several bottles of sodas. She picked up two six-packs of Pepsi and moved back into the kitchen. She was startled to find Brittany and Justin standing in the kitchen, locked in an embrace.

Brittany was standing still and Justin had his arms around her, kissing her and hugging her tight. For a moment, Anna couldn't decide whether Brittany was a willing or unwilling participant in the kiss. Then she decided it didn't matter. Brittany was very young and Justin was too old for her. Besides, Anna was certain that Justin drank.

Anna put the Pepsis down with a bang on the counter and said, "You two better get back to the party."

Brittany jerked away from Justin and he rocked back on his heels and fell backward, breaking his fall on the kitchen counter. He managed to recover his balance by pretending to lean back and put his elbows on the counter. He grinned at Brittany and said, "That was quite a kiss."

Brittany blushed and seemed about to say something. Then she turned and ran out of the kitchen. Justin laughed aloud and called out, "That's right, knock 'em dead and then scamper away."

"She didn't knock you dead," Anna said. "You've been drinking too much."

"You're wrong," Justin said. "I haven't been drinking enough. Been trying to put a good face on and behave myself, but from now on I'm going to be myself." He turned and began looking in the cabinets.

Anna went back to the side porch and carried out two six-packs of 7-Up. When she returned she said, "How about a 7-Up?"

"Where's the brandy?"

"You drank it all," Anna said. "The cooking sherry, too."

Anna decided right then and there that she would have to tell Aunt Jessica about Justin. She hated to do it because she liked Justin, but he obviously had a big problem with alcohol. And if he was acting like that around Brittany, Aunt Jessica should know.

Chapter 24

Brittany ran back to the living room, Justin's kiss still on her lips. Her face felt flushed and she wondered if people could tell that she'd just been kissed. But no one paid any particular attention to her and everything seemed about the same as it had been. Only she was different.

As she walked around the room, refilling people's drinks and offering them cheese and crackers, she relived the magical moments.

Justin started following her around early in the evening, telling her how cute she looked in her ballerina costume and asking her to dance. At first, she didn't pay much attention because Justin was always kidding around with everyone. He called her mother Lady Jessica and when her sister walked through the room he always sang the first lines of "Willow, weep for me . . . weeping willow tree."

She'd always supposed he was more interested in Willow — everyone else was. But this evening was different. This evening Justin wanted to talk with her and he told her a lot of silly jokes and laughed a lot. She laughed, too.

Then he suddenly got very sad and said, "Can I talk to you, Brittany? I mean *really* talk to you?"

"Sure, Justin." Even then she thought he might talk about Willow or a girl back home or something.

Justin took a long drink of his punch and leaned back against the living room wall and said, "I think you're the best one of the Winstons. All together, I mean. The smartest, the nicest, the most sympathetic, and the funniest."

Then he smiled and she smiled back. That was when she realized that he was actually interested in her. Or at least, he might be. "So what about it? You want to be my girl?"

"*Your girl?*"

Justin nodded his head. "I'm crazy about you." He reached out and touched her face, tilting her chin upward and asked, "Are you crazy about me?"

Brittany stared at the handsome young man. How old was he? Nineteen or twenty. And she was soon to be fifteen. That wasn't such a big difference, was it? But was she *crazy* about him? She was too honest to say yes and she certainly had no intention of saying no.

Justin didn't wait for her answer. He seemed to accept that she'd meant to say yes. " 'Course if you're my girl, you've got to help me."

"Help how?"

"Come into the kitchen with me. Help me find something," Justin answered. He took her hand and led her into the kitchen.

Once there, they stood looking at the closed cabinets and Justin asked, "Are you psychic?"

"Maybe, a little," Brittany answered. She was not exactly worried about being out here in the kitchen with him but the whole thing was taking on a definitely strange feeling. She found herself yearning to be back in the living room talking with Teddy. But that was silly. Justin was much more interesting than Teddy!

Then he'd said, "Pick a cabinet."

She pointed to the second to the left cabinet, having no idea what he was looking for. He opened the cabinet and looked in, then shook his head and said, "Pick another cabinet."

She tried to pull her hand away. "What are we looking for?"

He turned to her and smiled. He really did

have a wonderful smile and he was darling when his hair fell onto his forehead like that. In many ways, he was the best-looking of all the men in their lives — even better-looking than Lars. And he liked her!

"I think we ought to get back to the party," she said.

That was when he pulled her close to him and kissed her. She was so surprised that it took her a minute to react and by that time Anna was in the room, calling out to them. That's when she pulled away and Justin almost fell. In all, it was a less than perfect first kiss but it *was* a first kiss.

Justin was crazy about her, she thought. He'd told her so and then he'd taken her in his arms and kissed her. If Anna hadn't come in and thrown him off balance, it would have been the most romantic thing that ever happened to her. And even if the last few minutes were awkward, she was glad it happened.

She held her head a little higher and smiled brightly at Lars and Carlos who were talking together. They were both very attractive. Maybe they would be the next to declare their love. At that moment, Brittany felt like anything at all could happen. It made life exciting and she loved that.

"Come here, Britt," Teddy called her over to the fireplace where he was talking with an older couple she didn't know. "Tell these folks about the fireplace. They were asking me a lot of questions I didn't know the answer to."

"It's Pennsylvania flagstone," Brittany began. "The original owner came from Pennsylvania and he insisted that nothing else would do. They brought it out here by train in 1911 when the house was built."

"You are so lucky to live in this wonderful house," the woman who was wearing a clown outfit said.

"Yes, I am," Brittany agreed.

"But it's so large," the woman went on. "I should think you and your sister and mother would rattle around in it."

"We don't rattle," Brittany said. "We enjoy it and we have some college students who live with us."

"Boarders — isn't that darling. So old-fashioned. It makes the house so — authentic. I'm in your mother's painting class and she invited us all to the party. I didn't really want to come until someone told me about her house. Your mother is a lucky woman."

Brittany smiled and then said, "I think I hear her calling me right now." She smiled sweetly at Teddy and said, "See you later." She walked over to the piano where Willow was playing and singing.

Willow had a nice voice and she could play the piano almost as well as Brittany. She enjoyed being the center of attention at a party but she didn't like to practice. Brittany thought she sounded a little rusty tonight.

As Willow finished singing, she motioned for Brittany to come and sit beside her and play. Brittany shrugged her shoulders and slid onto the piano bench. It would make her mother happy and it didn't really take much effort. She took over the accompaniment and that made Willow's voice sound stronger because she only had to concentrate on one thing at a time.

First, she started out with "Wind Beneath My Wings." Teddy stood beside the piano and actually joined in on the chorus of "A Whole New World." When they finished, Brittany said, "I've done my bit. I'm out of here."

Teddy said, "What have you been doing? I didn't see you around much."

"I was around," Brittany answered. "And you just saw me play the piano for my sister. Wasn't that nice of me?"

"Very sweet," Teddy said. "What else?"

"What do you mean what else?"

"I mean, what else have you been doing?

You look like the cat that ate the canary."

"I've eaten canapés, cheese balls, cucumber sandwiches, chocolate cookies, and some other stuff," Brittany answered. "But absolutely no canaries."

"You're not telling, huh?"

"There's absolutely nothing to tell."

"There — you're doing it again!" Teddy said. "You're actually licking your lips."

"That's silly," Brittany said as she turned away quickly to hide her smile. She had no intention of telling Teddy that Justin kissed her because he would find some way to ruin it for her. But she couldn't help wonder what he would say if he knew.

Chapter 25

Anna came into the kitchen from the laundry room about ten on Saturday morning and Aunt Jessica was waiting for her. Her aunt asked her to sit down and have some tea.

Anna took a cup of tea and said, "I wanted to tell you that I think Justin has been drinking a lot. He's drunk all your brandy and cooking sherry and I really think it's a problem."

"Justin?" Jessica stirred her tea absentmindedly and said, "I suppose he might have sampled the sherry. Young men do that sort of thing. I'll ask him to replace it. But you can't tell about the brandy. We keep it on the tea cart all the time. Anyone could be drinking that." She sighed and said, "I'll lock up the liquor."

"Aunt Jessica," Anna said, "I wasn't going to tell you, but Justin was drunk last night and I caught him kissing Brittany in the kitchen."

"Brittany? That's ridiculous. She's only fourteen."

"He was kissing her and when I came in, he sort of staggered. I know he's drinking too much and I've seen him before when I thought he was drunk. I think you should do more than lock up the liquor."

Jessica nodded and tapped her fingers on the table. "I suppose Brittany enjoyed the attention?"

"She ran when he let her loose. I think she may have been frightened."

"You don't think she encouraged him?"

"No, I think Justin drinks too much."

Jessica nodded and said, "I'll call his parents this afternoon. He's underage and they need to know why I'm asking him to leave. Perhaps they're smart enough that they'll do something about it. I'll suggest he may need treatment. I'll insist he leave right away."

Anna said softly, "That will be good." She supposed it would come out that it was her fault that Justin was leaving and she hoped that Brittany wouldn't be mad at her. But at least she'd managed to keep her cousin out of trouble.

"Now I want to talk to you about something more pleasant," Jessica said. "You have a birthday coming soon so I thought we'd have a party on Tuesday or Wednesday evening and on Sunday we'd run you home."

"To Saint Olaf's?" Anna's heart rose in joy. "For the festival?"

"Yes, I've been meaning to do it sooner, and then I read about the harvest festival in a magazine. Your parents must think I'm very neglectful but I've been so busy." Jessica stirred her tea and said, "I don't think you've been very happy here, dear, and I'm sorry about that."

"I'm happy, Aunt Jessica. I'm doing exactly what I came to do."

"I know you're accomplishing your *goals*, dear, but I would like to see you happier. Would you like to invite your friend Joe Andrews to your birthday party?"

"Oh, no, please, Aunt Jessica."

Jessica smiled sadly and asked, "Ashamed of us?"

"No, it's nothing like that. But he isn't really a friend. He's a big star and he takes time to help me. That's all. And you'd have to invite his wife and his daughter. And I don't even know them. Besides . . ." She let her voice trail off. Joe was leaving college next week and going to the Jets. There would be a formal announcement in the papers on next Thursday. But it wasn't Anna's place to tell his decision.

"So whom should we invite to your party?" Jessica asked.

"Do we have to have a party?"

"Oh, yes, you'll be sixteen and that's a very big event in a girl's life. Are there any girls at school who are your friends?"

"Not really." Anna blushed and wished with all her heart she could get away from this embarrassing conversation and get back to her work.

Jessica looked worried. "How about some of Willow's friends? You must have met several nice girls through Willow?"

Anna didn't know what to say and so she said nothing.

The spoon began to hit the side of Aunt Jessica's cup and her mouth tightened. Anna sighed, knowing that Willow would get another lecture and then Willow would dislike her even more than before. It was all so hopeless.

"Very well. We'll celebrate your birthday at dinner tonight. Just the four of us. Unless you reconsider inviting the Andrews family. Now, I want to give you my special birthday gift today. We're going shopping and I have an appointment with Joel to have your hair cut at five this afternoon."

"What about supper for the boarders?" Anna asked.

"While we're shopping, Willow and Brittany are getting supper and Dan volunteered to do the dishes this evening. It will be a small group anyway." Jessica frowned. "Carlos went to New York City for a few days so that leaves Justin, John Johnson, and the Zimbalist boys."

"Are you going to get some other boarders?" Anna asked.

"No, I don't think so," Aunt Jessica said slowly. "I'm so busy with my painting, and some of the boarders are so unpleasant. Funny, I thought university students would be very easy to deal with. That Victoria was a horror and John Johnson is so stingy I can barely talk to him." Jessica shook her head and said, "Ah, well, we don't have to do it forever, you know. I'll talk to Justin about leaving. But not today. Today, we buy you some new clothes and get you a wonderful new haircut. Let's go."

Anna always felt as though she was swept away by Aunt Jessica's energy. Her aunt was so different from any of the relatives she had in Saint Olaf's. She was so enthusiastic and so young in so many ways that there were times when Anna felt she was older than her aunt. And yet, she knew that Jessica had done a lot of things alone that other women would find difficult if not impossible.

She dreaded shopping, but her aunt made it easier than it had been with the girls. She started out by saying, "Now, the challenge is to find clothes that are tall and sophisticated and still look young. Right?"

"I suppose so."

"And the problem with your last shopping trip was that Brittany tried to get you to wear cast-offs and Willow tried to put you in little Miss Muffet outfits. Right?"

"Right." By now, her shopping trip with her cousins seemed almost funny and if Jessica wanted to believe they had tried to help her and failed, that was obviously better than the truth. The truth was her cousins couldn't wait to get rid of her.

Aunt Jessica took her to Hunsaker's again but this time they went to the third floor. "This is where I find things," she confided. "Let's look around and see what we can see."

Anna was stunned at the elegance and she knew the prices would be very high. She said, "I bought my last clothes in the budget department."

"You must promise me you'll never do that again," Aunt Jessica said. "Budget departments may be all right for small people but you have a figure for good clothes. Magnificent shoulders, slim waist, and long legs. If you weren't so interested in sports, you might have been a model."

Anna laughed. Sometimes her aunt was as imaginative as Brittany.

"I'm not joking," Aunt Jessica said. Then she tipped her head to one side and said, "Let's see, you're a spring when it comes to colors, aren't you? So we want to stay away from muddy colors and go for the light, clear shades. Not too pastel, of course, because of your height, but light and clear — definitely."

Aunt Jessica went over to a rack of dresses and picked out three and said, "Start with these. Don't look at the price tags. They're none of your business. It's your birthday, and you need one beautiful dress. And don't hide in the dressing room. Come out and show me. No. I'll come in with you so you can't cheat by looking at prices."

Anna had never been in such a large dressing room. There was a three-way mirror and two chairs. Aunt Jessica sat down in one and said, "Now, no peeking. I'm watching you."

The first dress was a light blue-gray silk with long, full sleeves and a very straight skirt. Anna put it on and stared at herself in the mirror. The dress was a little tight but it did look good. She was startled at how different she looked. It was almost as though she were a different person in that dress.

"Too small," Jessica pronounced, "and a little too old but the color is perfect. Don't you like the color, dear?"

"Maybe they have a larger size?"

"You *do* like the color," Aunt Jessica nodded approvingly. "I can see that underneath all that shyness there's a beautiful woman just waiting to come out and meet the world. Don't blush, my dear. You will be beautiful when you come into your own."

Anna tried on seven more dresses before they found one they could agree on. It was a simple gray-green silk and linen two-piece dress with a long skirt that hit Anna mid-calf. The top was cut like a Russian soldier's blouse with a high neck and full sleeves and a wide waistband. It could be worn open as a jacket and came with a mandarin orange shell underneath. Best of all, it had slits on both sides of the long, thin skirt so Anna could walk.

"One dress, I think," Jessica said. "You may need something else later but school clothes are most important. So, we're off to the sportswear department."

"Aunt Jessica, you don't have to do this," Anna said weakly. "I like my school clothes."

But she could hardly wait to get home and try on her new dress again. The reflection in the mirror fascinated her.

"You can wear your dress tonight," Jessica said. "It's perfect to go to dinner. And you can wear it on dress-up dates."

Anna, who was standing behind her aunt, couldn't resist smiling at Jessica's determination to believe that she was a normal high school girl who went out on dates with boys all of the time.

In the end, Aunt Jessica managed to buy one pair of Levi's, three turtleneck sweaters, three blouses, and a half-dozen T-shirts in the sportswear section. Then she took Anna to another store called City Girl, which had tall sizes, and said, "These things will fit you fine but they're not as stylish. We'll have to choose carefully. And no horizontal stripes. Never try to hide your height. Be proud. Stand proud."

"Yes, Aunt Jessica." By this time, Anna was in mild shock. She had never dreamed of having so many clothes but her aunt wasn't finished yet.

She purchased a soft beige-and-gray tweed blazer, a gray pleated skirt, and a beige sweater set. Then she found some sea-green leggings and a huge overblouse she said were perfect for school. "I couldn't wear those to school," Anna protested.

"Willow does," Aunt Jessica answered and that was the end of that conversation.

Black stretch pants, gray stretch pants, and a second pair of Levi's with a two-inch-wide leather belt. These pants were baggy and very stylish; to be mixed and matched with a yellow-and-white striped shirt, a yellow sweater, a huge black overblouse, and a soft apricot-colored turtleneck sweater.

The tall shop had shoes in her size, and Aunt Jessica insisted on buying her new black and navy flats as well as a pair of low-heeled shoes in metallic green to wear with her dress. When it was time to total the bill, Aunt Jessica sent her to the car and so Anna was never exactly certain how much her aunt spent but she knew it was a very, very great deal.

Eventually, Aunt Jessica came out of the store with the clerk who was carrying a lot of bundles and Anna jumped out to help. As she took the packages from Aunt Jessica and her aunt opened the trunk and began putting all the clothes inside the car, Anna said, "I know you spent too much, Aunt Jessica. I'm really sorry."

"Sorry?" her aunt said. "Why not be happy? You're a beautiful girl with a whole new wardrobe. And now we're going to get that haircut. Then it's going to be time to sing 'Happy Birthday.' "

Chapter 26

Brittany was surprised when her mother insisted that they wear dresses to dinner but in a way, she enjoyed dressing up. She chose her long black dress and piled her red curls on top of her head, letting several strands hang down around her ears. She put on a pair of black sequin earrings that dangled and an artificial flower behind her ear.

When she got to the bottom of the stairs, her mother was waiting. She frowned when she saw Brittany and said, "We're only going to Perontino's. I think that shawl is a bit much."

"You're wearing black," Brittany pointed out. Her mother was wearing a simple black knit dress and jacket with a strand of pearls and pearl earrings. Brittany thought her mother looked nice — boring but nice.

Willow was also all dressed up. Her strawberry blond hair was fanned out over her shoulders and she looked gorgeous, as always.

Brittany barely looked at Willow. She was used to having her sister look perfect. It was Anna who startled her.

Anna came down the stairs last and she was wearing a soft gray-green dress with big sleeves and an orange belt. She was wearing darker green pumps and most importantly — earrings. Brittany could hardly believe her eyes. Anna Goethe — her awkward, bashful, basketball-playing cousin, was actually wearing shoes with heels and earrings. The earrings were small silver buttons and Anna looked pretty uncomfortable in the shoes but she was making it down the stairs without falling on her head.

"Your haircut is great," Willow said. "Did Joel cut it?"

"Yes," Anna said and smiled quickly.

"Did you lighten it?" Willow asked with amazement.

"Just in front a bit," her mother broke in. "Doesn't she look great?"

"Great," Brittany said, and she shifted her shawl slightly and lifted her head higher. She was tired of being short and red-haired. If she couldn't have beauty like Willow's, she might at least have been given height like Anna.

"We are all remarkable-looking women," her mother said, as though reading her younger daughter's mind. "Each with her own particular beauty and sense of style. We'll probably stop traffic in the streets." Then she laughed as she saw Anna's face and said, "Not to worry. That's just something my grandmother used to say. We won't even be walking on the streets."

Dan came out of the kitchen to admire them and said, "You are all a great-looking bunch of women. Anna, you look specially good tonight." But it was Willow he kept looking at and she played it for all it was worth, smiling at him and flirting until Brittany felt like screaming.

"Let's go, I'm hungry," Brittany said. She was a little surprised at how difficult it was to get them moving but they were soon in the car, and then to Perontino's.

"May I take your coats, ladies?" the maître d' asked and they all gave up their coats easily. Brittany didn't like her coat because it looked too juvenile. Willow's was a dark blue dress coat, which Jessica discarded last year, and Anna was wearing a dressy black cape of Jessica's. Only Brittany was stuck with a three-quarter-length school coat of serviceable khaki wool. Life definitely wasn't fair.

Over their menus, Brittany studied Anna more closely. No — she still wasn't pretty. She would probably never be really pretty but she was nice-looking in a different kind of way. Her hair was cut short, like a boy's except she had very long bangs that were blown-dry to curl around her face. Anna *did* have pretty eyes, Brittany decided.

She smiled twice during dinner and that was interesting because when she smiled, Anna's face looked very different. She looked almost pretty then. Brittany wondered if everyone looked so much better when smiling. If so, she was going to practice smiling more. She would start this evening.

She smiled at the waiter when she ordered the chicken with lemon sauce. She smiled at another waiter who walked by their table. In fact, she smiled so much at him, that he came over to their table and asked, "Do I know you?"

Brittany shook her head and said, "No, I don't think so."

"Can I get you anything?"

"No thanks."

He went away looking so confused that she decided to concentrate her smiling on guests at the restaurant. There was one man of about thirty who was sitting alone, reading a newspaper, and Brittany decided to test the magnetic power of her smile. Even though he was reading, she smiled steadily at him until he looked up. Then he smiled back, folded his newspaper, and stood up.

As he walked toward their table, Brittany wondered what he would say or do. Was he so drawn to her smile that he would ask for her name or phone number? Could he tell from that far away that she was as young as she was? It was kind of exciting and kind of scary to watch him cross the restaurant.

When he got closer to the table, she decided he was definitely too old for her. He was closer to forty than thirty and he was kind of mussed-up-looking anyway. His jacket was old and his shirt wasn't pressed very well. Still, his attraction to her proved that she had magnetic powers and that was something.

"Hello, Jessica," the man said. He didn't seem particularly surprised to see her.

"Oh, Burt!" Jessica was obviously surprised and pleased to see him. Her mother was smiling widely now and she looked prettier because of it.

"I thought I recognized you when you came in," the man said, "but you only have two daughters. Right?"

"Right," Jessica sort of laughed and said,

"My daughters, Willow and Brittany. And this is their cousin Anna. Won't you join us?"

"No, thank you," Burt answered. "I just wanted to say hello and take a closer look at all these charming young ladies." As he said that, he winked at Brittany and she understood that he'd been watching the table all along. It was his interest in her mother that drew him over, not her magnetic smile.

"See you tomorrow," Jessica said as he walked away.

"You could have introduced us," Brittany complained.

"But you know him," Jessica answered quickly. "You met him at the Halloween party. He's Burt Hawkins, my painting instructor. He's a well-known painter as well."

"I met so many people at the Halloween party," Willow said in a bored voice. "Was he wearing a George Washington outfit?"

Jessica smiled at the idea. "No, he was wearing a goatee and beret and carrying a brush and pallette. It seems he's already living his secret ambition. Which reminds me, he's bringing his art appreciation class through our home on Friday afternoon. I hope you'll clean up your rooms."

"I thought you gave up house tours when

you started the boardinghouse," Brittany complained.

"We don't have so many boarders anymore and Burt — Mr. Hawkins — asked me as a special favor."

When they were finished with dinner, three waiters brought a beautiful chocolate cake to the table and sang, "Happy birthday, dear Anna." There were sixteen candles in the cake and Anna blew them out without even trying.

"I guess with lungs like yours, you'll always get your wish," Brittany said.

Anna looked up, surprised, and said, "Don't you get your wishes?"

"Not often," Brittany answered in a sad, little voice.

"Brittany, that's enough," her mother said with a slightly amused voice. "This is Anna's party and I'll thank you not to try and upstage her."

"We could put the candles back in and Brittany could wish," Anna suggested. "Willow, too."

"Nonsense," Jessica Winston said with a grim look. "Now cut your cake and enjoy your evening."

On the way home, Brittany asked, "So what did you wish?"

"It's supposed to be a secret," Willow said.

"I won't tell," Brittany answered. "Come on, Anna. What did you wish?"

But Anna was looking out of the car window at the stars that sprinkled the dark sky and she just pretended that she didn't hear her cousin.

Chapter 27

They piled into Teddy's mother's van at six o'clock in the morning and started out across the long, flat highway toward Saint Olaf's. As they drove, a light dusting of snow covered the ground, and Willow snuggled in between Carlos and Dan in the middle seat.

"Cold?" Dan asked.

"A little," she answered and smiled up at him. It was fun being between the two of them and she was glad that things worked out so that Teddy and Brittany were in the backseat and Anna was up front with her mother.

Carlos leaned forward and asked, "Is that a windmill?"

"Yes," Anna answered. "Out here there are lots of windmills and some of them have their own generators as well."

"And they're growing wheat?"

"Wheat, corn, soy," Anna answered

promptly. "Of course a lot of it is pigs and dairy. Some sheep, too."

"I knew there was something I liked about you right away," Dan teased. "You're a cowgirl."

Anna laughed. Willow was startled at the sound. Her cousin's laugh was low and throaty and beautiful. She realized she'd never heard her laugh before. Willow guessed her mother was thinking the same thing because she turned her head sharply and looked at Anna.

"You are in a good mood," Carlos said. "You are glad to be going home?"

"Oh, yes!" Anna said and then quickly added, "Of course, I love Madison but home is . . . home."

Willow wondered what could be so special about a lot of flat, black dirt, and red barns, and open sky. As far as she could see, everything was boring out here in the country. But Anna looked excited and happy.

"How about you," Willow asked Dan, "are you lonesome for the prairie? Does this make you homesick?"

"Not really," Dan said. "I'll go back to Wyoming some day but I kind of like city life and Madison. In fact, I like it so much I'm thinking about switching my major."

"To what? I thought you loved farming."

"To architecture. Living in your house has shown me how much I love beautiful houses. You'll never know how much it has meant to me to live in your house."

"And you'll never know how much it's meant to us to have you there." Jessica laughed as she spoke from the front seat. "No more squeaky stairs and dripping faucets. You're the only one of our boarders who has been worth the trouble."

"Mother!" Willow said. "What about Carlos!" She tucked her arm through Carlos's arm and smiled at him. "My mother didn't mean that."

"Your mother meant it and I am desperate to make it up to her," Carlos said cheerfully. He leaned forward, withdrawing his arm from Willow's as he talked into the dashboard mirror to Jessica. "You'll have to accept my invitation now to soothe my hurt feelings. Come to Mexico for Christmas. Give *me* a chance to be your favorite boarder."

Jessica laughed and shook her head. "I'll tell you one thing, you'll never be my *least* favorite."

"Everyone who is glad Victoria is gone, raise a hand," Brittany shouted. She raised her hand first and everyone followed suit.

Anna laughed and this time her laughter seemed to fill the car.

Willow called out, "Everyone who is glad Justin is gone, raise your hand." This time, no one raised a hand and there was a silence that made Willow uncomfortable. She said, "Well, *I'm* glad he's gone. He was always trying to hug me."

"Yeah, you hated that," Brittany said sarcastically.

"At least I didn't let him kiss me like some people did," Willow retorted. Then she caught herself and said in a more grown-up voice, "Justin had a problem and he's solving it. That's admirable. Mom, are you going to let him come back when he finishes the rehab program?"

"No, I think he'll do better somewhere else," Jessica answered.

In the backseat, Teddy said, "I wonder who will be next."

"Next to go?" Brittany asked.

"Yes. It's sort of like that old movie, *And Then There Were None*. Your mother doesn't seem interested in replacing anyone either. I think I'll have my ten dollars before Christmas."

"She's not closing the boardinghouse. She's

just keeping the easy boarders," Brittany said. "Actually, I'd just as soon John Johnson go tomorrow."

"That's the serious one?"

"Stingy," Brittany explained briefly and then she yelled out, "Everyone who votes for John Johnson to go next raise your hands."

Willow raised hers and the others laughed.

Then Anna called out and said, "Look, there's the church. There's Saint Olaf's and it's just fifteen minutes to ten. It took us less than four hours. We made good time." She pointed to a small stone church on a slight hill. It had a pointed roof and a white steeple. There were lots of cars parked all around it.

Anna squirmed in her seat, acting nervous and excited as she said, "We need to hurry to get seats. We may need to split up. People come from all over the state for this festival."

Jessica pulled up close to the door and said, "You guys get out. I'll find a parking place. And, Anna, if you get a chance to sit with your family or friends, you run right along. Don't worry about us. All right?"

Anna was out the door and practically running up the church steps. Everyone else piled out and Dan moved into position to get into the front seat and said, "I'll go with Jessica. Save us seats if you can."

"No, you go with the girls," Carlos said. "I'll go with Jessica."

The two young men were obviously in a contest about who could be the most considerate. Willow realized her mother had hurt Carlos's feelings by praising Dan so much and she was angry at her mother's lack of consideration. But Jessica just waited for them to decide who would stay with her. She had that look on her face — the one where her eyebrows were raised and she seemed to know something you didn't know. Willow found the look infuriating and, if she were telling the truth, she found the fact that both men wanted to wait a little annoying, too.

Finally, Willow decided she would have to decide for them. She said, "Dan, you stay with Mom. Carlos and I will go and we'll save you seats."

"I'll stay with Jessica," Carlos said firmly.

"So will I," Dan answered.

"Oh, for Pete's sake," Brittany said. "You guys go on in. Teddy and I will stay with Mom. The three of you can sit together and we'll sit together. We'll all meet later."

"Come on, you two," Willow said. "Don't make me feel bad. Anyone would think you preferred my mother's company to mine."

"This is not about a popularity contest,"

Brittany said to Willow in a very superior voice. "This is about a politeness contest. Carlos thinks he's the politest man in the world and Dan thinks he's the most considerate. So they're both being silly and keeping us from getting anywhere at all. Makes me think we should have invited the Zimbalist boys. They don't compete. They stick together."

Carlos and Dan did look as though they felt silly then and Willow was dismayed that neither her mother nor her sister was any more sensitive to their feelings. Willow took each by the hand and said, "Come on, you guys. Let's go get seats before it's too late."

They climbed the low hill and made their way into the church. Once inside, Dan said, "Looks like we have a problem."

Then Willow saw Anna at the front of the church, waving her hand and motioning for them to come up on front. "Anna's got seats for us," Willow said. She couldn't get over how outgoing and happy her cousin looked in this setting. It was like seeing two different Annas. Really — about four Annas. The Anna she saw at school was always awkward and out of place but the worker Anna usually looked relaxed and content. The dressed-up birthday girl had looked grown-up and attractive. Now, this Anna looked like a great big overgrown kid.

Chapter 28

The minute church was over, they had to meet all of Anna's relatives. There was a mother and father who looked like older, wiser versions of their daughter and three younger brothers who also looked like them.

Anna seemed happiest to be with her younger brothers and ran with them down to the booths as quickly as she could. Then Mr. Goethe said he had to go judge the animals and Mrs. Goethe invited Jessica to go with her to help with the "setting out."

Jessica didn't really seem to know what she was going to be "setting out" but she went off with Mrs. Goethe because it seemed the thing to do. The others drifted from booth to booth, looking at the displays of animals and produce.

"You didn't really let him kiss you?" Teddy asked Brittany.

"Who?"

"You know who? When and where?"

"In the kitchen on the night of the Halloween party. Is that what you meant by where?"

"Kissed you on the lips, I guess."

"You guessed right. I liked it, too."

"You would."

"I liked it just fine. Justin is a nice guy."

"Justin is a drunk."

"He's only nineteen. Only five years older than I am. Lots of people marry people who are five years older than they are."

"So now you're telling me you're engaged?"

"Of course I'm not engaged," Brittany answered. "Mom called his folks and now he's in a rehab center in Minneapolis. He hasn't even written to me."

"Why should he write to you?"

"I guess he'd have to write to me if we were engaged," Brittany answered. "Want to walk over to the barns?"

"So it turns out that you're even nutsier than I thought. In some ways, you're not even as smart as your sister. At least she knew enough to keep away from someone who smelled of vodka."

"Vodka doesn't smell. That's why he drank it. And I don't see why you're always picking on Willow anyway. You really don't like us, I guess."

"I like your mother," Teddy said. "And Anna. And I like you when I'm not mad at you. And I guess I'd like Willow if she ever really looked at me. She's always looking over my shoulder."

"Willow looks over everyone's shoulder. Don't take it personally."

"Did you really like it?"

"I don't know. Maybe. Or maybe I just liked the idea of it. I haven't been kissed that many times, you know. So I have no real way of judging."

"I could kiss you."

"That's ridiculous," Brittany kind of turned and looked at Teddy and shook her head in amazement.

"What's ridiculous?"

"Why would you want to kiss me?"

"You would have a bigger frame of reference," Teddy said.

"No thanks."

"Why not?"

"For one thing, I would be very self-conscious. For another, I'd rather kiss someone older. For another, I don't want to kiss anyone who is only helping me out — doing research."

Teddy seemed to consider all this and then he grinned and said, "Just thought I'd offer."

"Look at those goats," Brittany said. "Did you ever see goats like that?"

"Pygmy goats," Teddy answered. They stopped and leaned on the fence and looked at the tiny animals.

As they watched, their warm breath looked like frosty air as it was breathed out. Brittany was fascinated by the way it blended together in the cold air. Teddy's breath and hers was like one breath the minute it hit the air. She moved away from him, suddenly conscious of how close they'd been standing and she said, "I really like Carlos, you know. And I think he likes me."

"Carlos is too old for you."

"Now. But he won't be in a year or two. Willow doesn't think he's too old for her."

"Willow's wrong. Carlos is as interested in your mother as he is in Willow. And he's not really that interested in any of you."

"How do you know?" Brittany asked. Sometimes Teddy made her really mad because he acted like he knew everything.

"It's a guy thing," Teddy answered and then he laughed.

"What a sexist thing to say."

She turned to walk away from him but he reached out and caught her arm, drew her close to him, and pointed over to Carlos and the others. "Stand here and look. See exactly the way he is talking to Willow. Now fix that charming way he holds his head to one side and smiles in your memory. Can you remember that?"

"Of course I can remember," Brittany said. "I'm not dumb."

"I could argue that," Teddy teased, "but I won't. Now that is exactly the way he talks to you. You think he's flirting. So does Willow. But it's just the way he talks to women."

"That's silly," Brittany said. She jerked away from Teddy and called out to them, "Hey, we're over here."

But Willow and Carlos walked off by themselves toward the field just below the church where there were a group of tourists standing around in the cold, watching men chop wood. "Maybe Carlos is going to enter the wood-chopping contest," Teddy said.

"Why don't you enter it if you think you're so smart," Brittany answered.

"I'm too smart to chop wood when there's a pie-eating contest coming up. Let's go inside and see if the food's ready yet."

Teddy and Brittany walked through the wide open doors of a giant metal barn and looked around at all the small booths that lined the two sides of the barn and made a double row down the center. "Oh, look," Brittany said. "Look at those funny chairs." She led Teddy over to a booth near the door which had at least fifty wooden chairs stacked against the walls. Each chair was covered with fantastic wild patterns that had been hand-painted.

"I like them," Teddy said. He reached out to trace his finger along the paisley pattern of a nearby chair. It was covered with a design in gray, black, and red with lines and dots very carefully painted all over the surface. "It's sort of like pin-striping on cars. The artist saw a space and decided to decorate it."

"Look over there," Brittany pointed to another shop across the aisle. "That has the same kind of painting but on big furniture." They crossed over and Brittany said, "Look at that hutch. It's great, isn't it?"

"Rosemaling," a man who was obviously the owner of the hutch said. "It took me a long time to do the hutch. Only two thousand five hundred dollars."

"It's beautiful," Brittany said.

"But a little over budget," Teddy added.

The man laughed and turned away to talk to two people who looked as though they might have the money to buy it. "I guess all this painting is called rosemaling," Brittany said. "You wonder who has the time to do work like this anymore."

"Long winters on the farms," Teddy said.

They were walking slowly now, admiring all the handcrafted items that were for sale. Many of the booths were run by one or two people. A few had names of organizations on them. Brittany bought a small bowl from the Boy Scouts as a souvenir and Teddy bought a tiny replica of Saint Olaf's church from The Norway Club booth.

As the man was putting Teddy's little church in a bag, he said, "You kids going to take in the dancing?"

"What kind of dancing?" Brittany asked.

"Polka first. Later they'll do the kickapoo stomp."

"You're kidding?" Brittany said.

"Nope," the man assured her. "They've started the polkas already. I hear the accordians. Outside, behind the barn."

"Think you can learn the kickapoo stomp?" Brittany asked.

"No. I came to eat," Teddy said.

"Let's see if we can find the others," Brittany said.

They found Jessica working in a food booth

with Anna's mother, and she looked very much at home and quite happy. When Brittany said they were looking for the others, Teddy suggested that they eat instead.

Jessica said, "Good. I'll join you." She slipped an apron over her head and walked with them up and down the booths, selecting a little something from just about every booth.

By the time they sat down to eat, their plates were piled high with sausages, potato salad, barbecued beef, sauerkraut, pickles, and other wonderful things. Teddy was the first to take a bite of the lutefisk and he laughed as he said, "It's just salted fish. All my life I've heard about lutefisk but I'll stick to the sausages."

"Try the *lefse*," Jessica said. "I helped Mrs. Goethe make some and I think they're wonderful."

"They look like tortillas," Brittany said.

"But they're made from flour and water and potatoes," Jessica answered. "Much better than tortillas." Then she laughed and said, "Don't tell Carlos I said that."

After they'd eaten, they walked outside to look at the dancing before tackling dessert. There were so many tourists trying their luck at the polka that there really wasn't much to see so Jessica went back inside to help Mrs. Goethe. Teddy and Brittany decided to look at the outdoor exhibits.

After about an hour of looking at cows, goats, and pigs, they ran into Willow and Dan and Carlos who said they'd been participating in the cornhusking contest. Dan held up a blue ribbon that he'd won and said proudly, "You can take a boy out of the farm but you can't take the farm out of the boy."

"Let's go eat pie," Teddy suggested. "And cake and brownies and cookies."

"But it's all so fattening," Willow objected.

"No it's not. It's wholesome," Teddy told her very seriously.

It was difficult to know if Willow believed him or simply decided to pretend she did while she joined the others in a feast of delicacies. Whatever she believed, she managed to eat almost as much as Teddy did and he said he was proud of her.

After they'd eaten, Brittany decided she wanted to take her mother's picture so she asked Carlos if she could borrow his camera. "Of course, my darling," he answered. "I'll go warn Jessica she's having her photo taken."

Carlos walked over to the table where Jessica worked and reached out and touched Jessica's shoulder. Brittany couldn't hear what he was saying but she could see the slight bend of his head, the flashing smile, and the low, amused laughter. Behind her, Teddy said, "He talks to your mother the same way he talks to Willow, doesn't he?"

"Get out of my light," Brittany answered.

But later, Brittany happened to catch a glimpse of Carlos talking with Anna. He was standing with his head tilted and he was laughing and talking and smiling all at once. While he couldn't look down at Anna in exactly the same way, his whole posture and manner was as close as it could be to the way he had talked to Willow and her mother. When she saw that, Brittany had to admit that Teddy had been right. Carlos did flirt with all women.

Chapter 29

Anna was so happy. She had forgotten what it felt like to feel this good. As she looked out over the horizon, she felt she could really breathe for the first time since she'd moved away from Saint Olaf's. She felt free. She felt healthy and she felt strong.

During church, she enjoyed the smells and sounds of her childhood. At lunch, she was pleased at the way Aunt Jessica worked right alongside of her mother and the other women, and she was glad her mother told her to take her brothers on a walk instead of helping out.

She called to Tom and Mike and Olaf and they came running along with their dogs. They walked down the trail to the old mill and stood on the bank of the river and tossed small flat rocks out onto the water. She could still make them skip but each of the boys had grown better at it. It made her a little sad to see how citified she'd become and how grown-up they were getting.

Tom was the youngest and he was the one who asked the question over and over, "But why do you live in Madison?"

"I've told you. I want to play ball. To get a scholarship to college. To make something of myself."

"You can make something of yourself here," Tom objected. "Mom is something."

"Yes, of course."

"But you think if you go to Madison you'll be better than us." It was a child's lament — a refrain she'd heard the whole three weeks before she left for school. She knelt down beside her nine-year-old brother and hugged him close to her. "Tommy, don't start that again. I'm already in Madison and I'm not coming home except for vacations."

"You'll be back at Thanksgiving?"

"Not Thanksgiving but Christmas. I'll have two whole weeks at Christmas."

"How long?"

"Two weeks."

"No, how long till Christmas?"

"About a month — five weeks. Now, Tommy, let's not spoil today worrying about tomorrow. What shall we do next?"

"We have to eat," Mike said. He was the

hungry one. "They'll be expecting us. And then I have to help Dad in the judging and then we have to go home because we have chores before dark."

"Okay," Anna said. "Then we'd better have the contest now. I've got some great prizes for rock skippers. Any rock skippers here?"

It was a short contest with three equal winners. Her brothers forgot all about her and their loneliness when they received their dollar prizes. They ran back to the fair to spend their money as fast as they could.

Anna walked more slowly, breathing in the wonderful air of the countryside and letting herself enjoy her day. She was so glad to be here and she realized that she felt like a teenager again. At Aunt Jessica's she always felt so grown-up and so different from Brittany and Willow that she'd forgotten her own youth and hopes and dreams. I must be more careful of myself, she thought, and she wasn't quite sure what that meant but she believed she would find a way to feel more normal in Madison now that she'd been home and remembered who she was.

Soon it was time to say good-bye. She fought back the lump in her throat as she hugged her brothers but there were tears in her eyes as she clung to her mother. Her father, who seldom said anything to her except to give quiet orders, said, "You be a good girl, Anna. Don't shame us."

"Oh, she's a wonderful girl," Aunt Jessica rushed to defend her, not knowing that it was simply her father's way of speaking.

He nodded in acknowledgment of the compliment and turned away to walk to the car. Her mother wrapped her arms tight around her daughter and reached up and smoothed her hair, lamenting, "You look so grown-up with that short hair. Be sure and wear your cap in the snow."

Behind her, she could hear Brittany stifle a laugh but Anna didn't care. Here, in Saint Olaf's, it was Brittany and Willow who would be considered "citified" and that wouldn't be a compliment. Nevertheless, she knew her cousins would find a way to get along. Anna smiled as she imagined Willow driving the young men wild at the church social.

"I'll wear my cap," she promised her mother.

"And don't spend too much on foolishness," her mother said with a worried little voice.

Anna flushed. She had known that wearing the new jeans and yellow sweater was a mistake. At least Aunt Jessica permitted her to wear her old tennis shoes. "The clothes were a birthday gift from Aunt Jessica," she said.

Her mother frowned, obviously wondering how she would ever repay her husband's rich relatives. Anna was glad she didn't know about all the other clothes tucked away in the closet at home. "Best you come by the house before you leave," her mother said.

Anna nodded. "We will."

"We have a long trip," Aunt Jessica protested.

But her mother was already climbing into their car and they were soon moving down the highway. As they watched the car recede, Anna said, "I'm sorry, Aunt Jessica, but now that she knows the clothes were a gift from you, she'll load you up with jams and jellies and probably a ham and other stuff. It's her way."

"What if we don't go there?" Aunt Jessica asked softly.

"Please," Anna said. "They wouldn't rest easy until they paid you back. So let's just drop by for a few minutes."

She couldn't tell her aunt the truth — that not accepting the invitation would be considered very rude.

"Well, let's get going," Jessica said. She reached up and put her arm around her niece. "This day has been a total success so far. I should think a nice ham would be the crowning glory."

"Thanks," Anna said gratefully.

"Do you know what's been the best about this day?" Jessica asked.

"No."

"Seeing you so happy," Aunt Jessica answered.

"I agree one hundred percent," Brittany said.

"I agree one thousand percent," Willow added. "You have a beautiful laugh, Anna."

"I agree one million percent," Carlos said. "Now if I can just persuade you to come to Mexico for Christmas, my dear, with your charming aunt and her daughters."

"Oh Mother, are we going?" Brittany and Willow asked in one breath.

"I told Carlos we would go for a few days *before* Christmas," Jessica answered. "Four or five days."

"You won't leave before school is out?" Teddy asked.

Jessica smiled at Teddy and shook her head, "Before I've seen your play? Of course not. Besides, Burt Hawkins has invited me to a faculty party. I promised him."

"Like a date?" Brittany asked in amazement.

Jessica raised her eyebrows in mock surprise and said, "I should say it was more or less like a date. Long black dress but no shawl. I'll leave the fringe to you, my dear."

"I don't think that's very funny," Brittany pouted. She didn't much like the idea of her mother going out on a date but she wasn't exactly sure why. Her mother was entitled to a life of her own. But somehow, it didn't seem fair that Willow had all those boys after her and now her mother was going to date. When would it be her turn?

"We can ask your parents for permission for you to come to Mexico with us," Jessica said to Anna.

"Please don't," Anna said. "They would never permit it and it would worry them to have you ask."

"I suppose you'd just as soon have the whole two weeks at home anyway, wouldn't you?"

"Oh, yes," Anna said. "It looks so beautiful, doesn't it?"

In the backseat, Brittany drew her knees up under her chin and stared out the window at the low, flat landscape. "What's so beautiful?" she whispered to Teddy.

"It's beautiful in a plain kind of way," Teddy mused. "But not exactly exotic. In Mexico you might see pyramids or snakes or something. You'll like that."

Brittany smiled at him. He seemed genuinely happy for her, now that he knew she would be here for his play.

might see pictures or statues or something.
Would like that."

Brittany smiled at that. He started point
Andy know nothing anything but know the
would be nice for is play

Chapter 30

On Wednesday after their trip to Saint Olaf's, the first real snow fell and Madison was covered with a three-inch layer of white magic. Jessica drove all three girls into school that morning and they detoured into the city so that they could see the capitol building and the university under the white carpet.

"I love it," Brittany pronounced. "Teddy and I will be skating right after school. Don't wait dinner for me."

"Teddy has practice," Jessica reminded her. "Why don't you take Anna to the pond?"

"Sure," Brittany's voice was flat but the silence that hung over the car betrayed their discomfort over their cousin. It wasn't that Anna looked so bad anymore. In fact, with the new clothes, she looked fine, but she was still silent and stood around looking awkward. She just wasn't much fun.

"I'll go with you, too," Willow offered. "But I'm going to wear my new skating outfit."

"Don't you think a red short skirt is a little fancy for an after-school outing?" Jessica asked with a smile.

"I didn't get many chances to wear it last year," Willow answered promptly. "There wasn't enough ice. So naturally, I want to get some wear out of it."

"You want to show off those cheerleader legs," Jessica teased.

"That means we have to go home and wait around while you dress," Brittany complained. "I want to go straight to the pond."

Willow turned to her cousin and explained, "The pond isn't really a pond. It's a large shallow bowl that's a lawn in the summer, and they flood it in the winter to let it freeze so everyone can skate. It's great fun. Music and trees and everything."

"I have no skates," Anna said quickly. Then she added, as though for double insurance, "And I have homework."

A slight flicker of a frown crossed Jessica's face and she said, "You're off the hook today, Anna, but we'll get you skates this week. And the girls want to include you."

"Oh, yes," both sisters said in unison and Willow had to bite her lip to keep from laughing. Anna looked a lot better but she was still a lump when she was around strangers. She certainly didn't add anything to the party.

"Look at the library," Brittany said. "There's already a path beaten to the door. Can't keep students down I guess."

Everyone knew Brittany was just making conversation to keep things running smoothly but they chimed right in, talking about the stone buildings and how much fancier they looked in the snow. Jessica said she would pick them up right after school so that they could get to the pond early, and all day long Willow looked forward to wearing her red skating costume out onto the ice.

That afternoon, when Willow and Brittany arrived at the pond, there were already about a hundred people skating. Most were college students and the girls didn't see many kids from Madison High.

"Guess we should stick together," Willow said.

"We make a great pair," Brittany complained. "You look like an Olympic champion and I look like the clown at the Ice Follies."

"You're the one who chose to wear new baggy purple pants," Willow laughed. "Come on." She started out across the ice, laughing at how awkward she felt. It had been almost a year since she'd been on skates and she felt like a beginner. But it wasn't any time at all before she was at home on the ice and began having fun. She'd always had a natural talent for skating but was never good enough to really work at it. Nevertheless, she was probably the best skater on the pond today and that felt good.

Brittany followed along behind her, not trying to keep up as Willow whizzed around and around on the ice, doing some of the twirls and small jumps she'd learned a few years before. She knew she made a pretty picture on the ice with her long strawberry blond hair and her short red costume, and she was pleased to see the eyes of so many young men following her as she went through her paces.

"Come on," she called out to Brittany. "Try this," and she twirled and did a light jump simultaneously.

"I see some friends," Brittany said and skated away.

Willow looked over to a group who were laughing and talking together and recognized several of them. Her heart began to beat with excitement as she saw the blond head of Lars, standing out in the crowd. So Lars was here this afternoon. She would do a few more rounds on her own so everyone could see how good she was and then she'd join them. She skated by, twirling as she waved, calling out, "Hi, guys."

By this time, the ice was getting pretty slushy from the day's activity so she knew it would be wise to slow down a bit but she couldn't resist going around really fast just a few more times. As she raced, she imagined that Lars and the others were watching her speed and grace with admiration. But she was going too fast to see if their attention was really on her.

Someone turned on a loudspeaker and began blasting skating music onto the pond. The music slowed to waltzes and several young men asked her to dance. She shook her head and headed for her school group. They were still talking and drinking hot coffee and when she skated up to them, Deirdre, who was on her cheerleading team, asked, "How can you stand the cold? We're all going."

Willow was amazed.

Deirdre shrugged. "We're *cold*. We would have left already except for Lars. He really wants to skate."

Willow looked directly at Lars and said, "I'll take you home if you'll dance with me."

"Sure," Lars grinned. "That would be great." Then he added, "I could have taken my mom's car if I'd thought ahead. I'm sorry."

"You're sorry and I'm freezing," Deirdre said. "No hard feelings, pal."

"Maybe Brittany wants to go with you," Willow said.

Deirdre shook her head quickly, "We're not going straight home."

Willow gave her a look that said she would remember this refusal to help her and turned to Lars with a big smile. "Shall we dance?"

They danced slowly at first, skating round and round the pond with their arms linked and testing their ability to stay synchronized to the music. Lars was a good skater, and he was easy to be with. Though they ran around with the same kids at school, Lars didn't go to many parties or activities, sometimes because he was working and Willow wasn't sure why not at other times.

Willow loved the music. She loved dancing and she lost herself in the physical rhythm of what they were doing. She was having a great time and that seemed to be enough. After a while, she was confident enough that she said, "I'll show you how to do some other things if you want."

"Sure."

So she taught him how to dance while she skated backward and to lead her so she wouldn't run into anyone. Then she taught him how to lift her off the ground. By the time they'd skated together for an hour, they had a little routine they could go through. Lars was strong and could lift her easily, and she looked so good that she could make the rest work.

Soon, they just skated side by side. She placed Lars's arm around her waist and they went round and round. Finally, he said, "The ice is so slushy, it's time to go."

She leaned her head onto his shoulder and asked in a soft voice, "I wanted to get to know you better but I forgot to ask questions."

"What did you want to know?"

"Why you run around with us all but you really don't. Do you prefer being alone?"

"Not really," he answered. "I have a job and I have to help at home and I have a lot of homework. I'm just kind of busy."

"Why do you have a job?" Willow asked. Then she felt foolish.

"For money," Lars answered simply. "I work to earn money."

They were standing still and he had his arm around her waist. The sun had gone and the sky was getting dark. She knew if she just stood there and smiled up at him he would get the idea to kiss her. She just knew that he was going to kiss her any minute now.

She took a deep breath and smiled at him. He smiled back and said, "You look pretty, Willow. Exercise makes you happy, doesn't it?"

"I guess so."

"You could come running with Anna and me sometimes," he offered. "I'll bet you're a fast runner, aren't you?"

"Not really." He wasn't going to kiss her. The magical moment dissolved because he was so . . . so unromantic!

"We'd better get going," Lars said. "Do you know where Brittany is?"

"Probably in the car," Willow answered curtly. "She asked for the keys and I just hope she didn't run down the battery."

She skated over to the table where her things were, untied her skates, and slipped into her boots. Lars did the same and followed her to the car. As they walked, he said, "You're a great skater."

"Thanks for dancing with me," Willow answered.

"I liked it," Lars said. "But I really like racing better. I can hardly wait until the river freezes. There's nothing I love more than skating long distances out in the country. Maybe you and Anna would want to come with me some Sunday?"

"Maybe." By now, Willow's teeth were chattering and she felt as though she would never be warm again. She could hardly wait until she got home, took a hot bath, and climbed into her warm bed. She really wasn't interested in planning another ice-skating activity — especially one with Anna as a chaperon.

When they dropped Lars off at his house, Brittany asked, "Well, did you make out with Mr. Dreamboat?"

"Mr. Dreamboat is basically dull," Willow said. "He's more interested in athletics than romance."

"Did he ask you to the New Year's Eve ball?" Brittany seemed to ignore her first answer. "Did he kiss you?"

"No. No."

"What did he do?"

"He admired my athletic ability. He invited Anna and me for a long skate in the country some Sunday. He didn't do much."

Brittany tucked her knees under her chin and said mildly, "It sounds like progress."

When Willow didn't answer, Brittany went on, "Of course, you're used to men falling at your feet so you were probably insulted because he didn't. But Lars is your basic nice guy and probably won't ever *fall* at anyone's feet. But he might like you a lot, you know."

"When I get a steady boyfriend," Willow said, "he will be romantic and exciting. He won't be a best buddy like your Teddy."

"Teddy's not my boyfriend," Brittany said. "And you don't need to get mad at me just because Lars didn't fall all over you. I didn't stop him."

"You're just defending him because you like him a lot," Willow answered. "I don't want to talk about him anymore." She didn't add what she was thinking — that she wanted someone who was romantic and exciting in her life and she was going to find that special person.

Chapter 31

Willow knew that Carlos was always flirting with Brittany and Jessica and even Anna, but she was certain that he paid her a lot of special attention. She thought Carlos was romantic and exciting or as close to it as she would find in Madison. One afternoon, soon after she'd skated on the pond with Lars, she came home from school and found Carlos in the living room reading a book.

He was alone so she dropped onto the arm of the chair beside him and asked, "What's so interesting?"

He frowned slightly and then closed the book, keeping his place with his thumb. "Beautiful Willow, how wonderful to see you. Home from school early?"

"No. It's the regular time. Only the house is emptier than usual, that's all. Where is everyone?"

Carlos shrugged and said, "I have been sitting here, reading while the world passes me by. Now you are here to entertain me. That's a delight."

"Mom's probably painting," Willow said. Then she smiled and said, "I don't think she's as interested in her painting as her instructor. I saw them together in town yesterday. They looked like they were having fun."

"Your mother is a beautiful woman," Carlos said. "It is natural that she would have many admirers. I am certain you have many admirers yourself."

Willow shrugged. "I suppose. But not so many as all that."

Carlos laughed and tilted his head, moving away from her slightly to ask, "What about your school — your classmates. That young man who runs with Anna is an admirer of yours, isn't he?"

"Maybe." Willow frowned slightly. Since they'd skated she'd barely seen Lars. Anyway, Carlos was the one she was *really* interested in, she decided. And Carlos was sitting right beside her.

"And there's poor Dan," Carlos teased. "He can't take his eyes off you. And I'm sure there are others. Aren't there?"

"There's Tim and John and Marty," Willow

admitted. "But they're all so young. I'm only interested in older men." She took a deep breath and almost added, *Like you.* But she didn't have the nerve.

"The trouble with older men," Carlos said, "is that they are older. Not so much fun, you know. Gray hair and walking canes can be attractive but they definitely slow you down."

Willow laughed because she knew it was a joke but she wondered if Carlos was really trying to tell her that he was too old for her. As she leaned over him, she searched his face for any signs of his love for her. But all she saw was a very handsome young man. He wasn't too old. He might be twenty but she was almost seventeen. That really wasn't any difference at all.

As she looked at him, Willow had an irresistible urge to reach out and touch his face. She would just like to feel the texture of his hair, or let her fingers run down his cheek. She blushed, just thinking of how forward he would think she was.

"Do you want to watch your soap?" Carlos asked.

Willow was startled by the question. "No. I never watch soap operas."

Carlos looked confused and said, "I thought you were watching it yesterday."

"That was only because I was with Brittany," Willow explained. "I'd never actually turn one on. They're too silly."

"I see." His face was without expression and she wasn't sure what he meant.

"Do they have soap operas in Mexico?" Willow asked.

"Oh, yes," Carlos laughed. "We have all sorts of modern conveniences. Cars, showers, television, and airplanes. Even rock and roll."

"Rock and roll." Willow repeated. "Do you know how to dance?"

"Certainly," Carlos replied.

Willow's heart leaped with joy. She would invite Carlos to the New Year's Eve ball! Since it was her school dance, it was perfectly all right for her to ask him.

She leaned closer, breathing rapidly. She was about to ask him if he would like to go to the New Year's Eve ball with her. She wanted with all her heart for him to say yes.

"Willow!" Her mother's voice called her sharply from the dining room. "Come in here and help, please."

Carlos jumped up and so did she. She blushed and said, "I'd better go."

"I'll explain," Carlos said quickly.

"Nothing to explain," Willow answered just as quickly and she turned from the room.

Her mother was plainly very annoyed with her and she said, "I thought you were going to help Anna tonight. The poor girl's in there all alone."

"The poor girl!" Willow said. "You always talk about how poor Anna works so hard but *you* don't stick around much, do you?"

"I will from now on," Jessica said grimly. "You were practically sitting on his lap."

"I was not! I was sitting on the arm of the chair."

"You do *not* raise your voice to me, young lady. And *do* behave like a young lady. Is that clear?"

"It's clear that you're always picking on me," Willow answered. "You always think the worst about me. You let Brittany do what she wants, and you talk all the time about how good Anna is but you never have anything nice to say about me."

"I have nothing nice to say about the behavior I just witnessed," her mother replied.

"You don't know what you're talking about!" Willow shouted.

"Go to your room." Jessica shouted back.

Suddenly, Willow was very aware that Carlos could hear every word of this quarrel. Her mother was treating her like a child and she was responding like a child and Carlos was witness to the whole thing. How could she ever get him to take her seriously if this scene went on. She drew herself up and said in a very clear and very dignified voice, "I am going to my room now. I don't want to discuss this again."

She turned and went to the staircase. Carlos was standing at the bottom of the stairs looking very concerned and he said, "Willow, I will talk to your mother. I will explain that it was just . . . nothing."

"Please," Willow said, "please don't discuss this with me or my mother ever again. Let's just forget the whole dreadful scene."

"But it was nothing," Carlos protested. "I can explain."

"Promise me you won't." She reached out and touched his arm. "Promise me."

He shook his head and said, "Whatever you say, but it is all nonsense. A tempest in a teapot." Then he laughed and added, "I learned that expression in England. Good expression, right? A tempest in a teapot."

Willow didn't even bother to ask him to explain what he was talking about. She was going to her room and she wasn't going to come out until she'd totally forgotten this mortifying scene.

Chapter 32

John Johnson gave his notice on November 20. Everyone was polite but no one tried to talk him out of his decision to move. He was very pleased to report that he'd found a job that enabled him to have a free room. "As a night clerk at the hotel," he explained, "I can sleep in any vacant room in the afternoons after I get my studies done. And of course, most night clerks learn to sleep in their chairs at the switchboard."

"Do you get free food?" Brittany asked. "From the kitchen leftovers, I mean."

"Brittany!" her mother said sharply.

"How did you know?" John Johnson wasn't offended by the question. He was proud of his cleverness and went into a long, detailed explanation of how hotels often had so much food left over. After two desserts, he went directly to his room to pack.

244

When he left the table, Brittany said, "Count on Johnson to have dinner before he packs. Did he ask you for a refund on this month's rent?"

"I'll discuss it later if you wish," Jessica said quickly. "I'd rather not have any more talk about money at the dinner table. If you don't mind."

After supper, Dan offered to help Anna clear the table but Jessica said, "No, thanks. Tonight I think that the Winston family will do the honors."

All the boarders left the room and Jessica said, "Let's get this done and then have a little talk."

As they carried dishes in, Brittany said to Willow, "Notice how cranky Mom is lately?"

"Notice? She sent me to my room on Monday, as if I were six years old," Willow answered.

"I have a theory," Brittany said.

"What's that?"

"That's when you think something but you can't prove it," Brittany answered.

"You really do think I'm stupid, don't you?" Willow was just a little bit angry and quite hurt.

"That was a joke, dummy," Brittany explained.

"There you go again, I'm not a dummy."

"My theory . . . my theory is that Mom is thinking of getting married and she wants to make sure we're model children for our new stepfather."

"She wouldn't?"

"She might. A lot of widows do. I read this magazine article that says happily married people tend to remarry within three years. It's been exactly three years."

"Who could she marry?" Willow asked.

Brittany shrugged, laughed, and put the last remaining olive in her mouth. "Carlos maybe."

"That's ridiculous!"

After the kitchen was clean and the dishwasher was loaded and running, Jessica sat down at the kitchen table and said, "Sit here, girls, we'll have a family meeting."

"Good night, Aunt Jessica," Anna said.

"Oh, no," Jessica said quickly. "Sit down, Anna. You're part of our family now."

So they sat down and waited for Jessica to tell them whatever was on her mind. While she waited, Willow's mind raced against the possibility that Jessica might actually be interested in Carlos. But the idea was so sickening that she couldn't even seriously think about it. Nevertheless, she was trapped in her own circular thought and had a hard time following what her mother was saying. Something about Thanksgiving.

" . . . so you see, I thought it would be nice to have a few others in for Thanksgiving dinner. I've invited Mr. Hawkins, my painting instructor. You remember him. You met him in the restaurant and at the Halloween party." Jessica seemed a little nervous as she spoke.

"Is he going to be our new stepfather?" Brittany asked.

Willow relaxed. Of course, it was the man she'd seen her mother with the other day. It had nothing to do with Carlos. Carlos was her own true love. Or at least — he would be her own true love once he realized it.

"Don't be ridiculous," Jessica snapped. "Mr. Hawkins just happens to be alone on Thanksgiving and I thought he'd enjoy a family festivity. Carlos will be in New York and the Zimbalist boys will be home. So that just leaves Dan with us. Which brings up another subject."

"Aunt Jessica," Anna said timidly. "Do you think I could go home for Thanskgiving?"

Jessica seemed about to object and then she said, "I don't see why not. We can manage here, of course. It's just that I enjoy having you around, dear."

"I know our original agreement said I'd only get the two weeks at Christmas," Anna said, "but you really don't need me and I'll give you a refund on my wages."

Jessica laughed and shook her head, "Anna, Anna, you're always trying to give me a refund on those wages. And I know you save every penny so you obviously need the money. No refunds allowed."

"So you're inviting our new stepfather to Thanksgiving dinner," Brittany said. "Anyone else?"

"That's up to you," Jessica answered, completely ignoring the jibe about a stepfather. "Do you want to ask Teddy and his folks over? We haven't entertained anyone in a long while."

"No, I don't," Brittany answered quickly. "I'm not such good friends with Teddy anymore."

Jessica shrugged and said, "If you change your mind before Tuesday, let me know. Anyone else?"

When no one suggested any other guests, Jessica went on. "I really wanted to talk to you all about closing the boardinghouse. Now that John Johnson is leaving, we're down to four boarders and it hardly seems worth the effort." She frowned and said, "It was never really *worth* the effort, but it was kind of interesting."

"You wouldn't!" Willow wailed.

Jessica smiled at her older daughter, "I realize that would eliminate two of your admirers, but Carlos is definitely too old for you and you don't seem the least bit interested in Dan."

"You couldn't just put them out on the street," Willow protested. "It wouldn't be fair." She didn't bother to point out that there was really less than two years' difference between Carlos and Dan. What made twenty so much older than almost nineteen? She just repeated her first objection, "You promised them and now they'd have no place to go. You couldn't be that cruel."

"I don't know," Jessica said. "They're not a lot of trouble but I kind of miss my quiet house with just the . . . just the four of us." She leaned over and patted Anna's arm. "You have a home here as long as you want it. All the way through high school and college, I promise you that."

Anna smiled and shook her head. "I couldn't do that, Aunt Jessica. I already feel guilty because there isn't enough work to do. I couldn't just accept *charity*."

Jessica sighed. "Well, the Zimbalist boys aren't any trouble and I like Dan and Carlos."

Then she looked directly at Willow and said, "But you mustn't make pests of yourselves, girls. Those fellows are college men who need to get their work done. And you shouldn't assume that just because they live in your home, they are your private property."

Willow colored and couldn't think of anything to say that wouldn't sound foolish, so she said nothing. She wished her mother would understand once and for all that she was grownup now and didn't need to be reprimanded like a baby. She certainly knew that Dan didn't think she was a pest. And as for Carlos, she knew Carlos loved having her around. He'd invited her to Mexico, hadn't he?

Chapter 33

Brittany sat in the third row, center front for *The Good Ship Grease*. Though she was nervous about the whole thing, she was glad they had good seats. At least she would be able to see the look on Teddy's face and know how he was doing. Maybe she could send him some courage by mental telepathy. But first she would have to get some.

As she waited for Teddy to make his entrance, Brittany felt a knot in her stomach. What if he made an absolute fool of himself? She didn't think three more years of high school would be long enough to live it down.

Her mother seemed very confident that things would turn out all right and she kept up a constant line of chatter with Teddy's mother, who wore a very distracted and frightened expression. At one point, Brittany noticed that

Mrs. Myers's knuckles were literally white as she gripped her chair handle.

She didn't blame his mother. This whole undertaking seemed medium to definitely ridiculous to Brittany. Of course, she hadn't told Teddy that. She'd simply clapped him on the back and said, "Break a leg."

Teddy laughed but Brittany wondered for the hundredth time why anyone would say such a thing to a performer who was just going onstage.

She was prepared for the fact that Teddy was the last one of the cast to come onstage, but she wasn't prepared for exactly how long it would take. By the time Teddy tap-danced his way onto the middle of the stage, the others in the cast were over their nervousness and singing loudly. You could barely hear Teddy and it almost broke Brittany's heart to see how uncomfortable he looked up there on that huge stage.

The curtain went down on the first act about two minutes after he got onstage and Brittany, for one, was very happy to see it drop. Even if it didn't help Teddy, it might give *her* time to regroup. She stood up quickly and raced to the back of the auditorium where she stood in line at the drinking fountain and listened to people's comments. Mostly, the comments were favorable but no one said anything at all about Teddy. Brittany didn't know if that was good or bad. But she did know that the water sloshing around in her stomach wasn't such a great idea, after all.

Her mother and Teddy's mother and Willow found her in the foyer and Jessica said, "Didn't he look wonderful?"

Brittany stared at her mother. Was she kidding? Couldn't she see how nervous Teddy was? How uncomfortable he looked? Couldn't she see the terror in his eyes? Brittany shuddered. In this next act, Teddy was practically the sole performer. He had two dances, a song, and a long monologue. There were a few pretty girls onstage but mostly, it was just Teddy.

"I think I'll stay out here," she whispered to her mother.

"That's ridiculous," her mother whispered back. "He's doing fine."

"He was terrible!"

"He was fine," Jessica said. "For Pete's sake, don't say anything to his mother. She's worried sick."

Unconsciously, Brittany moved closer to Mrs. Myers. Jessica's determined cheerfulness was driving her nuts. At least Mrs. Myers was a realist. She reached out and put her arm around the older woman and hugged her lightly. "Hi."

"Hi, Brittany. Pretty grim, wasn't it?"

"So far but I think he'll get better."

Mrs. Myers shook her head. "I'm glad his father didn't come. We had a big fight over whether or not we should be there to support our son. But Dennis just couldn't bear to watch. He has an ulcer, you know."

"I know," Brittany said. Her own stomach was turning itself over and over and she wondered if it was possible that she might have an ulcer. But fourteen-year-olds didn't get ulcers, did they? Then she reminded herself that she was almost fifteen. In January, she and Teddy would be fifteen. Maybe by then Teddy would be ready to grow up a little.

The lights were dimmed and Jessica took Brittany's hand very firmly so that she would know she had no choice but to go and sit down again. As they walked back to their seats, Willow whispered, "He's really bad, isn't he?"

"Give him a chance," Brittany snapped. But Willow wasn't even listening. She was flirting with two senior boys who were walking ahead of them.

Brittany looked around, hoping she would see Lars somewhere in the crowd and she spotted him over on the left. She said to her sister, "There's your boyfriend."

"Who?"

"Lars — your dream man. Remember?"

"Oh, Lars," Willow shrugged. "I thought *you* were interested in Lars. I never was."

"Then how come you trip all over yourself to talk to him every time you see him?" Brittany asked.

"I'm nice to everyone," Willow said and tossed her strawberry blond hair. "But I really think Lars is too young for me."

"I suppose you think Carlos is exactly the right age," Brittany challenged.

Before Willow had a chance to answer, the lights went out and the curtains opened. There was Teddy, standing all alone, in the middle of that great big stage. Brittany wanted to close her eyes and scrunch down in her chair, the way she would if she were watching a horror movie, but she didn't want Mrs. Myers to notice anything odd. She forced herself to sit straight with a smile on her face.

Teddy looked a lot more comfortable onstage this time. He was wearing a funny pair of baggy Levi's and a bright-colored baggier shirt with a cap turned backward. He began to dance in a kind of break dancing that Brittany had no idea he could do. If she didn't know better, she would have thought she was watching some professional teenager on television.

Teddy's feet moved easily and his body bent to and fro as though he was having a great time. She was surprised and pleased at how well he could move. Now if he could only sing.

Teddy's voice started out too soft and someone in the back of the hall yelled, "Can't hear."

Brittany saw his throat tighten in fear and she knew he was getting scared again, but he widened his smile and opened his mouth and really belted out the lyrics of his song. He was loud. He was carrying a tune and he kept the beat. As far as the quality of his voice, Brittany thought he probably needed a lot more work. Nevertheless, he was a lot better than she expected.

And his dancing was really wonderful! After he sang, he really opened up and did a solo. Brittany was simply amazed at how well he played the character of Greasy George, tugboat captain extraordinaire. He was fast and he was funny. In his last number, he was joined on stage by three beautiful girls and he pretended he couldn't make up his mind which one to chase faster. He ended up running round and round in a circle until he kind of melted into the floor and the girls grabbed his arms and legs and dragged him offstage.

By the time Teddy's part was over, Brittany was so proud of him that she almost didn't want to sit through the rest of the play. She'd seen the leads — Bill Crawford and Lorilynn Jones in two other school musicals and while they both had good voices, they were boring. In fact, if it hadn't been for Teddy, it would have been just another boring school play. But Teddy had talent and he had made all the difference.

At the end of the show, Teddy got the most applause. When he came out at the end to take his bow, the audience hooted and stamped their feet and called out, "Yeah, Myers!"

Brittany was pleased because it had all turned out all right. Teddy took a real risk when he'd tried out for the play and the risk paid off. She was proud of him.

After the bows, a lot of people pushed up onto the stage and into the makeshift dressing rooms on the gym floor. Willow and Brittany followed the crowd and when they got to the dressing rooms, Teddy was surrounded by a large group of people. Perhaps the most surprising thing was that Lorilynn Jones was standing beside him.

Teddy moved away from Lorilynn and came straight toward Brittany when they walked into the room. "How'd I do?"

Brittany reached up and hugged him. "You were great — really great."

Hugging Teddy was a new experience and she felt awkward about it. She wasn't quite sure how long she was supposed to stay in his arms and she also wasn't quite sure why he felt as solid as he did. Funny, she'd known Teddy for years and she'd never really noticed before that he had muscles that made his embrace seem a lot like a man's embrace.

Brittany flushed and was glad when Willow tapped her on the shoulder and said, "Break it up, Britt. My turn."

Brittany moved back and Willow stepped up to fill her place in Teddy's arms. As she watched them, she noticed that Teddy was getting taller. He used to be her height but now he was taller than Willow. Funny how you could be with someone every day of your life and still be surprised when they changed. Funny and kind of scary.

Willow stayed very close to Teddy and he looked pleased to have her there. He kept his arm around her waist and looked over at Brittany and winked. She laughed out loud. Teddy had finally gotten Willow to stop looking over his shoulder and look directly at him — what's more, he looked as if he liked it.

Soon, a crowd of kids who were Willow's

friends and either juniors or seniors circled them. Some of them were people who walked by Brittany and Teddy every day at lunch and never spoke but they were speaking now, acting as if everyone were an old friend. Teddy seemed to enjoy his newfound success but the look on his face told Brittany he didn't take it very seriously. And he was careful to acknowledge his real friends. When Jason and Mitch came by, Teddy turned away from Willow and two of her cheerleader friends to speak to his buddies. Brittany was proud of Teddy for that — she knew it cost him.

Lars came up behind Brittany and said in a low, soft voice, "Hi, Britt. I guess you're pretty proud of your pal, huh?"

"Oh, Lars, did you see him? He was wonderful, wasn't he?"

She turned and smiled up at the handsome senior. Any other time she would have been so flustered just to be in his presence that she'd probably stumble and make a fool of herself, but tonight she was just too proud of Teddy to be self-conscious.

"He was great. Too bad Anna couldn't stay, isn't it?"

"Yes, but if she hadn't left yesterday, she would have missed her cousin who's in the Army. He's stationed in the Philippines and they used to be really close." Then she let her voice trail off and she said, "I forget you and Anna run together. She must have told you all that. Right?"

"Right. Can I buy you guys a cappuccino? You and Teddy and Willow. Your Mom and Mrs. Myers, too?"

"You must be rich," Brittany said. "That's a lot of cappuccinos."

"Got my Christmas bonus early," Lars said. "Come on. Let's ask the others."

"Sure thing, Peterson," Teddy answered. "I'll see if my mom wants to come along." Then he looked just a little shy and said, "You sure you don't mind?"

"I invited everyone," Lars answered. "It's okay."

So the whole party ended up going to the Javanese Java on Front Street. The place was filled with college students as it always was but they found a table in the corner and crowded around it. Brittany was wedged between Lars and Teddy, and Willow sat across from them, making beautiful eyes at the boys. Brittany thought that her sister's flirting was a lot like an addiction — she just did it automatically even if she wasn't interested in the people she was flirting with. Brittany shook her head and reminded herself to tell Teddy that. Although at the moment Teddy, who usually saw right through Willow, looked as though he was enjoying her silly behavior.

Everyone laughed and had a good time. Mostly they talked about Teddy's great success. At one point in the evening, Lars asked, "So I know you're planning to go into show business, Myers. What's next?"

Teddy looked a little nervous and his mother looked very, very surprised. He looked directly at his mother as he answered, "I've known for a long time that what I really wanted to do was make people laugh. I thought for a while I might be a writer but then I decided to try dancing. I like dancing better."

"And you're better at it," Brittany said. "Those poems you wrote were really awful."

"They were song lyrics and they weren't awful," Teddy answered crossly.

Brittany took a deep breath and stopped herself before she answered him. She saw no reason why they should spoil this wonderful evening by wrangling over some silly old poems he'd written in the sixth grade. Besides, she knew Teddy wanted to appear grown-up and successful in front of Lars and Willow, and going back and forth like a couple of babies would surely spoil that image. "You're a great dancer," she said.

Teddy looked directly at her as though to ask her why she'd changed her usual habit of arguing with him. Then he smiled slightly and tipped his hand to his forehead in a mock salute. Turning to Willow, he said, "So did you do any double flips or anything lately?"

Willow was looking over his shoulder again and obviously didn't hear what he'd said. Teddy grinned his crooked grin at Brittany and said, "I knew it was too good to last."

"Look, that's Carlos," Willow said. Then she frowned and said, "He's with some woman."

"Imagine that," her mother said dryly.

"He's never mentioned any women friends," Willow said. She seemed really surprised and disappointed. Then she brightened and said, "He's just helping her on with her coat. I think he's coming over here."

Unself-consciously, she reached up and fluffed out her long, strawberry blond hair and then smiled into the distance. When it looked as though Carlos might be passing them by, Willow raised her hand and called out, "Carlos. Carlos, we're over here."

He seemed delighted to see them and came right over to their table, seating himself between Mrs. Myers and Jessica. "Who's your girlfriend?" Brittany asked.

Carlos laughed. "You are my only girlfriend, Brittany, my love. You know that." Then, when he saw the look on Willow's face he added, "You and your beautiful sister." Turning to Jessica he said, "I'd ask how you managed to find two such wonderful, beautiful, clever daughters if it weren't obvious that they get all their good looks and brains from you."

"So you're not going to tell us who your lady friend was," Jessica teased her boarder. She had long since become immune to his flattery.

"That, my dear Jessica, was my psychology teacher. She gave me a D on my last paper and I invited her out for a cup of coffee to discuss my work. A dismal failure, I fear — my paper, not the coffee. But enough of that." He turned to Teddy and said, "Your face portrays your pride. You did well, yes?"

"I was awesome," Teddy answered simply.

Instead of laughing, Brittany added, "Simply phenomenal." She launched into a long description of Teddy's success. The others added bits and pieces and Teddy just sat back and let them talk about how well he did. Finally, Brittany turned to him and asked, "Don't you ever get tired of hearing yourself praised?"

"Not really," Teddy admitted. "I was kind

of scared and now I'm proud. Why shouldn't I enjoy my success?"

"You should," Carlos said, "you should." He rose from the table and said, "I must excuse myself. I have many things to do before our journey tomorrow. Tomorrow night, ladies. Are you ready?"

As Brittany and Jessica assured him they were ready, Willow said, "Will you take me home with you, Carlos? I have some things to do." Before anyone could object, she stood up and waved a hand, "Bye-bye." Then she bent over and kissed Teddy on the cheek and smiled. "You really were wonderful."

Willow was out of her chair and halfway out of the restaurant when Lars seemed to realize what had happened and he rose, saying, "I'll be right back. I want to ask her something."

Brittany watched as Lars caught up with Willow and stood talking with her. His handsome face was so earnest and intense that Brittany was dying to know what he asked. She wondered if he was asking her to the New Year's Eve ball. Most kids already had dates and she knew for a fact that Willow had turned down three invitations. Brittany guessed that Willow planned to ask Carlos to the dance while they were in Mexico.

Brittany sighed and stirred her second cup

of cappuccino with a spoon. Would the day ever come when she'd have three and four men asking her out at once? So far, she hadn't seen any signs of it. No one had asked her to the New Year's Eve ball.

Whatever Lars had wanted to talk to Willow about, he seemed sorry he'd brought it up. He walked slowly back to the table and his handsome face was as impassive as a mask. Brittany wanted to reach up and hug him, she felt so sorry for him. She wondered how he would react if she took him in her arms and said, "Never mind, I love you." She supposed he would think she was nuts. Anyway, with Teddy and their mothers here, it was out of the question.

Poor Lars. She was so mad at her sister for making him suffer in this way. When he came back to the table, Brittany leaned over and put her hand on his. "Thanks a lot for the coffee, Lars. It meant a lot to Teddy. Made it feel like a real celebration."

Lars smiled softly and said, "That's nice," but it was obvious that his mind was elsewhere.

Chapter 34

Willow snuggled into the small red sports car, and Carlos said, "Use your seat belt."

"I can't find it," she smiled in the darkness. Carlos reached across the car to show her how to use the seat belt and she looked up at him. They were very, very close.

She could see his dark eyes in the light of the streetlight and the outline of his handsome face. She was always aware of the cologne that Carlos wore, and that smell mixed in a wonderful way with the purr of the car motor and the softness of her own coat wrapped around her shoulders.

"Cold?" Carlos asked.

"A little," she answered. She hoped that he would take her answer as an invitation to take her in his arms.

"I'll turn on the heater," he promised.

"First, would you do the seat belt for me?"

So Carlos had to lean across her and fasten the seat belt in place for her. As he did so, she leaned back and closed her eyes. She was certain that he was going to kiss her. She was waiting for that kiss. In her mind she'd pictured this moment hundreds of times.

But Carlos misunderstood and said, "Go ahead and sleep if you want." Then he started the car and she was too embarrassed to open her eyes and tell him she wasn't sleepy. They drove home in silence and Willow felt like a coward but she never worked up the nerve to mention the New Year's Eve ball.

Once they were home, he practically rushed her into the house, claiming she needed her beauty rest for the day that followed. Willow went to her room and tried to sort out exactly what had happened. Finally, she decided that she was just too in love with Carlos to be her usual self-assured self. When she got around Carlos, her nerve failed her. It was as simple as that.

As she brushed her long, gleaming hair, she smiled at her reflection and promised herself that she wouldn't be such a coward next time. Anyway, it didn't much matter anymore. She'd turned Lars down for the dance and he was the only other boy she would be interested in going with. Carlos would just have to say yes.

The next morning, she looked all over the house for Carlos. Her bag was all packed and she was ready to go, but the plane didn't leave until seven that evening. And Carlos was nowhere in sight. She even went out for a walk, taking the route to town that Carlos would be most apt to drive by. But she had no luck and at lunch only Brittany showed up. Willow was discouraged and she sighed. "I hope it's warm in Mexico City."

"We won't be in the city," Brittany said. "The driver will meet us and we'll go directly out to the countryside. And it will be warm because it's a lower elevation. In Mexico, the elevation has more to do with the temperature than the latitude."

"You sound like a geography book."

"I listen. I don't just sit round and look in the mirror all day."

"What have I done to you?" Willow asked.

"Lars asked you to the New Year's Eve ball and you turned him down, didn't you?" Brittany asked.

Willow shrugged. "I turned four guys down."

"You think you're so powerful," Brittany said. "You go around making people feel perfectly miserable and you obviously don't care a bit."

Willow bit into a piece of toast and seemed surprised at the loud crunch the toast made. She pulled her head back and looked quizzically at the brown diagonal with the half-moon bite. "I wonder what makes some bread loud," she mused.

"You really like that — don't you? You think of yourself as some sort of femme fatale, some great heartbreaker or something."

"You sound jealous," Willow said mildly. "I have a right to go to the dance with whomever I please."

"Did you ask Carlos yet?"

"Not yet."

"What if Carlos says no?" Brittany's anger seemed to have dissipated and now she just seemed curious.

"Carlos won't say no."

"Then why haven't you had the courage to ask him?"

Willow frowned. Sometimes her little sister hit things so square that it hurt. She had *almost* asked Carlos that day a month ago when her mother sent her to her room for sitting on the arm of his chair. Since then, they'd almost never been alone. Though she never made an issue of it, Willow knew that her mother was the reason for that. But last night, when she *had* been alone with him, she'd lost her nerve.

Willow frowned just thinking about last night.

"So what happened last night?" Brittany asked.

"Get a life," Willow answered. She didn't have to explain everything to Brittany. She left the kitchen and went out into the yard to help the gardener shovel snow. She had nothing better to do so she might as well get some exercise. Besides, she would know if Carlos came in.

She worked for a couple of hours and then Dan came out and asked, "Want to walk into town?"

"Sure," Willow said. "I just need to comb my hair."

Dan reached out and touched her hair. He shook his head and said, "You don't need to do anything, Willow. You look great."

"Thanks," she said. "Now if I would just *act* great. Right?"

"You act fine," Dan smiled down at her. "Brittany on your case again?"

"Yes." Willow jammed her hands in the pocket of her denim jacket and picked up her pace. "It's cold," she complained.

"Little," Dan agreed. "Colder in Wyoming though. The wind really blows in Wyoming."

"What's it like?" Willow asked. She liked

Dan and it often seemed as though he'd been around forever. She didn't really think of him as one of the boarders — more like a friend or family like Brittany and Teddy. Usually, she didn't pay much attention to him. He was just always there, waiting, happy to talk to her a little bit. Never asking for much. When she was with Dan, she always felt she was all right just the way she was. Now, she was suddenly curious about his former life. "Big skies, you said," she prompted him.

"Big skies," Dan agreed. "Lots of wind and sudden, dark days that come up over the mountains and nearly freeze you to death. But beautiful just the same. Sometimes temperatures drop thirty degrees in two hours where I come from. Wind and cold kill in Wyoming."

Willow shivered. "I don't think I'd like it," she said.

"You can't tell," Dan said, companionably. "You're young but you're kind of tough in your own way. I think you'd get along fine in Wyoming. 'Course, I might decide to stay out here. Wisconsin's a good place for a builder."

Willow understood he was talking about a future that included her but she had no intention of letting him think she did understand that. She wasn't interested in Dan and she'd let him know that in many different ways. If he chose to dream out loud, she would simply ignore it.

In town, they stopped at the hardware store and bought some nails and then they went into Markey's Café for a hamburger and coffee. "I'll miss you," Dan said.

"It's good you can stay here during the holidays," Willow answered. She often gave him a deliberately indirect answer to his direct statements. If he minded, he never said so. In fact, he didn't usually seem to notice.

Dan nodded. "I'm going to paint the cellar and repair the roof fascia."

"Why do you always want to fix things?" Willow asked.

Dan grinned. "There's a lot in life you can't fix. So it's good to fix what you can. Right?"

"I guess so."

"Besides, your ma is obviously getting out of the boardinghouse business. If I'm handy enough, she'll probably let me stay on. Don't you think?"

Willow laughed and took another bite out of her hamburger. There was no sense asking Dan why he would want to stay on. The look of love was as plain as the nose on his face.

Chapter 35

They took a plane from Madison to Chicago and then a direct flight to Mexico City. They were there a little before midnight and by one in the morning they were through customs and tucked away in the backseats of the Montoya limousine that had been waiting for them at the curb. Their driver's name was Alejandro and he had been born on the Montoya ranch.

"Most of our help was born on the ranch," Carlos said. "Some leave, of course, and my mother helps some of the children with college educations. But most just live their lives on our land."

Once again, Brittany found herself wondering *exactly* how rich Carlos was. She had an idea that he was richer than anyone else they knew. "Why did you decide to live in a boardinghouse?" Brittany asked.

"I was majoring in psychology and I wanted

the experience of living with an American family," Carlos said. "You were as close as I could come to that."

"Aren't you majoring in psychology anymore?" Brittany asked.

"The future is unclear," Carlos said softly. "Let's not talk for a while. I think the others may be sleeping."

He then started giving Alejandro directions in Spanish and the two of them talked on and on. Brittany wasn't sure what they were talking about but she could hear the words *rancho* and *señora* from time to time so she supposed Carlos was getting news about home.

Brittany found the foreign language sort of comforting, and since she couldn't understand anything, she just let Carlos talk and give the orders without worrying. As they whizzed through the streets of Mexico City, she was amazed at how wide-awake everyone on the streets seemed to be.

They drove through one neighborhood where there were loads of people standing around talking and sitting in outdoor restaurants. Groups of musicians roved up and down the streets carrying trumpets. They were wearing fancy uniforms with brass buttons and wide felt hats that looked as if they were from old Western movies. "Mariachi bands," Carlos explained. "They play for tips if they don't find work. We're in an old section of town where the tourists love to come. Would you like to stop for supper?"

"Supper?" Jessica laughed and stretched. "I just woke from a catnap and it's two in the morning."

"We keep different hours in Mexico," Carlos said. "You'll have to observe our siesta hour while you are here. Then you can stay up all night with the rest of the Mexicans."

"Tomorrow," Jessica promised. "Tomorrow we'll all take a nap and we can go out."

"Tomorrow there will be a big fiesta at our home," Carlos said. "I am sure my mother has invited many of our friends to meet you."

"Do they all speak Spanish?" Willow asked. "I have a headache from trying to understand what was going on in the airport." Willow had completed two years of Spanish in junior high school and she obviously thought she was going to be able to speak and understand. By the pained look on her face, it was clear that dream was fading fast.

"Of course they speak Spanish," Brittany snapped. "We're in Mexico."

"Don't worry," Carlos said. "Nearly all educated Mexicans speak English. Many speak French, Italian, and German as well."

"My French teacher says Americans are lazy and ignorant about languages," Brittany said. "Do you agree?"

"I think Americans are wonderful people," Carlos said quickly. "They work hard and they accomplish a lot. Certainly, they can get the job done."

"But they're lazy about languages," Brittany finished for him.

Carlos laughed and said, "Brittany, you are delightful. But you will get me in trouble with my charming American guests." Then he leaned toward the window and said, "Look over there. You can see the cathedral of Guadelupe outlined against the sky. We'll visit that when we come into the city. I wish you were staying longer. Four days isn't enough."

"My eyes are burning," Willow complained.

"It's the smog," Carlos explained. "We have a big pollution problem in the city. Twenty-two million people live here, you know."

"Is it always like this?" Willow asked. She wiped her eyes with a Kleenex.

"Not always," Carlos answered. "Don't worry, where we are going there is no smog. Beautiful skies and warm weather. You will love it."

They were on a large highway now and the trucks and buses roared by them. There weren't any streetlights and it was too dark to see anything. Brittany noticed she was getting sleepy and she decided it would be all right to doze a bit. After all, they had four days to see the sights and there weren't many sights at two-thirty in the morning.

Brittany barely remembered being wakened and led to her room where she fell into a huge four-poster bed and dropped back into a deep, deep sleep. When she awoke, it took her a few minutes to figure out where she was. Certainly, there was nothing in the room itself to give her a clue that she was in Mexico. Her guest bedroom was furnished in traditional French furniture with rather formal dark woods and brocade drapes. It might have been a room from a magazine such as *House Beautiful*.

Brittany pulled on green pants and a green sweater and drew a pick through her tangled red hair. She followed a coffee smell down the hallway. Soon, she was in a beautiful large dining room with a table that was bigger than the one they had at home. There was no one there except a girl about her age who bowed and motioned for her to sit down.

Brittany sat down and looked around. Carlos obviously lived in a mansion. From where she was sitting, she could see outside to a large patio and garden and a long two-story wing of rooms. The house was a mixture of white and pink plaster and there were huge flaming-red flowering bushes growing up to the second-story balcony.

There were paintings of people she suspected were Carlos's ancestors on the walls and there were a few French landscapes. The furniture was French mahogany with deep peach brocade seats and there was a sideboard with a lot of silver bowls and teapots along one wall.

Soon, the maid brought her a cup of delicious coffee with heavy cream and sugar in it. Brittany took the fragile china cup in her hands and sipped the coffee. She closed her eyes in appreciation. Never had she tasted anything more delicious. It was almost like cocoa but it was unmistakably coffee.

The maid was asking her questions and she could only shrug and open her hands wide to indicate that she didn't have a clue what the girl was saying. She wished she could communicate because there were questions she would have liked to ask. Finally, the girl disappeared and returned with an older man. The man was wearing a white cotton shirt and pants and had a red scarf around his neck. His skin was dark and lined and Brittany decided he was probably a gardener, not a house servant.

"You eat egg?" the old man asked.

"Oh, yes," Brittany agreed.

"Three egg?" The man held up three fingers.

"Two eggs," Brittany held up two fingers so the girl could see.

"Tortilla? Bread? Rice? *Frijoles?*" Then the man laughed and shook his head. "No *frijoles* — beans."

"Bread, please," Brittany answered.

The man disappeared then and so did the girl. Brittany amused herself by drinking coffee and trying to find a family resemblance in the portraits that lined the walls. She didn't think any of them looked like Carlos, but they had so many mustaches and beards and looked so old-fashioned it was hard to tell.

Soon, a plate with two fried eggs, beans, rice, and hot sauce was placed in front of her. Then a basket of small loaves of bread arrived as well as wonderful fresh orange juice. Brittany thought she had never eaten a better breakfast.

As she was finishing up, a tall woman of about fifty came into the room. Brittany's first impression was that she was the most dignified woman she had ever seen and one of the most beautiful. She wore her graying hair pulled back in something that was halfway between a ponytail and a bun and looked very sophisticated. Her dress was a beautiful silk print dress that Brittany just knew was European. She smiled briefly and formally held out her hand. "You are Brittany, no? I am the mother of Carlos. They have all gone to the pyramids and I waited to take you. Are you still hungry? You are finished? Good, we will go to the ancient ruins."

"Thank you, Mrs. Montoya," Brittany said. "I'm sorry I overslept." Her watch told her it was after eleven.

"You are on holiday," Mrs. Montoya said. "Time is not important. And I have seen the ruins many, many times." When she smiled, she looked a little bit like her son and some of her formality loosened a bit.

Brittany was shy around Mrs. Montoya and she wasn't sure why. On the ride through the countryside, the older woman pointed out trees, shrubs, and landmarks and gave Brittany a mini-tour. Brittany asked polite questions and wished she'd worn a dress instead of pants. She also wished she'd thought to change into a cotton bouse. The sweater was hot in the noonday sun.

Mrs. Montoya must have sensed her discomfort because she had her driver turn on the air-conditioning. As the cool air blew into the backseat, Mrs. Montoya asked her, "And my son, he has a girlfriend in the United States?"

"I don't think so," Brittany answered. Then she added, "My sister has a crush on him, but I think he is too old for her."

Mrs. Montoya nodded. "He *is* too old for her. And your sister would not find life in Mexico compatible."

Brittany heard steel in the older woman's voice and she knew that as far as Mrs. Montoya was concerned, the subject was closed. Was she supposed to tell Willow that she had no chance? Somehow, she didn't think that Mrs. Montoya would bring up a subject such as her son's love life unless it had a purpose. She suspected that she was supposed to warn Willow not to be serious about Carlos. Maybe that was the way Mrs. Montoya did things — politely but firmly.

They were driving through a small town now and Brittany looked at the dirt streets, the bright colored signs, and the bicycles leaning against buildings. Mrs. Montoya ordered the driver to pull up at a central square and said to Brittany, "This is market day. Let us see if we can find you a souvenir of your trip, my dear."

The town was dusty and not prosperous. The square had a bandstand right in the center and there were makeshift booths clustered round the bandstand. Some of the market day stores were simply tables with no roof covering at all. The stands displayed an amazing variety of goods.

Brittany felt a little self-conscious walking through the market with Mrs. Montoya who looked so rich but her hostess didn't seem to notice the flies, or the barefoot children. She held her head high and sailed past the stalls with flowers, onions, and canned goods until she came to a stall with cotton shirts.

"Buenos días, María," Mrs. Montoya said to a young woman with three small children who crowded around her in the tiny stall store. Brittany couldn't understand a word of what was said after that but the two women conversed at length. While they talked, Brittany looked at a large collection of embroidered shirts and blouses, bright colored ponchos and silk scarves with fringe that were hanging from the racks that lined the inside of the stall.

There were a few long dresses and even one pair of brightly embroidered white cotton pants. Many of the shirts were made of dishtowels and flour sacks and Brittany made a mental note to take a flour-sack shirt home to Teddy.

Mrs. Montoya had Maria pull down several blouses but none seemed to suit her. She finally decided on a white cotton shirt that was hanging on the highest rack of the store. Brittany thought it was probably a man's shirt because it had long sleeves and she supposed that Mrs. Montoya was preparing to buy it for her. She was too shy to argue so she just stood around and waited while the two women carried on their business.

Maria used a hook to lift the shirts off the tall racks and bring them down to street level. Mrs. Montoya took one blouse after another and looked at it critically, shaking her head in dismay at the workmanship and saying something in a sharp voice to Maria. Eventually, Maria dug into some boxes that were under the table. She brought out two other shirts that were a soft beige color.

Mrs. Montoya apparently liked these better. She turned them over and inspected the stitching and then shook her head, in agreement. The shirts were wrapped in plastic and Brittany and Mrs. Montoya were out of the store and back in the air-conditioned car within minutes.

As soon as they were outside town, Mrs. Montoya rapped on the glass and told the driver to pull over. "You can change over there." She pointed to a large cluster of cactus just off the road.

Brittany would have liked more privacy but she was definitely ready to get out of the hot sweater. She stepped out onto the highway and walked the short distance to the cactus plants. Then she very quickly skinned off her sweater and pulled on the cotton shirt. Once she put it on, she realized how beautiful it was. The cloth felt almost like silk, it was so soft and there were tiny embroidered flowers along a back yoke. The sleeves were long and flowing and Brittany decided she liked it better than any of her other blouses.

Once back in the car, she said, "Thank you. I really love this."

"This is the best and purest cotton we grow. The work is not as good as it was," Mrs. Montoya said. "When I was a girl, everything was by hand and everything was beautiful. But now we are a modern nation with machines and our craftsmanship is disappearing."

"The fabric is so soft," Brittany said.

"It is handwoven," Mrs. Montoya said. "This cloth is unbleached and it comes down from the mountain towns and the village women sew it. Unfortunately, the embroidery work is done by machine."

"How odd," Brittany murmured. "Hand-woven cloth. Is it really cotton?"

"Yes. They grow the cotton in hillside fields and pick and spin it themselves. The color is natural. Your sister's blouse is browner than yours, did you notice? And you will be very happy that is so in the noonday sun. Mexico is a sunny landscape, no?"

"Mexico is beautiful," Brittany said. She ran her hands along her sleeves and said, "And I love my shirt."

When they arrived at the ruins, Jessica, Willow, Carlos, and several people she didn't know were all sitting on a blanket, just beginning to picnic. Carlos jumped up immediately and ran over to his mother, kissing her on both cheeks and inviting her to join them.

She smiled in amusement and asked, "On the ground?"

"We will find you a chair," Carlos said.

"I will return home," Mrs. Montoya said. "I do not care to see the ruins today." She kissed her son on the cheek and turned to Jessica and said, "Mrs. Winston, you have two delightful daughters. I have enjoyed Brittany."

Brittany thought her mother and sister looked absolutely beautiful in the sun. She sank down beside them and began to chatter, "We stopped at market and Mrs. Montoya bought me this shirt. I have one for you, Willow. Have you seen the ruins? What time did you wake up? What did I miss?"

They ate sandwiches and drank Cokes and then Carlos took Brittany, and two others who'd arrived late, on a tour of the ruins. Jessica and Willow stayed behind with a young man who had a guitar and said he could only play American songs because he'd eaten too much American cheese. But as they walked away, he began to strum and sing in Spanish.

"That's 'La Paloma,' " Carlos said. "The most common song in Mexico. Especially for beautiful tourists."

"It sounds beautiful," Brittany said.

"It is," Carlos assured her. "And the ruins will be beautiful, too." Then he laughed and said, "However, I think your lovely mother and sister had about all the ruins they wanted to see today. Your charming relatives begged off the afternoon tour."

After two hours tramping around in the hot sun, Brittany knew exactly why her relatives begged off the tour. The pyramids were actually a lot like old, tall stone bleachers with tiny, tiny steps to walk up. As they climbed to the top of yet another pile of stones, Brittany said, "This has all been wonderful."

Carlos reached out and caught her chin in his hand and looked down at her with laughing eyes. "You are marvelous, Brittany. Don't ever lose that wonderful enthusiasm for life."

"Oh, I never will," Brittany promised him.

When she got back to her mother and sister, who were packing up and getting ready to go back to the ranch, Willow caught her by the arm and whispered, "What did he say to you?"

"Who?"

"Carlos — what did he say?"

At first she didn't know what Willow was talking about and then she figured out that her sister must have seen Carlos reach out and touch her. For one brief, glorious moment, Brittany realized that Willow was jealous of her. She considered telling her some big story but the look on Willow's face stopped her.

Out here, in the bright sun of Mexico, Willow looked young and a little scared and very, very vulnerable. *She really cares about him,* Brittany thought and it wasn't a happy thought. How could Willow take Carlos seriously? "He just told me to keep on enjoying life," Brittany said. Then she added, "But his mother told me he was not going to marry an American girl and that you wouldn't like Mexico. And I kind of have the opinion that what his mother says goes. If you get my meaning."

"It's too early to think of marriage," Willow said and then she smiled quietly. If his mother was warning Brittany then that must mean that she saw something going on between Carlos and her that she thought was important. That was a very good sign.

Chapter 36

Willow dressed carefully for dinner, selecting her dark burgundy pants and white lace blouse. Her mother would think the blouse was too seductive but she didn't care. She wanted to look as grown-up and pretty as she could on this first evening in the home of her wonderful love — Carlos Montoya.

She used a lot more blusher than usual but kept the lipstick in a light hue and selected her dark blue mascara to highlight her eyes without making them look too made-up. True, the blouse was a little low cut and the satin camisole under the lace was even lower cut but the sleeves were long so she thought the total effect was ladylike enough.

She met her mother in the hall who took one look at her and said, "Get a shawl or change your blouse. Those are your choices."

"Mother!"

"Let's not have a scene. Get something else on. That's an order."

So Willow went back to her room and rummaged through her clothes once again, trying on everything she'd brought and she didn't like anything. Finally, she selected a simple blue silk dress. She was furious with her mother, of course, but she didn't dare cross her. Jessica was an easygoing parent, but Willow knew that she was capable of grounding her if she disobeyed her.

When she saw how the other women were dressed, she knew her mother would be certain she was right. Despite the fact that Willow believed she would have looked better and more grown-up in the white lace, she could see that the other women were dressed rather conservatively and even formally.

Mrs. Montoya was wearing a dark blue silk dress that was so long it was almost floor length, and the wife of a Mexico City lawyer was wearing a black high-necked dress with a full skirt. There were several other women in the room — all older than Willow and all wearing clothes her mother would definitely approve of. Willow yawned and hoped that she would soon be able to get Carlos off by himself. Parties full of old adults like this weren't a lot of fun.

Willow was pretty much trapped with the women most of the evening. They laughed and told stories and talked about their shopping trips to the States and to Europe. They were especially sympathetic to Jessica and thought it was a shame she was such a young widow. "And soon your girls will marry and you will be totally alone," one woman lamented.

"My girls are a long way from marriage age," Jessica said quickly. "Brittany is fourteen and Willow is sixteen. In our country, most young women don't marry until much, much later."

"Of course not," the woman answered swiftly and then she smiled and added, "unless they fall in love. Love must find its way, no?"

"No," Jessica said and turned to Mrs. Montoya, asking, "are the flowers from your garden?"

"I'm not certain," Mrs. Montoya answered, "Lupe takes care of the flower decorations. If you like, I'll call her and ask."

"Please, no," Jessica said. "Wherever they are from, they are gorgeous. But then, Mexico is called the land of flowers, isn't it?"

"Yes," Carlos answered as he joined the ladies. "And the land of sunshine and 'our third world neighbor,' and many, many other things. But now you have seen a bit of my Mexico. I am delighted to share it with you."

"I'd like to see the gardens," Willow said directly to Carlos. She was aware that it was a bold thing to say but she really didn't care. She was bored with these ladies.

"Of course," Carlos bowed slightly and looked very pleased at her suggestion.

"I would also like to see the gardens," Jessica said. "How about you, Brittany?"

"Sure."

And so the four of them spent an hour walking up and down the rows and rows of flowers, vegetables, and trees that made up the Montoya gardens. It turned out that Carlos knew a great deal about plants, and he entertained them with stories about many different flowers.

Pausing by the poinsettia plants, he said, "Here they are. The Mexican flower that has become your Christmas symbol. Did you know the poinsettia is Mexican?"

When they said they didn't, he added, "It's named after an American though. During the reign of the Emperor Maximiliano and Empress Carlotta, Mexico was under Napoleon's rule. Did you know it was once a part of the French empire?"

"No," Jessica admitted. "I don't think we

get much Mexican history in our schools. At least in Wisconsin."

"To go on with my story," Carlos's voice was smooth and pleasant as he talked but Willow thought she detected just a faint note of exasperation about the fact that his American friends knew so little about Mexican history.

"There was a Captain Poinsett who was attached to the American Embassy and the flower was named after him. Legend has it that the Empress Carlotta had a crush on him. Of course, that is only gossip. Historical gossip, but gossip."

As they walked back to the house, Carlos said, "Tomorrow will be fun. We will go into the city of Oaxaca and then I will take you to Dona Epedia's for lunch. They have parrots there." Then he laughed and added, "Not for lunch — for decoration. And then we'll go to the village for a fiésta tomorrow evening. *Las Posadas.*"

Willow was a little cheered when she heard what he had planned for tomorrow. At least they would be out touring again and there was a good chance that she could be alone with him. Sometime during the day or the evening, she would surely find a way. She would tell him how much she cared for

him and perhaps he would say he loved
her. She would surely get him to kiss her.
And she would ask him to the New Year's
Eve ball. She was certain she could manage
that.

Chapter 37

The parrots were wonderful — great big birds with bright red, green, and purple wings and orange bodies. Though they flew all around the outdoor restaurant, they never flew over the high walls into the countryside. "Why don't they just run off?" Brittany asked.

"Their wings are clipped," Carlos explained. "They can't fly very far or very high. Besides, they wouldn't get very far. It's better for them to stay inside."

Brittany frowned and bit into another delicious tortilla chip. It was hard to think of anything living its whole life in such a small space, even a space as beautiful as this one. As she looked around the restaurant, she saw tall red bushes serving as fences in every direction. The flowers on the bushes were brilliant scarlet and had a papery look, as though they were not quite real. "What are those bushes again?" she asked.

"Bougainvillea," Carlos pronounced the word slowly. *Boo gan vee yah.* He seemed to enjoy the role of host very much and he explained things well. He was careful to help them select food they would enjoy and had been very good about pointing out the beautiful sights on their three-hour drive to Oaxaca.

Once in the city, they'd spent the morning wandering up and down the lanes of the largest outdoor market in Mexico and everyone purchased a lot of souvenirs in the market and tiny stores that lined the streets. "Oaxaca is a big city now," Carlos said. "But when I was a boy it was much smaller. The market was right off the center square and most of the vendors were Indians down from the mountains."

"You sound like that was a million years ago," Willow teased and tucked her arm in his.

Carlos smiled down at the beautiful girl and said, "It seems like a million years ago. I've been in Europe and the United States and my own country has changed a great deal. Even Christmas has changed. In those times the Indians brought orchids and bromeliads down with tree moss to sell for Christmas decorations. Now the people import plastic Christmas trees and Japanese lights."

"It still seems pretty old-fashioned to me," Brittany said. "Look at that guy over there selling that fruit on a stick. We don't have that in Madison."

"You do have mangoes though," Carlos said. "I saw it in the supermarket one day. But the fruit was picked too young and wasn't sweet." They stood beside the man who was jabbing sticks into rich, warm mangoes. The fruit was larger than an avocado but shaped the same and when it was peeled, had a yellow-orange color that was just beautiful. They watched in fascination as the man peeled the fruit with a paring knife, never letting the peeling drop until it was all done. Then he quickly cut petals into the fruit and held it out to Willow. It looked a little like a soft orange pinecone.

Carlos handed the man a coin and they all walked on.

The stalls were very close together and there were so many smells and sounds that Brittany had a hard time taking it all in. The sound of Spanish washed around her and though she couldn't understand a word of it, it was beginning to sound less foreign.

They moved from stall to stall, looking at

piles of tomatoes, avocados, potatoes, and herbs. Wherever they went, people called out to them, urging them to purchase their wares. They walked quickly through the section of the market where people were eating at low benches and stalls. Smoke from the cooking meat and the sting of chilies burned their eyes.

When they got to the section of the market that sold flowers, everyone slowed down and walked up and down the stalls, marveling at the amazing variety and beauty of the flowers that surrounded them. Most of the blooms were unknown to Wisconsin gardens and Brittany thought she had never in her life seen such wonderful roses. There were piles and piles of lilies that smelled so sweet it was almost like a strong perfume.

"Should we take some home to your mother?" Jessica asked.

Carlos smiled and quickly shook his head. "Flowers are very common in Mexico. She has her own gardener and he brings her blooms as good or better than these every day."

"I'd like to get your mother something," Jessica persisted.

Carlos wrinkled his brow and thought and then said, "She would like some tamales. The Oaxaca women make them special for Christmas. They're sweet, with raisins and nuts."

So they purchased two dozen tamales, which were wrapped in plastic and carried back to the limousine as though they had been the most expensive caviar. Each time they made a purchase, Carlos or his driver would carry it back to the car and then be back for more.

From the market they went for a long, slow *comida* at Dona Epedia's restaurant in one of the older parts of the city. As they sat in the beautiful garden, looking up at the bright blue sky that was framed by the scarlet bougainvillea branches, Brittany was suddenly struck by the thought that she was a long, long way from home.

Even though her mother and sister were with her, she felt the foreignness of the place where she was and she realized that there were millions and millions of people living on this planet and that everyone was different from everyone else. Somehow, the thought was a little frightening and she shivered.

"Are you cold?" Jessica asked. "Did you bring your coat for tonight?"

"I'm fine," Brittany said. "I think I'll walk about a little bit." She rose before anyone could object and walked over to the swimming pool where she looked down into the clear, cold water at her reflection. She saw her face looking back at her and it seemed to her that her face was somehow changed, somehow more grown-up than it had been three days ago. The bright red hair that tumbled around her pointed chin no longer seemed the most important thing about her. No — now she saw that the most important thing about her were her green eyes. Were eyes really the window of the soul? She wished she had someone she could talk with about ideas like that.

Brittany sighed and asked her reflection when she would find someone who was truly her own. She wanted a boyfriend who was honest and true and someone who would listen to her and her ideas. She wanted someone to really share things with. "When?" she asked her reflection in the swimming pool. "When will he appear?"

The answer seemed to be whispering in the soft papery blooms of the bougainvilleas. It was a strange and magical answer but it was clear as a bell. The wind whispered back to her, "He's already here. Your own true love is already here."

She was surprised by the clearness of the message and wondered if she should be worried about hearing things. On the other hand — if you asked a question out loud and got an answer out loud — that was perfectly normal.

The main thing is to figure out who the voice was talking about, Brittany told herself. And even as she thought the question, she knew the answer.

She'd been crazy about Lars Peterson for a long, long time and now that he'd been turned down by Willow she had a chance. When she got back to Madison, she would ask Lars to go to the New Year's Eve ball with her. Why not?

Chapter 38

It was cold when the sun went down and Willow was glad she was wearing a jacket and scarf. Most of the villagers wore only silk shawls and some had bare feet. That seemed funny to Willow and it seemed even funnier that Carlos, who always seemed so bundled up in Wisconsin, was only wearing a sweatshirt and Levi's here in the village of San José del Valle.

As for herself and her mother and sister, the cool night air of the village seemed plenty cold and they kept their jackets and scarves wrapped tight around them. Willow stuck as close to Carlos as she could as they made their way down the tiny, narrow streets toward the church. There were hundreds of people, and it was a small community. Carlos led the way, holding her hand, and she held onto Jessica who held Brittany's hand. The four of them formed a snake line in the darkening evening.

"How many people live here?" Brittany shouted.

"Mostly they're tourists from Mexico City," Carlos shouted back. And then he saw someone and began to yell and pull them along toward a group of very citified-looking young people. Willow wasn't very happy about meeting any more of Carlos's friends. She wanted him alone tonight — or at least alone with Jessica and Brittany. There was only one more day on the ranch and then another half day in Mexico City and they would be going home. Willow was determined to go home with a date for the New Year's Eve ball.

This group was seven young students from Mexico City. All the young men attended the University of Mexico. Two were American, one was German, and the others were Mexican. They immediately crowded around the three Winstons, offering to show them the church, to bring them refreshments, and generally behaving in a very charming manner.

Willow loved the attention and laughed and asked, "Is everyone in Mexico this polite?"

"No. Some people work for a living," a short, dark young man with deep-set, serious eyes said. "These people who are in the procession tonight worked all day in the fields.

They haven't time to flirt with pretty *gringas*."

"Listen to Miguel," one of the Americans said. "He's pulling his revolutionary rap on the girls." The two Americans laughed and a tall fellow with sandy brown hair took Willow aside and said, "Miguel comes from the richest family in Mexico. Richer than your friend Carlos even. And he just plays revolutionary when he thinks it will go over with the girls. He'll say anything to get you away from Carlos."

That set the pattern for the evening. They watched the villagers and tourists as everyone waited for the procession to begin. The boys vied for their attention and most of the competition was between Miguel and Carlos. Each took up a post beside Willow and each tried to outdo the other with compliments. After a while, Willow began to feel as though she was just a handy prize for their contest and though she usually liked attention, she didn't really enjoy this game.

She turned to the American boy behind her and he returned her gaze steadily. "Do they always compete like this?" she asked.

The American laughed. "We play baseball and they flirt with girls."

Willow smiled and sort of dropped back a bit to talk with the American but Carlos took her arm and said, "We want to stay together.

It's easy to get lost in a village this size."

"I won't get lost," Willow protested.

"Of course not," Carlos smiled and bent his head toward her. "You are my guest and I will make sure you are safe."

Willow understood that Carlos was telling her that she had to stay with him. On the one hand, she resented the restriction, on the other, she was pleased that he wanted her close by. The villagers were pushing a bit now and the crowd seemed to have grown thicker.

Miguel called out, "Willow, Brittany, come with us. We'll climb to the top of the wall and see better."

Willow shook her head. If Carlos wanted her by his side, she would stay by his side. Brittany made a move to go with the Mexico City students and both Jessica and Carlos reached out and pulled her back. She laughed and stayed put, which told Willow that she was a little bit afraid of the crowd as well.

Finally, the procession began. The church doors opened and a long line of children carrying candles walked down the church steps and into the street. Perhaps there were two hundred children in all, ranging from three to twelve. They each carried a candle that they held close to their chests so that their faces showed. Some of the children were dressed in their best dresses of satin but many wore simple cotton clothing that was no different from their daytime wear. They were not lined up according to size so some were tall and some were shorter but to Willow, they were all beautiful. As they passed by, their little faces glowed in the candlelight and they looked like angels marching along.

"Aren't they sweet!" she said. She leaned back just a little to be closer to Carlos. It felt good to have his warmth near her and she wished he would put his arms around her. Of course, he would never do such a thing in front of the others, but she could still wish it. She closed her eyes and tried to imagine what this evening would feel like if it were just the two of them and Carlos was holding her close.

She shivered and woke from her dream. It really was very cold and she was wondering how much longer this procession was going to be. She didn't want to ask though because Carlos was obviously trying so hard to please them. It would be terrible to seem ungrateful and the village was certainly picturesque.

"How much longer?" Brittany asked. "I'm freezing."

"I thought Wisconsin girls could take the cold," Carlos teased.

"This is different," Willow chimed in. "It

seems different from home. Here, it was so warm all day that the night is a real shock."

"In Wisconsin it's psychological warfare," Brittany said. "Mind over mittens or something. You start getting ready for winter about Labor Day. Here, you only have winter at night. That's weird."

"It snows in Mexico City from time to time," Carlos said. "But the snow melts when it hits the ground. Or soon after."

"I wonder if it's snowing at home," Willow said. It was the first thought she'd given to Wisconsin since they'd started on the trip. Wisconsin seemed a million miles from this small village in a remote part of the Mexican mountains.

"I hope so," Brittany said. "Teddy and I are entered in the ice sculpture contest again this year."

"Maybe this year you'll win a prize," Jessica encouraged her daughter. Since third grade, Teddy and Brittany had been contestants and they'd never so much as received an honorable mention.

"Yeah," Brittany agreed and dug her hands into her jacket pockets. She wished she had a cap because her ears were cold. "It's how you play the game though, you always tell me that." She and her mother laughed happily.

"The fiesta is beginning," Carlos said.

"I'll get us some chocolate and bread," Carlos said. "Brittany, I need some help."

Willow and Jessica waited in a sheltered place between two trees as Brittany and Carlos pushed their way to the stall that was selling refreshments. Willow wished he had asked her to help him but she understood. Carlos was always sensitive to the feelings of others and his friends had certainly paid a lot more attention to her than to Brittany. He was just trying to make it up to her. She smiled as she thought of what a nice person Carlos was. And she knew he loved her — she just knew it.

"Penny for your thoughts," Jessica said.

"Not thinking," Willow answered. "I'm just freezing, that's all. "

"Are you having fun?" Jessica asked.

"Of course, aren't you?"

"I was until we hit this cold snap," Jessica grumbled and tried to turn her collar up around her ears. Just then, a woman came by selling shawls like the ones the women in the village wore. Jessica bought four of them. The woman seemed very pleased with her sale and scampered away.

"I think I made her evening," Jessica said. Willow and she laughed as they wrapped the shawls around their necks, shoulders, and up over their heads. When they were finished, Willow asked, "How do I look?"

"Like a citizen of San José del Valle," Jessica pronounced. "And I don't really care how I look, my ears are warm for the first time in hours."

Willow wondered if she should take the shawl off when Carlos returned. She was certain that her hair was her best feature and she didn't really feel right covering it up. On the other hand, it was cold and the shawl was just temporary.

She could see that they were at the tables now and she watched as Carlos laid down some money and handed Brittany a sweet little pottery tray with a jug and four tiny cups on it. Then he picked up two loaves of decorated bread and they hurried back to Jessica and Willow.

When Carlos saw their shawls, he nodded and said, "*Rebozos*, good idea."

"We got you one, too," Willow offered.

Carlos thought that was the funniest thing he had ever heard and he laughed and laughed. Willow didn't think it could possibly be all that funny and she watched in dismay as Carlos practically doubled over with amusement at the idea that he would wear a *rebozo*.

"We were just trying to be nice," Willow said.

He wiped the tears of laughter from his eyes and said, "Yes, of course you were. But we will take the *rebozo* back as a souvenir." He pointed to the tray Brittany was holding. "We need to drink this before it gets cold," Carlos said. He tipped the pitcher and poured hot chocolate into four cups.

They drank quickly and Willow said, "It's the best chocolate I ever had." She held out her cup for more.

As Carlos poured, he said, "You're supposed to break the cups when you finish. They were made especially for the festival."

"No!" All three Winstons reacted immediately.

Carlos laughed and said, "I thought not. That's why I got the tray and pitcher as well. Completes the souvenir set. If you like, we can get a wreath made of these chocolate cups for you to hang on your door back in Wisconsin. They probably have a few here and there are lots in the Mexico City market."

They ate one loaf of bread, which turned out to be stuffed with white raisins, almonds, and some small candies that seemed a bit like jujubes. They drank more chocolate and milled around the churchyard for a while, talking a few minutes to the group from Mexico City before they left, and then Carlos said, "Time to go back to the ranch. It's a three-hour drive and it's almost eleven now."

"I must find one of those wreaths made from the tiny cups," Jessica said. "Come on, let's go look."

"I'm tired," Willow complained. "You and Brittany go. Carlos can stay with me."

Jessica shook her head. "Either we all go or we wait till we get to the market in Mexico City."

"We may have a better selection in Mexico City," Carlos said. "This festival is so popular now that the best things are sent to the city for higher prices."

Willow sighed. Once again, she had failed to get Carlos alone even for a few minutes. If this kept up, she would have to ask him to go to the dance with her mother and Brittany watching. And as for ever kissing him — it was beginning to look as though it was impossible to kiss anyone in Mexico.

Chapter 39

Brittany dreamed of Wisconsin and that seemed a waste of time to her. When she woke the next morning and looked around her guest room, she realized it was her last day at the ranch. She quickly pulled on her Mexican cotton shirt and Levi's and practically ran down the stairs to the garden.

In the garden she stretched her arms open wide and turned round and round, drinking in all the delicious colors of Mexico. The scarlet bougainvillea plants were so strong that the first day they were practically all she could see but now she'd learned that there were layers and layers of colors to enjoy.

She walked over to the small fish pond with no fish and admired the bright green lily pads and the yellow green water. She tried seeing her reflection in the pond, hoping that she might have more communication from her "voices" about her true love but the water was too murky to see anything except the pond itself. It was pretty though. The green water looked sharp and bright against the white and blue tiles. And the blue tiles were accented with orange and yellow and pink tiles, making the whole thing seem like a fiesta.

"You like the garden, yes?" Mrs. Montoya asked. She had slipped up behind Brittany as soundlessly as a butterfly.

"It is gorgeous," Brittany said.

"And were you thinking of some young man at home?"

"Just a friend," Brittany said quickly. Actually, she had been thinking about Teddy, wishing he were here. There were so many things she could talk with Teddy about that she'd never think of discussing with Willow or her mother.

"This friend is in your school?"

"Yes. He's been my best friend since kindergarten," Brittany said, "but he's not a boyfriend."

Mrs. Montoya smiled at her and asked, "He is a boy and he is a friend. So he is a boyfriend, no?"

"No." Brittany shook her head. "I do have

a boyfriend though," she offered the older woman. "His name is Lars and he's very tall and very blond and very nice."

"And very handsome?" Mrs. Montoya was still smiling.

"Yes. He is very handsome but that's not the most important thing about him. The most important thing is that he's nice. I'm going to the New Year's Eve ball with him," Brittany confided. Then she looked away quickly. It wasn't quite a lie to say she was going with Lars. She was going to ask him as soon as she got home and maybe, just maybe, he would say yes. Still, it wasn't technically true and Mrs. Montoya was the sort of person who made you feel that it was good to be absolutely, technically true.

"Two young men," Mrs. Montoya nodded and linked her arm in Brittany's. "That's the way it was when I was a girl. Always best to have several suitors. That way, one is never disappointed."

Brittany opened her mouth to correct Mrs. Montoya but the older woman smiled and said, "Now, go and have breakfast and then we will drive to our oldest friends, the Beltrans. Their daughter Luisa is going to marry Carlos one day."

Brittany stopped and stared at Mrs. Montoya. "Is Carlos engaged?" she asked.

Mrs. Montoya nodded and smiled. "Carlos has been engaged for three years now. She is a few years older and went to Europe to college. She is a brilliant girl. Studying medicine, you know." Then Mrs. Montoya frowned slightly and said, "By the time my son finishes his college education, she will be a medical doctor."

"How old *is* Carlos?" Brittany couldn't believe that anyone as nonserious as Carlos could have been engaged at seventeen. So either they were wrong about his age or his mother was wrong about his intention to marry Luisa Beltran.

"Twenty. Luisa is twenty-three. But they are serious about each other in their own way. They also knew each other as children and perhaps they were also best friends. You look troubled, my dear. Surely you are too sensible to be in love with Carlos? He is too old for you, you know."

"I know," Brittany responded. But she couldn't help feeling sorry for Willow. Wait until she heard that Carlos was engaged!

Chapter 40

Anna came in from taking a long walk and her mother said, "Some boy called." Her mother frowned and waited for an explanation.

"Who was it?" Anna's first thought was that it might be Teddy and that something terrible had happened to the Winstons on their flight to Mexico.

"Lars Peterson. He wants you to call him."

She couldn't imagine what Lars was calling about, and her hands were shaking as she dialed the phone. Lars picked it up on the second ring, and she told him hello and waited.

"Are you having fun?" Lars asked. "I went running this morning and I missed you."

Anna was just plain confused by this conversation. What did Lars want and why had he called. "Is there anything wrong?" she asked.

"No," Lars said. "I was just thinking about you and I called. That's all."

"How did you get my number?"

"Dan gave it to me."

"Oh." Again, Anna waited. There had to be more to this call than this but she couldn't imagine what.

"You're sure there's nothing wrong?" Anna asked.

"Everything's fine," Lars said. "Oh, and I was thinking you might go to the New Year's Eve ball with me. Will you?"

"Go to a dance?"

"Sure. Have you ever been to a dance before?"

"No. I don't know how to dance."

"That doesn't matter. No one really dances anyhow. Look Anna, I really hope you'll say yes."

A lot of thoughts rushed around in her brain. For one split second she thought maybe this was a joke and the person on the other end of the line was an imposter. But it was definitely Lars's voice. Then it occurred to her that he might be making a joke and she discarded that immediately. He would never, never be so cruel. So he must want to take her to the dance. She thought of how pleased her Aunt

with him. If he noticed, he didn't say anything.

As they bid their guests good-bye, Mrs. Beltran said, "Perhaps you will all return soon for a wedding. No?"

"Are you getting married?" Willow asked Carlos directly.

He laughed and said, "Perhaps one day. And when I do I will certainly invite all the beautiful Winston ladies to the wedding. Of course, I may be attending your wedding first, lovely Willow. One never knows about these things."

"I won't marry for a long time," Willow said.

"Good," Jessica said and then she laughed and added, "I don't want either of my daughters rushing into commitments. I want them to be free and strong and wonderful — just the way they are right now."

Jessica put her arm around Willow and squeezed her shoulder. "Now we'd better be going or we'll miss our tour of the anthropological museum."

"I'd love to come with you," Carlos protested. "I never imagined letting you go alone."

"We have your driver," Jessica said. "And you have so little time with your mother. We'll see you in January. January seventh, you said?"

So Carlos hugged and kissed everyone

good-bye and the three Winston women went down the hill by themselves. As they came to the bottom, Willow asked, "You knew I wasn't carsick, didn't you?"

"Yes, I did," Jessica answered. "But I didn't know what to do about it. I hope you don't mind that I practically forced poor Carlos not to come with us today."

"Poor Carlos!" Brittany said. "I don't see anything so poor about Carlos. He's a big flirt, if you ask me, and he was really cruel to Willow."

Jessica said slowly, "I don't think he's even aware that he's flirting. And if he is, he obviously thinks women like it. What's more women *do* like the attention, don't they?"

"But Willow believed him," Brittany was not going to let go of her indignation that fast.

"Willow believed what she wanted to believe . . . and Willow is certainly a flirt herself," Jessica answered.

Brittany said, "Everyone's in love with Willow — even Teddy."

Jessica laughed and drew her younger daughter into a hug. "You have a lot to learn but then, you have plenty of time to learn it. As for Willow, she's certainly getting her share of attention and I'm not sure she's treating the young men in her life much better than Carlos treated her. Not intentional, mind you, just thoughtless."

Willow turned to them and said, "Would you two mind not talking about me as though I've disappeared. I'm still here, you know."

"I know," Jessica said. "And I'm proud of you for that. You're tougher than you look, my dear. That's good."

Willow turned and looked out the window at the whizzing landscape. That's what Dan had said to her just before she went on this trip — something about how tough she was. She didn't understand it then and she didn't really understand what her mother was talking about now. She didn't feel tough. She felt just awful but she knew she would get over it.

Chapter 43

Flying into Madison on Christmas Eve morning was exciting and when Dan met them at the airport, he said, "You all look really great. Have a good time?"

"Great," Willow said quickly. Her smile seemed a little forced to Brittany but it looked as if Willow was determined to recover quickly. Willow went to a pay phone where Brittany could see her talking to someone. She's calling Lars, Brittany thought, and she couldn't resist feeling just a little sorry for herself. Of course Lars would be delighted to hear from Willow and of course she would go to the dance with him and of course, they would have a great time.

Dan caught the suitcases as they circled the roller belt and Jessica and Brittany stood back from the crowd. Brittany said to her mother,

"Now Willow is asking Lars to the ball and I don't have a date."

"The New Year's Eve ball? Why not ask Teddy?"

"I couldn't," Brittany answered. "I wanted to go with an older man."

"Teddy will be an older man someday. Seems to me he's grown up a lot this year." Jessica reached forward and took her suitcase from Dan, saying, "Now we're just missing the blue leather overnight case. The one with the gold trim."

"You're not helping," Brittany complained.

"I can't think about dances right now," Jessica said. "We've got people coming tonight and we need to get the decorations out. Could you and Willow pick up the poinsettias and the tree? I'm sure Dan will help me with the things around the house. I wish Anna were going to be with us. I miss her."

"Sometimes I think you like Anna better than you like me."

"Sometimes you and Willow seem so — so self-centered," Jessica admitted. "It's not that I love her more — there's no question of that — but she *is* helpful and considerate."

"And I'm not?"

Jessica sighed and said, "Brittany, I'm tired and so are you. I don't want to have an argument in this airport about boys or about who I love the most. It used to be just Willow but now your jealousy has extended to your cousin. You really ought to start growing up."

"I am grown-up," Brittany answered and she picked up two bags and started marching toward the car. "It's because I'm so grown-up that I have a problem about the ball. I *need* an older man for the ball."

Jessica didn't even answer her. And Willow looked so unhappy when she came back from the telephone that no one even asked her what was wrong. Dan put all the luggage in the trunk and Jessica sat up in front with him. As they climbed into the backseat, Willow whispered in a very dramatic voice, "Lars has a date. He wouldn't break it."

"Did you really ask him to?" Brittany whispered. Sometimes her sister's self-confidence and self-centeredness produced remarkable results. Brittany was never sure whether she admired the results or disapproved of them. But she was impressed.

"Of course I asked him to. I thought he'd want to." Willow frowned and shook her head a little. "He said he would *never* do that. He seemed really surprised that I suggested it."

"So who are you going to ask next?" Brittany asked.

"No one," Willow answered. "I'm just going to stay home."

"So will I," Brittany said. "It will be easier that way."

In a way, Brittany was glad to drop the idea of the New Year's Eve ball. Worrying about dates and dresses seemed like a lot of trouble and what was the sense of going with someone you didn't like?

Willow stretched and yawned and said, "I'm going to take a long nap this afternoon."

"I was hoping you and Willow would pick up the poinsettias and tree while Dan and I did the last-minute things around the house," Jessica said.

"I did it all yesterday," Dan said. "I figured you women would want to rest a bit before the party so I just took it on myself to fix everything. You can change what you don't like, but the tree's there and so are the poinsettias and all the glasses are clean and the silver's polished. We just have to make the salad and pick up the lasagna at six P.M. I can do all that."

Jessica reached over and hugged Dan, saying, "You are truly wonderful, Dan. You're a real sweetheart. Isn't he?" She turned to the girls in the backseat and her eyes commanded them to be appreciative of all he'd done.

"You're really great," Brittany said. "Thanks."

"I think you're wonderful, too," Willow said. "I always say, charming words can only go so far. Eventually, actions are what count."

Dan blushed and was obviously so pleased by Willow's praise that Brittany wondered if he was safe behind the wheel of the car. She looked at her sister and wondered why she couldn't see what was as plain as the nose on her face. If she wanted a date for the New Year's Eve ball, he was sitting in the front seat, driving their car.

Brittany decided to give it a little while and then tell Willow to invite Dan to the ball. Just because one sister didn't have a date didn't mean they both had to stay home.

The Christmas Eve party was a small get-together for a few friends and it was just the right way to usher in the Christmas celebration, Brittany decided.

The house looked beautiful and the food was simple but good. The company was fun. Teddy and his folks came and so did an older couple who had been friends for years. Two foreign students from Japan who were in Dan's classes at the university were invited and they were obviously happy to partake in a real American

Christmas celebration. They wandered all over the house, looking at the Christmas ornaments and decorations.

Burt Hawkins, Jessica's painting teacher and new boyfriend, was there, and for the first time, Brittany got a chance to really study him. He did indeed seem to be a nice man who was obviously very taken with her mother. At one point, Brittany went to the kitchen to dish out ice cream and he followed along to help. As he put the little crystal dishes on the tray he asked, "So how am I doing?"

Brittany pretended she didn't know what he was asking and said, "Fine. I think we need a couple more."

"No. I mean, how am I doing? You've been studying me all evening, trying to decide if I measure up. How am I doing?"

Brittany laughed and said, "You're doing fine. You must think I'm the weird sister, right? I mean, I was flirting in that restaurant that night. You must think that's a little strange?"

"I thought you were practicing your magnetic smile. I didn't think of it as flirting exactly, more as a scientific experiment."

Brittany nodded. "You're right. Are you always so smart?"

"I'm pretty smart," Burt Hawkins answered

comfortably. "I hear you are, too."

"Smart enough to know you're trying to get me to like you so my mother will," Brittany answered. Then she reached out and put her hand on his arm. "You don't have to try so hard. I think she does like you. I think she's been lonely long enough."

For a moment, she was worried that he would think she'd overstepped the boundaries of good taste. That was an expression her mother used quite often and he seemed to be about the same age, but he just looked grateful for the encouragement. He picked up the tray with the ice cream and said, "Thanks for the encouraging words, Brittany."

Everyone was supposed to have brought an inexpensive gift to the party and after dessert Jessica passed a basket around and everyone drew a number. Number one was Teddy who picked out a gift and unwrapped it and claimed he'd always wanted this wonderful bottle of bubble bath.

"Don't get too attached," Jessica warned. "The next number gets to take your bubble bath or keep his own present until the next guy gets a turn."

"I have number ten," Burt Hawkins said. "I guess that makes me the luckiest guy in the room."

Brittany had number six and unwrapped a huge chocolate bar that Dan, who was number seven, promptly took from her and gave her a pen and pencil set. The favorite gift of the evening was a stuffed yellow duck wearing a pearl necklace. It had five different homes before Burt selected it as his final choice of the evening and bestowed it on "our charming hostess, Jessica."

The gift exchange was fun although Brittany suspected that it might have been confusing for the Japanese students. Mr. and Mrs. Myers spent a lot of time trying to explain it to them but Brittany thought they looked even more bewildered after the explanation.

"Now I think it would be fun to sing, don't you?" Jessica passed out the family carol books, which were once her mother's, and everyone sat or stood around the piano while Brittany played Christmas carols.

After about three songs, Willow looked up and smiled and said, "This is the best caroling we've ever had at the Winston house."

"You always sound wonderful," Jessica told her daughter and reached out and smoothed Willow's strawberry blond hair. Then with the other hand, she reached out and patted Brittany's shoulder and said, "You do, too, Britt."

"But it's Teddy and Dan who make the difference," Brittany observed. And it was true. Teddy's voice was better than she'd ever noticed and Dan had that rich, warm baritone. It made the singing warmer and stronger. And the singing made the evening more perfect than she'd ever remembered a Christmas — at least since her father died.

Brittany looked around the beautiful living room with the fire roaring in the Pennsylvania fieldstone fireplace and she really saw and appreciated the beauty of her home. She spoke her thoughts aloud, "We saw some great houses in Mexico but none any better than this one. I even like the furniture better. It's more modern and interesting."

"To the modern and interesting Winston family." Burt Hawkins raised his wine glass in a toast.

Some people decided to leave, and by the time Jessica showed her friends and the Japanese students out, Willow had persuaded Brittany, Burt, Teddy, and Dan to keep singing with her. Jessica and the Myers sat on the couch and chatted about their Christmas and Jessica's trip to Mexico. Brittany could hear enough of her mother's conversation to know that she had really enjoyed getting away.

She overheard Mrs. Myers ask Jessica if she would like to travel more and heard her mother say, "Yes. That's one of the things that Burt and I have in common. We'd both like to see more of the world. Of course, until the kids are older, it will have to be short trips but . . ." Jessica's voice trailed off and she looked at the fire.

"Time to go home," Mrs. Myers said.

"I'll drive Teddy home," Willow and Dan offered the same thing at the same time. They both laughed at their simultaneous answers.

"Best to go to bed now," Mrs. Myers said. "Santa Claus can't come until the smoke's out of the chimney."

"That means she's tired," Teddy said but he stood up and said good night without any more arguments. Instead of walking to the door with his parents though, he grabbed Brittany's arm and pulled her into the hallway.

"What's up?" Brittany asked.

"This," Teddy said and he pointed to a sprig of mistletoe taped to the ceiling under the first landing. Then he took her in his arms and kissed her.

Brittany was so shocked that it took her a minute to react at all to the kiss. Somehow, she'd just never expected to be kissed by Teddy and so her primary response was surprise. She didn't pull away immediately and she supposed that was because she was too surprised. Finally, she did push him away and she asked, "What are you doing?"

"Kissing you," Teddy said. "You're under the mistletoe."

"You put me there," Brittany argued. "I didn't even know it was there."

"You know it's there now and you haven't moved," Teddy said and he took her in his arms once more, kissing her again. This time, she could feel that this was a serious kiss. He wasn't just kidding around, he was actually kissing her as though he found her an attractive girl — a girl he liked to kiss. And what's more, she enjoyed it!

Then Teddy's mother's voice came from the living room, calling him to join them. He grinned and kissed the top of Brittany's forehead and said, "Good night, Britt. Merry Christmas."

"Merry Christmas." It wasn't a very clever reply but it was the only reaction she could think of.

Chapter 44

They awoke on Christmas morning later than usual because everyone was still a little tired from the Mexico trip, but by nine o'clock the family was having coffee and unwrapping presents, just like the old days.

There were some expected gifts: ski sweaters and ski boots for the girls, school clothes, and a new robe for Jessica. There were also some surprises that delighted and pleased as they were unwrapped.

Willow bought Brittany new music videos and Brittany bought Willow a videotape and book on jazz dancing. She explained, "I thought with your voice you might like to try out for school plays in the spring. After cheerleading, I mean."

For Dan, there was a huge book on the architecture of Frank Lloyd Wright and a new Swiss Army Knife.

Jessica was pleased with the lace shawl that Brittany purchased for her in Mexico, and seemed just as pleased by the navy sweater that Willow chose from Hunsaker's Department Store.

Perhaps the biggest surprise was two tiny boxes tucked in the branches of the Christmas tree. The boxes were identical and each girl opened her gift to find exquisite gold earrings. Brittany's earrings were large hoops with tiny, lacy filigreed work. Willow's earrings were much smaller, daintier hoops attached to studs shaped like flowers.

"I got them when we were in the Oaxaca market. When I bought mine. Remember?"

"How?" Britanny demanded. "We were always together."

"I said I had to go back and have mine repaired." Jessica laughed and said, "I loved actually putting one over on you. Are you surprised?"

Dan said he would cook Christmas breakfast alone and insisted that they sit down and wait to be served. Brittany wore her earrings to breakfast and she jumped up several times to look in the mirror and proclaim that she looked like a gypsy princess. Willow tucked her earrings back in their box and said, "I'll save them till a special time."

"You will have many special times," Jessica promised her daughter.

Willow looked at her mother and sister and said, "I really thought he liked me. I guess it was very foolish and self-centered of me but I couldn't quite imagine that he didn't. Even after I heard about his girlfriend from Brittany I believed I was the special one."

"You are special," Brittany said. "Everyone knows that."

"We are all special in our own way . . ." Jessica began. Both girls were happy when Dan came in with the eggs and Jessica broke off her sermon.

Teddy came over in time to have his second breakfast of the morning and show off his new Christmas watch. "It tells time in six different parts of the world at once," he said. "So if your Japanese friends come back and want to know what time it is in Tokyo, I can tell them."

Teddy seemed to be in a very good mood and he laughed and joked with everyone, as though everything was just exactly the way it always was. Brittany could barely look at him she was so shy.

He talked Willow and Dan into playing Monopoly with him. There wasn't any way Brittany could really get out of it, so she ended up spending most of Christmas Day afternoon on the floor in front of the fire playing a game. About three o'clock she went bankrupt, and Willow said she was bored and wanted to watch TV. Dan claimed he had to start on his studies, and so Brittany and Teddy were left alone.

"Want to take a walk?" Teddy asked.

"Where to?"

"We could walk downtown," he offered. "Look at the decorations. We could go to a movie if you want."

"A walk, I guess," Brittany said. Teddy seemed pretty normal. More or less like his old self. She supposed that things would go back to normal now and that the surprising kisses of last night would never be mentioned again. However, Teddy did a surprising thing when they walked into the hallway. He took her coat off the hook by the door and actually held it for her.

She stared at him. He held her coat open, waiting for her to slip into it. She asked, "What are you doing that for?"

"What?"

"Holding my coat?"

"Good manners," Teddy answered.

"You never held my coat before," Brittany said.

"You're older now," Teddy answered. "Not

a kid anymore. I hold coats open for non-kids."

She shrugged and slipped into the coat, buttoning it tight under her chin. Then she said, "Thanks."

"You're welcome," he answered. He seemed very comfortable.

"You don't have to hold my coat all the time," Brittany said. "It makes me nervous."

"Okay, I won't," he answered mildly. "We could have a signal. You could sort of nod your head if you want me to hold your coat and shake it like this if you don't."

They were walking past Teddy's house now and she laughed out loud. This was more like the old Teddy, the guy who made her laugh. "And no more kisses," she said. She wished she hadn't brought the subject up, but the words sort of tumbled out of her mouth before she could control them.

"I liked kissing you," Teddy said and then he added, "but maybe we could work out a second set of signals. You could tap your feet or wiggle your ears or something."

"You really are silly," Brittany laughed.

Then he did something that was as strange as holding her coat. He reached out and took her hand and held it. Even though they were both wearing gloves, she felt a kind of electric spark move between their hands and she was surprised once again at how good his touch felt to her. She thought about taking her hand away but she simply walked down the street with him, holding hands.

"Listen, Britt," Teddy said, and his voice was serious, "this is going to take some adjustment but not much. We're still friends but we're older. So now we're friends who date. That's a big difference in some ways but in most ways it will be the same."

Brittany's mouth went dry and she said, "You seem very sure of yourself. Why do you think we're dating?"

"We're walking downtown holding hands," Teddy said. "That's a date, isn't it?"

"I'm not sure what it is," Brittany answered honestly. "But I never planned on having you as a boyfriend."

He squeezed her hand. "I know. That's why I waited for you to grow up a little. You're getting there."

"I'm a lot more grown-up than you are," Brittany protested. "I've certainly had a lot more experience than you." Then she thought about the last few months and she reviewed her experiences. What had she really done? What had she learned? She'd flirted with Justin and been kissed, but that wasn't anything to brag about. She'd had a crush on Lars and not gotten anywhere at all with him. She'd had a crush on Carlos and that was nothing but fantasy. And through it all, Teddy had been there — her best friend. He'd been waiting for her to grow up, he said. She laughed in surprise and said, "Maybe I am growing up."

"You are," Teddy said. "You've been different ever since you came back from Mexico. More solid. Not so fantastical. Fantastic but not fantastical."

"So you've been . . . interested in me all along?" Brittany couldn't keep sneaking looks at this new Teddy who was walking beside her. "I always thought you had a crush on Willow."

"No. I have a crush on you. Have had since kindergarten."

He stopped and looked at her. She looked up and noticed how tall he was. When had Teddy grown that extra three inches? And when had he become so handsome? His eyes were the same deep blue, merry eyes she'd always known but they were framed by dark brows and lashes. His smile, which was still a crooked grin, now seemed to light his whole face with love. "Are you nodding your head?" he asked softly.

She nodded and he drew her close to him, touching her eyes, her cheeks, and her lips with light kisses. She sighed and said, "We're standing on a street corner. People can see us."

"It's almost dark," Teddy answered.

"My mother would have a fit if she saw me kissing you on a street corner," Brittany said. Even so, she did not pull away. It felt so strange and so good to be in Teddy's arms.

"You're right," Teddy agreed. "So we can go to the movies, can't we?"

Brittany laughed and said, "I'll call home. But I don't think I'll tell Mom that we're on a date. I think I'll break it to her gradually."

"Not too gradually. I wanted to ask you to the New Year's Eve ball," Teddy said. "Will you go with me?"

Brittany had the feeling that the ground was shifting under her feet. Nothing was quite the way she thought it was and nothing would ever be quite the same again. She was torn between surprise and delight and a certain amount of pride in Teddy for turning into such a special person. "Yes, I will," she said.

"Good," Teddy said. "We can double-date with Lars and Anna." Then he frowned and added, "Unless that would bother you?"

"Lars and Anna? Did Lars ask Anna?"

"Yes, I thought you knew." He took Brittany's chin in his hand and turned her face toward his. He looked deep into her eyes and said, "We don't have to go with them. I can find someone else. It's just that he's a senior and has a car."

"It won't bother me," Brittany said. "I was just surprised. My life seems to be full of surprises today."

"Good surprises?"

"Very good." Brittany smiled at her new boyfriend and said, "Let's call home and then get in out of the cold."

Chapter 45

When Willow heard that Anna was Lars's date, she frowned thoughtfully as though she were trying to solve a puzzle. Finally, she shook her head and asked Brittany, "Do you think he felt sorry for her?"

"According to Teddy, he just naturally thought of her as his second choice. According to Teddy, Lars and Anna have a lot in common. I can only tell you what Teddy thinks."

Willow sighed. "Do you think there's a lesson here?"

"Sort of," Brittany admitted. "At least I think we both underestimated Anna. And overestimated Carlos. And I overestimated Justin, that's for sure. I don't know — maybe the lesson is just to appreciate what you've got or something."

"What kind of a lesson is that?" Willow laughed and shook her head. "If we just went around appreciating what we had, we'd never get anything better."

"I didn't really need anything better," Brittany said and she drew her knees up under her chin. "I just was always looking for Prince Charming and there he was — the boy down the street."

The phone rang and Brittany answered it. Willow heard her tell someone that she would pick them up in an hour. When Brittany hung up she turned to her sister and said, "I told Anna we would pick her up at the bus station in an hour. And I also said we'd help her pick out a dress. Are you up to that?"

"Sure," Willow answered. "Just because Anna gets to play Cinderella doesn't mean I'm stuck in the part of the wicked stepsister, does it?"

And so the three of them spent the afternoon tramping all over Madison looking for the perfect dresses for Brittany and Anna to wear to the New Year's Eve ball.

Willow gave advice, helped push through the racks, and actually had a good time. From time to time she thought about Carlos, or she thought about Lars, and she got a funny little knot in her stomach, but it wasn't nearly as bad as she had expected.

They didn't find dresses, though, and that

evening they talked Jessica into letting Willow drive into Chicago to shop there. It was Willow's first big trip in the car and she felt very grown-up and proud as she maneuvered her way through the downtown city streets.

As they pulled into a downtown parking lot, Anna said, "I've never been to Chicago before."

"It's a great city," Willow promised her. "We'll find you something spectacular to wear."

Anna smiled timidly and followed her more cosmopolitan cousins up and down aisles until they came upon a wonderful bright hot pink dress for Brittany. The dress was very unusual with only one shoulder bared and a diagonal cut neckline. The skirt was a drop waist, also cut on the diagonal and the hem was uneven, coming to several points ranging from Brittany's knees to mid-calf.

"It will show off my red hair," Brittany claimed, as she modeled the shimmering satin top with the bright organza skirts. "Now I need some pink shoes with sequins and I'm ready to go."

Willow smiled at her younger sister in the outrageous dress. It was certainly too old for Brittany and it would never be exactly what you could call "in good taste," but it was all

Brittany and she loved it. "You look great," Willow said.

"Teddy will probably think it's a weird dress," Brittany said as she studied her reflection thoughtfully. "But the important thing is that I feel comfortable. Right?"

"Right," Willow said and held out the charge card to make the purchase. "Now we've got to find something for Anna."

"Something plain," Anna said softly.

"Something to show off your great figure," Willow said. "Plain but pretty."

Anna looked at her cousin as though she wasn't quite sure whether Willow was making a joke or not. Willow felt ashamed as she looked into Anna's clear blue eyes. Impulsively, Willow reached out and hugged Anna and said, "You are pretty and I'm glad that Lars invited you to the New Year's Eve ball."

"But you're not going with us," Anna said softly.

"No," Willow admitted. "I don't have a date."

"That means you wish Lars had asked you again," Anna said.

"How did you know he asked me?" Willow answered the question with a question.

Anna shrugged. "I expected him to ask you. When he asked me I wondered about that and then I decided he probably asked you first. Did you turn him down because of Carlos?"

"Yes," Willow answered. "But all that seems like a long time ago. I'm not interested in Carlos at all anymore."

"I will ask Lars to take you to the New Year's Eve ball," Anna said suddenly. "Before, when you weren't so nice to me, I thought it didn't matter. But now that you are so nice, I see it matters. We'll go home now and I'll call him."

"No," Willow said in a clear voice. "We'll pick out your dress and then we'll pick out mine. I'm going to the ball with Dan and that's the truth."

"I'll tell Lars he *must* take you to the ball," Anna said.

"I could never break a date with one fellow to go with another," Willow said with conviction. "It would be against my principles. Dan will take me to the ball and that's that. So you've got to go with Lars and that's that. Now let's find the dresses."

Later, when Anna was in a dressing room trying on a simple blue dress, Brittany asked Willow, "Did you really ask Dan? When?"

"Not yet," Willow said. "But I can count on Dan." Then she smiled and shook her head and said, "On second thought, I think I'll go call him right now. I'm through taking things for granted."

She was back in time to admire Anna's blue dress. "You look very sophisticated in that," Brittany said.

Anna frowned at her reflection. "I'm not sophisticated."

"Don't worry about that," Willow interposed. "The dress makes you look like a winner and you are a winner, aren't you?"

Anna smiled and nodded her head. "I am a winner."

As their cousin was taking off the new blue dress, Brittany asked, "So good old Dan said yes?"

Willow nodded. "Dan said he'd love to go to the dance with me. And I'm grateful."

"Dan's a nice guy," Brittany said. "Not that he wouldn't jump at the chance to go to the dance with you. Everyone knows he's crazy about you."

"He is a nice guy," Willow said thoughtfully. "I guess I just always took him for granted but I realized when I called him how happy I am to know I can count on him. I like that feeling of being able to count on someone, Britt. Is that awful?"

"That's normal," Brittany answered. "Carlos was certainly no one to count on."

"It wasn't Carlos's fault," Willow said quickly. "And by the time he gets back to Madison I'll be totally over him. I'm certain of that. I just misjudged the situation, that's all. But with Dan, I will always know where I stand."

"Now we have to find you a beautiful dress," Brittany said. "You're a winner, too, you know."

Willow looked at her little sister and smiled and said, "You've been nice to me lately, Britt. Thanks for everything."

"I've always been nice to you," Brittany started to object and then she laughed and said, "You're welcome."

Chapter 46

"I want Carlos back," Willow said quietly. "And by the time he's sixteen Addison I'll be—I'll have—Adam, I guarantee it. She. I just misjudged the situation the first time, but this time I will know where I want..."

"Now we have to find you a beautiful dress," Jessica said. "We've—Willow, how you know..."

Willow looked at her little sister, the darling...

Anna's heart was beating too fast when she came down the stairs. She'd never felt more uncomfortable than she did in the long blue silk gown with the loose sleeves. And the dangling sequin earrings, which Willow insisted she wear, made her feel as though she was dressed up for Halloween.

Jessica insisted on taking pictures of her on the staircase and later she lined all three girls up in front of the fireplace to take more photographs. Dan stood beside her, looking very handsome in his tuxedo. Anna noticed that he had shaved his mustache. She decided that was probably at Willow's suggestion.

When Lars and Teddy arrived, Teddy did all the talking and that was good. They walked out in a group and they were at the door of the limousine before Lars actually said anything at all to her. What he said was, "You have a good Christmas?"

"Great," Anna answered. "It was good to see the boys and my folks."

"I'm glad you came back early," Lars said. "I like running better when you're there."

She smiled and said nothing. He had said exactly the same thing to her at six-thirty this morning. After all, what did they have in common except the ability to run fast and an interest in sports.

Once in the limousine Brittany turned to Lars and asked, "Doesn't Anna look great?"

"Yes."

Anna wished she could open the car door and jump out. What could he say when she was sitting right beside him and Brittany asked such a direct question. And what made her cousin ask such embarrassing questions anyway? Didn't she know that Lars would rather be going to the ball with Willow?

It was a short ride to the Madison Hotel and they were there before Anna could recover from her embarrassment over Brittany's question. When Lars tried to help her out of the car she looked at him and said, "I can manage."

Lars flushed and said, "Of course you can." He stepped back and she got out of the car with two steps onto the sidewalk. Then she turned and watched as Dan helped Willow out.

Willow had lots of full skirts to manage but she put so much emphasis on her need for help and attracted so much attention to her skirts that by the time she got out, Lars, Teddy, and Dan were all helping her. Somehow, they entered the hotel with all three men surrounding Willow and Anna and Brittany trailing behind.

Brittany looked at Anna and muttered under her breath, "She'll never change."

"She has changed," Anna said mildly.

"Not enough." Then Brittany called out to Teddy, "Teddy Myers, you get back here. You're supposed to be *my* date."

Teddy turned and grinned at Brittany as though he were a kid caught stealing cookies and came right over to her. "I didn't know you cared," he said.

"You *did* know I cared," Brittany retorted, "and you did it anyway. You've always liked Willow best."

"I've never *liked* Willow best," Teddy said. "But sometimes I get taken in by all that spun sugar and golden light. Like a moth to a flame."

"Can't you be serious for a minute?" Brittany said. "This is supposed to be our first real date." Her voice sounded a little hurt.

Teddy smiled and put his arm around her

waist. "It is our first real *formal* date," he said. "The first of many. And we are going to have a wonderful time. We'll dance the night away. We'll fly in my plane to New York City for breakfast on top of the Empire State Building. We'll do whatever your heart desires."

"I'd like to have dinner," Brittany said. "And I'd like you to talk to me during dinner. At least some of the time." Then she added, "You can talk to Anna, too."

Teddy looked over at Anna and grinned. "She thinks I'm safe with you but she doesn't know, does she, my dear? You haven't told her about the love letters I've been slipping into your locker at school or the way I wait around outside your gym locker, waiting to see if I can walk you home."

Anna frowned and said, "Don't tease Brittany."

All this while, Lars stood by her side and said nothing. She could barely look at him because she was so shy and she felt so very awkward. When it was time to sit at the table, the waiter held her chair for her, relieving Lars of the duty.

As the six of them ordered and ate dinner, Teddy and Brittany and Willow and Dan laughed and talked about Christmas, about school, about their plans for the future, and were obviously having a wonderful time. By the time dessert came Anna was desperate to join in the conversation but simply couldn't think of anything at all to say.

Teddy tried to help her out. "You have your first game on Tuesday?"

"Yes."

"I ran into Coach Contraro in the barbershop," Dan said. "He was bragging about you to the men in the barbershop. He really thinks you'll take the state championship."

"She will," Lars said.

Anna flushed. Here she was all dressed up and on her first date and the only nice thing her date could think to say about her was about her sports ability. She bit into her cake and said nothing more. What more was there to say?

There were several other groups who had the same idea they'd had and were eating in the hotel dining room before the dance. Several couples stopped by the table to speak to Willow and Lars. When Willow introduced Dan as her date to one of the girls on the cheerleading team, the girl looked very confused and asked, "You didn't come with Lars?"

"My cousin came with Lars," Willow said. "I came with Dan." She linked her arm through Dan's and smiled at him.

"But I thought . . ." the girl began.

"You were mistaken," Willow said smoothly and stood up. "Time to go, don't you think?" The whole party quickly got to their feet and they practically ran out of the dining room.

Once outside, Willow giggled and tucked one arm through Dan's and another through Anna's and said, "A rude question deserves a rude answer. Right?"

Brittany insisted on a table in the corner of the room that was closest to the bandstand and they claimed it by putting their bags and wraps on it. Then Brittany and Teddy and Dan and Willow went onto the dance floor to dance. "I'm not a very good dancer," Lars said. "I should have told you that."

Anna smiled and shouted over the music, "I can't dance. I did tell you."

They sat together for several dances, drinking Cokes they didn't want, looking at the people on the dance floor, and listening to the music. Finally, Brittany and Teddy came over and Brittany said, "You guys can't just sit there all night. Dance."

"I can't dance," Anna said. "But Lars can."

"Then come on and dance with me," Brittany said and took Lars's hand. "Teddy's tired anyway."

So Teddy slumped beside her, talking a mile

a minute about nothing in particular and Anna sat in her chair, staring out over the sea of dancers, wishing with all her heart that she were anywhere else at all. Finally, Teddy asked, "So, are we having fun yet?"

"You are," Anna answered.

"But you and Lars look like a couple of fish out of water. I had no idea he was so shy."

"He's very popular," Anna said. "I don't think he's shy."

"He's shy and so are you. You really can't dance?"

She shook her head. "Not at all."

"These dances are sort of like dribbling a ball up and down a court. You don't think you could just stand up and pretend you're doing your thing. Maybe make up the Madison jump or something."

"I can't," Anna said. "I never should have come. I knew I'd be miserable but I didn't know I'd be totally frozen. Poor Lars."

"He'll survive," Teddy said. "But I think you should at least get up and walk around some. You look paralyzed. So does he."

Eventually Brittany and Lars came back to the table and Brittany said, "Now he's warmed up. Now it's your turn."

Lars held out his hand but Anna shook her

head and said, "I really can't dance. Not even a little bit."

"We could walk," Lars offered. "The hotel has a gallery and some other things to see."

"Why don't you ask someone else to dance," Anna said. "I don't mind sitting alone."

Lars looked very solemn and said, "I don't want to do that, Anna. I want to be with you."

Anna stood up and said, "Let's just walk around the room. We can watch the others dance and maybe move a little farther away from the music."

Lars held her hand as they walked, and they gradually made their way toward the other end of the room where the music wasn't quite as loud. At one point, they passed Willow and Dan who were dancing very close to each other. Lars said, "Willow seems to be having a good time. I think she really likes Dan."

"I'm sorry," Anna said.

"Sorry? I think it's nice when people find people they really like, don't you?"

"You wanted to take Willow to the dance and now you're stuck with me," Anna said. "I shouldn't have come. But Willow wouldn't break her date with Dan. She said it was against her principles. Anyway, here we are and I'm sorry."

"I think we need to talk," Lars said. "You sound like you think I didn't want to take you to the ball but I did. I asked you, didn't I?"

"You asked Willow first."

"Yes, I did," Lars said. They were standing in a very dark corner of the ballroom now and the music was almost soft. For the first time all evening, Anna could hear Lars without straining and he was talking in a normal voice.

"I asked Willow first because Willow is the kind of girl you think about when you think about dances. When she said no, I actually gave the whole situation some thought and I came up with the idea of asking you. I thought you might turn me down but you didn't. And I'm glad you didn't."

"I'm better on a ball court than in a ballroom," Anna said.

Lars laughed and said, "So am I. I may not be as good a basketball player as you are, but I'm a lot better basketball player than dancer. And I'm better talking about sports than the romantic stuff that seems to go along with a dance."

Anna was actually beginning to breathe again.

Lars smiled and said, "Teddy and Dan just go right along with the whole program but it's not my program and I wouldn't know how to do it if I tried. You saw how awkward I was when I tried to help you out of the car."

"I was the one who was awkward," Anna said. "I should have let you help me."

"You can get out of a car all right," Lars said. "I knew it and you knew. It was just that you looked so beautiful in that dress that I was feeling even more shy than usual. Trying to do the right thing."

He thinks I look beautiful. Anna marveled at the naturalness of his statement. *He really thinks I look beautiful.* She smiled at him.

"I mean, I've always known you were beautiful," Lars said. "I see that every day but the dress did something different. Your eyes looked different or something."

Should she tell him it was Willow's mascara? No. She would just stand there and enjoy the compliment. It was the first time in her life that anyone had actually said she looked pretty. No — not pretty — Willow was pretty. He actually thought she was beautiful.

"You look different, too," Anna said. "And you acted different and I thought you really wanted to be here with Willow. So that made me shyer than usual, I guess. You know, I'm really pretty self-confident when I'm sure of my ground," Anna said. "At home. In class. On the ball court. Running with you in the mornings. Those are all easy places for me."

"Couldn't we just pretend we were in an easy space?" Lars asked wistfully. "Or maybe we could make an easy space just for ourselves right here."

The bells began to blow and the whistles went off, signaling that the New Year was there. Anna looked around at all the people who were hugging and kissing and wondered what she was supposed to do next. She couldn't quite look at Lars but she was aware that he was right beside her.

He was taller than she was. Not much, but an inch or two, and he was standing so close to her that she could put her arms around him if she wanted to. Anna frowned and stepped back. What kind of a thing was that to think?

"What did I say?" Lars looked very worried.

"Nothing," Anna admitted.

"Why did you back away?"

Anna shrugged. "I guess I just noticed how close we were."

"I thought it was nice. I was going to kiss you."

"You were?"

"Maybe," Lars admitted. Then he laughed and said, "At least I was working up the nerve to try and you moved away. Now what do I do?"

"Try again," Anna answered and she added, "I'll help."

She stepped closer and he put his arms around her and kissed her lightly on the lips. It was her first kiss so she had no way of knowing whether it was a truly wonderful kiss or just seemed that way to her, but she was happy.

They stood together, with their arms locked around each other, keeping out other people from their magic circle and waiting until the bells and whistles subsided. Eventually, the band started playing again. This time, the music was definitely more romantic and slower. Lars began to sway a bit with the music and Anna swayed with him. She felt very relaxed and easy about being in his arms. She enjoyed his touch, enjoyed having him close and she was wishing that he would kiss her again. It occurred to her that she was tall enough that if she wanted to kiss him, all she had to do was reach up just a little bit.

After their lips met a second time, Lars said, "The music is slower now." He still had his arms around her waist. "We could just stay here and dance in a little circle. A nice safe circle. Okay?"

And so they did that. They spent the last hour of the dance in the darkest corner of the room with their arms wrapped around each other, moving to the music and pausing from time to time to kiss again.

About one-thirty in the morning, her cousins and their dates found them still dancing in the corner. "We've got to go," Teddy reminded them. "The limousine price goes up at two."

"We have time to toast the New Year," Brittany said. She looked absolutely radiant, as though she had the best time of her life. She turned to Teddy and said, "You get to make the first toast."

So Teddy poured sparkling cider into all their glasses and held his high. "To Cinderella," he said. "The girl who grew up enough to find her Prince Charming."

Brittany laughed and drank down her cider, saying, "I do feel like Cinderella tonight. And I'm dressed exactly right for the part. Hot pink and sequins."

"What about me?" Willow laughed and smoothed her full-skirted organdy dress. "I'm certainly not going to play second fiddle to sequins. I'm the real Cinderella tonight." She smiled up at Dan who seemed as happy as she was. He bent his head a little and kissed her bare shoulder.

Anna smiled. "I do feel a little bit like Cinderella myself," she admitted.

"You are," Willow said. "We all are."

"I guess that makes us all Charming Princes," Teddy said. He then bowed to the girls and said, "Your golden pumpkin awaits you."

"We can't go until we make a toast for the New Year," Brittany argued. "And we get to make wishes, too. You first, Anna. An out-loud wish."

Anna held her glass up to the shining chandelier and said, "I wish to win the state championship this year."

Willow looked shocked but everyone else laughed and Lars hugged her, saying, "Cinderellas make great centers. You'll win."

It was Lars's turn to wish next and he said, "I wish to run faster this year so I can keep up with my girlfriend."

Brittany wished to find her true talent in life and Teddy wished for the lead in the school play.

Then it was Dan's turn and he turned to Willow, toasting her with his glass of cider and said, "I don't have to wish for anything. My dream came true this evening."

Willow looked up at him and smiled and said, "Thanks, Dan. And thanks for being so patient with me. As for myself, I wish to feel like Cinderella all year long."

"Why not?" Brittany asked.

And all around her, the others asked, "Why not?"

Romances

Dreamy Days... Unforgettable Nights

☐ BAK46313-6	First Comes Love #1: To Have and to Hold	$3.50
☐ BAK46314-4	First Comes Love #2: For Better or For Worse	$3.50
☐ BAK46315-2	First Comes Love #3: In Sickness and in Health	$3.50
☐ BAK46316-0	First Comes Love #4: Till Death Do Us Part	$3.50
☐ BAK46574-0	Forbidden	$3.50
☐ BAK45785-3	Last Dance	$3.25
☐ BAK45705-5	The Last Great Summer	$3.25
☐ BAK48323-4	Last Summer, First Love #1: A Time to Love	$3.95
☐ BAK48324-2	Last Summer, First Love #2: Good-bye to Love	$3.95
☐ BAK46967-3	Lifeguards: Summer's End	$3.50
☐ BAK46966-5	Lifeguards: Summer's Promise	$3.50
☐ BAK42553-6	The Party's Over	$3.25
☐ BAK45784-5	Saturday Night	$3.25
☐ BAK45786-1	Summer Nights	$3.25
☐ BAK44672-0	Winter Dreams, Christmas Love	$3.50
☐ BAK47610-6	Winter Love Story, A	$3.50
☐ BAK48152-5	Winter Love, Winter Wishes	$3.95

Available wherever you buy books, or use this order form.

Scholastic Inc., P.O. Box 7502, 2931 East McCarty Street, Jefferson City, MO 65102

Please send me the books I have checked above. I am enclosing $_____ (please add $2.00 to cover shipping and handling). Send check or money order — no cash or C.O.D.s please.

Name _____ Birthdate ___ / ___ / ___

Address _____

City _____ State/Zip ____ / _____

Please allow four to six weeks for delivery. Offer good in the U.S. only. Sorry, mail orders are not available to residents of Canada. Prices subject to change.   R594